It has been brought to our attention that you seem to be completely lost. If you wish to come to know what it is that constantly eludes you in life . . . I am your transport to seek within.

Kyle is young man with no future, and no past. Orphaned from a young age, he uses tough upbringing as an excuse for his lack of direction in life. But a mysterious parcel is about to change his view of himself, his parents, and the world in which he lives.

An old leather bound book, intricately embossed with creatures and strange beings, is left on Kyle's doorstep with no card or note attached. The book issues Kyle a personal challenge — to finish reading the book and face the innermost truth about himself, or forfeit any chance of finding his true destiny.

If this book was left on your doorstep and you had nothing left to lose, could you resist reading on?

BOOK OF DREAMS

Traci Harding

Voyager

An imprint of HarperCollins*Publishers*

Voyager
An imprint of HarperCollins*Publishers*, Australia

First published in Australia in 2003
by HarperCollins*Publishers* Pty Limited
ABN 36 009 913 517
A member of the HarperCollins*Publishers* (Australia) Pty Limited Group
www.harpercollins.com.au

HarperCollins*Publishers*
25 Ryde Road, Pymble, Sydney NSW 2073, Australia
31 View Road, Glenfield, Auckland 10, New Zealand
77–85 Fulham Palace Road, London W6 8JB, United Kingdom
2 Bloor Street East, 20th floor, Toronto, Ontario M4W 1A8, Canada
10 East 53rd Street, New York, NY 10022, USA

National Library of Australia Cataloguing-in-Publication data:

Harding, Traci.
  Book of dreams.
  Bibliography.
  ISBN 0 7322 7409 5.
  I. Title.
A823.3

Cover and internal illustrations by Mo Hine
Cover design by David Harding
Author photo by Terry Ludgate
Internal design by Christa Edmonds, HarperCollins Design Studio
Printed and bound in Australia by Griffin Press on 50gsm Bulky News

5 4 3 2 1   03 04 05 06

For Kyle,
my inspiration
for many a great
character.

And for
-the Canadian,
the one who forever
shows me new
worlds to change my
life.

ACKNOWLEDGEMENTS

I started writing this tale for my brother Kyle about ten years ago. It was to be a film script, but it was shelved and never finished. Then, it was to be made into a manuscript after *The Alchemist's Key*, but another Chosen trilogy came along, and once again *Book of Dreams* was shelved.

A year or so ago I was telling Kyle of my forthcoming projects when he asked, 'Whatever happened to my story?'

I must admit I felt a twinge of guilt. I considered that I owed Kyle a tale, having borrowed bits of his character for so many of the characters in my other tales, (Brockwell/Brian and Rhun in the Ancient Future Series and Wade Ashby in *The Alchemist's Key*). Thus I dug this half-a-film-script out of my computer archives, and found myself being tickled by the characters all over again. Yes, this one did have to be finished.

So, Kyle, here is your story, I hope it lives up to expectation, after such a long wait ... thanks for being so patient.

I must also thank the Matts who all contributed to the character of Kyle's best mate in this tale — Matt Burns, Matt English and Matt Wollaston.

Also to the girls behind Zoe's character, Marie-Claire Wollaston and Joey Ludgate, thanks girls.

On the research front thanks to Anne-Marie Mengel for aiding with land rights research and Rob Samson for help with researching indigenous Australian mythological animals.

My gratitude goes to Linda Funnell at HarperCollins, for taking a chance on our concept for the cover art for this book.

The beautiful creatures that adorn this cover were the creations of Mo Hine, a fabulous woman of extraordinary talent. Many, many thanks for the time, energy and imagination that you poured into this project.

A chug on the shoulder for my husband, David, for piecing this cover together, and kisses to my daughter Sarah Jane Harding, because she likes to look for her name in the front of my books — so there it is.

I must also say many thanks to Chez, for taking care of my Trazling site and my online newsletter, and hello to all those who frequent my message board. Thanks to Fiona at HarperCollins for maintaining my author site … we at the THC message board are very grateful for all your hard work.

As always, my thanks and praise to my editors Sue and Stephanie … here's to number nine, girls!

And last, but by no means least, blessings to my wonderful agent, Selwa Anthony.

CONTENTS

CHAPTER
ONE

LITTLE RICH GIRL

Four hours of torture to go before Kyle could hang up his smelly overalls and piss off to the pub.

He'd never wanted this job — he couldn't imagine who, in their right mind, would want to be a cleaner — but as his Centrelink officer had managed to place him in a position where he could work alongside his best mate, Matt, Kyle had decided he'd stick it out for a while. The money was okay and Matt seemed to be enjoying the work; but then, Matt usually enjoyed himself no matter what he was doing. Kyle wasn't too concerned about this 'bettering himself' fetish Matt was having. Matt would get over it like he always did, and then they could go back to being dope smoking, dole bludging bums and all would be right with the world.

The clock above the lunchroom door chimed six times to announce 6 p.m. — starting time. As Matt had yet to show, Kyle decided to grab another cup of coffee and catch a bit of the news.

The television ran twenty-four hours a day, as did the Nivok Industries building; there was always some member of staff hanging around the lunchroom no matter what the hour. At present, one of the older security guards was grabbing his tea break. He had his feet up on a table as he watched television.

'Hey, Charlie.' Kyle sat down opposite the guard, eyeing off a couple of pieces of cake in the old bloke's lunchbox. 'Your missus spoils you something awful.'

'There's an extra slice there.' Charlie's eyes remained transfixed on the news report. '*Anything* to stop you nicking mine.'

'God bless that sweet, sweet woman,' Kyle exclaimed, doing away with the plastic wrap.

He sat back with his cup of coffee to admire the look of the moist piece of orange cake before hoeing it down. His sweet tooth satisfied, Kyle's attention turned to the news broadcast. 'Hey!' He recognised the man on the screen. 'Isn't that God?'

'Yes, that's the boss. James Nivok.' Charlie glanced at Kyle as he reached for his tea. 'One of the wealthiest men in the world.'

'So what's he done to get on the news?' Kyle sipped at his coffee, noting the time was now ten past the hour.

'Some loony tried to attack his young niece at a Nivok Industries "do" last night.' Charlie shook his head in disgust. 'That's her there, Zoe Nivok.' He motioned to the young woman now featuring on the screen.

Kyle eyeballed the attractive, well-dressed female with contempt. 'I've seen her around.'

'*After last night's interruption*,' the report said, over the footage of Zoe Nivok, '*it was announced that a large expanse of land in far North Queensland, which has been tied up by the late David Nivok's will for twenty years,*

*will finally be made available for development.
It has been agreed between James Nivok of
Nivok Industries and the young heiress that on
her 21st birthday, when the land is released to
her along with the remainder of the family
estate, that the property will be signed over to
her uncle's company for the tidy sum of five
million dollars.'*

'Get-the-fuck-outta-here!' Kyle shot out of
his slouched position and leant forward in his
chair to hear the rest. 'That must be some hunk
of property.'

*'A price has yet to be set for Miss Nivok's
inheritance of nearly two-thirds of all Nivok
Industries.'*

'Sheesh!' Charlie shook his head, as the news
broadcast cut to another story. 'What I
wouldn't give to be a handsome twenty-one
year old again.'

Kyle grinned at the old man's folly. 'Your
missus was a much better catch.' His eyes
turned to the remaining piece of cake.

'Go on,' Charlie growled, warmed by the
truth of Kyle's comment.

As Kyle reached for his reward Matt came
charging through the large double doors of the

lunchroom, leaving them swinging in his wake. He was sporting a large video camera perched on his shoulder, and filmed Kyle scoffing down his cake as he approached.

'Where the hell did you get that from?' Kyle queried with his mouth full, knowing Matt was usually as broke as he was.

'Isn't it a beauty?' Matt circled Kyle as he zoomed the camera focus in on him. 'I got it on loan from my Uncle Max.'

'The quack?' Kyle recalled what Matt had told him of the man.

'That's right,' grinned Matt. 'He said I could borrow it for a couple of weeks ... see if I have any aptitude for it.'

'Oh, give me a break.' Kyle pushed the camera out of his face, and Matt ceased filming. 'You're going to be a cameraman now, is that it?'

'Yeah, why not?' Matt's face beamed with excitement. As always, there was not a doubt in his mind that this goal was achievable. 'Current affairs ... riots, bombs, *crime* ... wherever the news breaks.' He raised the camera to resume filming Kyle.

'Will you quit it!' Kyle shoved the camera aside, harder this time. 'If you want to film someone, go shoot your girlfriend ... she just inherited five million bucks. There ought to be a story in that.'

'My girlfriend?' Matt frowned, having to think about it.

'Up on ten?' Kyle hinted.

'Zoe?' Matt asked, as she was the only person he really knew on the tenth floor.

Kyle nodded, his brows raised for added assurance.

'Jeez, I knew she was inheriting some money, but *five million* ... sheesh!'

'That's what I said.' Charlie seconded Matt's amazement.

'You misunderstand me,' Kyle added. 'The five million is one tiny piece of what she's actually inherited.'

The double doors slammed wide as Mr Grego, the cleaning supervisor, stormed in, searching for his missing team. 'Are you two on *holiday*?'

'No sir.' Matt spoke up, knowing he would handle the situation more diplomatically than Kyle would. 'I —'

'Put that thing away!' Grego cut him off, referring to the camera. 'You've got to the count of five to get out of my sight, or you're both out of a job. One, two …'

Matt grabbed hold of the back of Kyle's overalls, thinking that his friend might hold their supervisor to his word.

'Three, four …' Grego counted down, as Matt hauled Kyle to the door.

Kyle paused at the exit to smile back at his boss.

'Five!' the supervisor roared, angered by the lad's defiance, but Kyle made sure to duck out of his line of vision by the appointed time. Grego let the incident pass.

The sound of the large rickety bin he towed always drove Kyle nuts. He hated hauling it around; he hated emptying trashcans. It was mind-numbingly boring work and, in his opinion, more degrading than not having a job. Tonight's rubbish round was even more depressing than usual given that he was forced to listen to Matt ranting and raving about his imminent media career. It wasn't that Kyle was the kind of person who would deliberately put a downer on a mate's aspirations, but Matt dreamt up a new job prospect for himself every second week. Kyle, on the other hand, had yet to think of a single realistic vocation that he could get enthusiastic about. He was a man of few talents. The skills Kyle possessed were useless in the regular workforce, and he would never, in all likelihood, have the skills to land a job which he would consider halfway acceptable.

They finished their round of the ninth floor and caught the lift up to the tenth. Matt retrieved his camera from the compartment of his cleaning trolley before the lift door opened.

'I wonder if she'll be working late.' Matt raised his brows in expectant enthusiasm.

'You're not seriously considering using that on the heiress to the Nivok Empire?' Kyle queried, thinking Matt naive. 'She'll have you up on harassment charges, just like the poor chump who got too close to her last night.'

'What poor chump?' Matt asked with fleeting interest, before waving off the answer. 'Zoe's cool, she'll dig it!'

Kyle opened his mouth to protest as the lift doors parted and Matt sprang into the hall to see if the lights in Nivok's private offices were on.

'Excellent,' Matt exclaimed, heading up the wide, plush corridor.

'Great!' retorted Kyle, put out by the fact that Matt had left him to haul the bin and the cleaning trolley. *Harassing the boss's niece ... that would be a fast way out of here.* As Kyle thought twice about the idea, his mood brightened considerably.

Zoe was seated behind her desk in the lavish, dimly-lit reception area out front of James Nivok's private office.

She had declined the offer of having her own office until such time as she decided whether she held any interest in the family business. If the truth be known, Zoe had pretty much decided already and was only humouring her uncle, who insisted that she be absolutely positive that she wanted to sell before he bought her out.

Although Zoe was still unsure of what she wanted to do with her inheritance, she was certain that the world of big business wouldn't enter into the equation. She didn't like the pressure, the office environment, or the thrill of the profit — that was her uncle's bag. After twenty years of waiting, James deserved to assume full control of the family company that he'd kept thriving and growing since the untimely death of her parents. As her guardian, James had also kept Zoe thriving and growing these past twenty years, and she had no desire to complicate his business affairs. Take the money and run, was more her way of thinking. She had extensive travel plans. And after she'd seen the world, Zoe hoped to have some clue as to what to do with the rest of her life.

A desk lamp shed light onto her fingers as she typed at her computer — the clicking noise of her long nails making contact with keys was the only sound to be heard.

The silence was shattered, however, as Matt came charging through the double glass doors, his camera mounted on his shoulder and rolling.

'It's the lovely Miss Zoe, heiress extraordinaire, sacrificing yet another evening to work late for her dear old Uncle James.' Matt grinned as he viewed Zoe through the lens.

Zoe didn't look, or act, much like your average executive secretary. Her designer, hippie-style clothes gave her a much zanier appearance than most of the female staff at Nivok Industries, and yet she always looked like a million bucks. Tiny wine-coloured braids fell amid her long, straight hair of deepest brown. Her large hazel eyes and luscious lips were painted in earthy tones, but unlike most females of her age, Zoe didn't use make-up to excess. Her body was tall and slender, which suited her flowing attire, and she had a scent that was subtle and intoxicating. Zoe's only apparent flaw, as far as Matt could readily assess, was a major lack of substance in the breast department. Not that this bothered Matt; he liked Zoe because she found him humorous.

'And how are we this fine evening?' Matt could tell straightaway that she was amused by his antics, although Zoe did her best to suppress her grin as she looked over the rim of her reading glasses at him.

'Very well, Matthew, and you?'

'Very well,' he confirmed, although his smile really said it all.

'You have a new toy, I see.'

Matt was about to commence his commentary on the camera's features, when Kyle backed in through the glass doors dragging the large bin and the cleaning trolley with him. He left the equipment parked beside the doors and went about his rubbish round as if Matt and Zoe weren't even there. He slammed the metal bins into one another as he emptied them, making one hell of a ruckus.

Zoe's head shrank into her shoulders. 'Is your friend all right?' she asked Matt on the quiet. 'He seems angry about something.'

'Yeah, work ... it's against his religion.' Matt circled round to capture Zoe's profile. 'But let's not talk about him. Let's talk about, say ... five million dollars.'

Zoe, having answered more than enough questions about her inheritance in the past few days, graciously declined. 'Let's not.'

Matt lowered the camera, gaping in awe. 'So, it's true then?'

Zoe merely shrugged, a non-committal grin on her face.

'Dear Lord.' Matt dropped down on one knee beside Zoe and took up her hand. 'Would you marry me? Please!'

'You're just after my money.' Zoe played along, pulling her hand away as she pretended to take offence.

'True,' Matt confessed, 'but your body would suffice.'

Zoe's jaw dropped, but she had to smile at his cheek.

'I hate to interrupt this very touching scene,' Kyle strode over to steal Matt's limelight, 'but I need you to open Uncle James' office, so I can finish up and get out of here.'

The contempt in Kyle's tone instantly rubbed Zoe the wrong way. She had encountered his kind before. Every underprivileged male she'd ever met immediately took her for a spoilt little rich girl to be despised — except for Matthew.

Matthew was the perfect embodiment of the 'boy next door'. His thick blond hair was a decent length, clean and well groomed. His blue eyes twinkled with a lust for life and, although his mouth seemed a bit large for his face, his smile was clown-like and he had the humour to match. What Zoe liked most about Matt, though, was that he was always so polite, considerate and sweet.

Unlike some, Zoe thought, as she gave Kyle the once-over.

This guy was Matt's exact opposite in every regard. Matt's work overalls were clean and pressed, while Kyle's uniform looked as if it hadn't seen a washing machine in a hundred years. Matt was tall and slender; Kyle was short and stocky. Matt bounced when he walked, whereas this guy thundered. Dark eyes, dark hair, dark demeanour: Kyle obviously had a major chip on his shoulder and he didn't mind letting everyone know it.

'It's Uncle Jim, actually,' she informed him in a snobby fashion, 'and he made it very clear that I was to let no one into his office. You've never asked to clean it before —'

'You're not here every night,' Kyle interjected. 'It's a once a month thing. It has to get cleaned sometime,' he appealed on a lighter note.

Matt knew Kyle was fibbing, but he was curious to see inside the bigwig's office; on the other hand, he didn't want to get Zoe into strife. As she turned to seek Matt's opinion, Kyle nodded and urged him on behind Zoe's back.

Matt wiped all expression from his face, except for half a grin. 'It won't take long,' he assured Zoe, before serving Kyle a look of caution.

CHAPTER
TWO

3 CHAPTER

GHOSTS OF YORE

Moonlight streamed into the office through the floor-to-ceiling windows overlooking the Sydney Harbour Bridge. By day, Kyle imagined, the busy harbour would be the highlight of the view.

As Zoe switched on the lights, Kyle's attention was drawn into the large, luxurious room.

'Well, would you check this out,' he commented to Matt, who was loitering by the door.

'What?' Zoe looked at Kyle, realising that she'd been had.

'Relax,' Kyle advised her, strolling over to the lounge area where he spied a remote control sitting in plain view on the coffee table.

'Don't you dare touch that.' Zoe moved to go after him.

But her warning only served to fuel Kyle's urge to make mischief, and taking the remote in hand he pressed the first button that took his fancy.

As a section of the farthest wall turned round to reveal a very well stocked bar, Kyle was tickled pink. 'Anyone for drinks?'

'Holy shit.' Matt finally got up the nerve to enter the room, and raising the camera up onto his shoulder he commenced filming.

'Give me that.' Zoe attempted to swipe the remote from Kyle's grasp, but he took a seat on the leather lounge to escape her.

'Get off there, you're filthy! And give me that remote.'

As Zoe leaned down to confiscate his toy, Kyle held it as far away from her as he could. In a desperate attempt to seize the remote, Zoe lost her balance and found herself on top of Kyle.

'Are you sure you wouldn't like a drink first?' Kyle chuckled, as she wriggled her way off him. 'Hey, that tickles.'

Zoe, not one to be played with for sport, straightened herself and with a very authoritative look on her face, she held out her hand towards Kyle. 'I'll take that, thank you.'

Kyle was almost inclined to comply with her request, but, pushing his luck, he raised his brows in a question and served Zoe a cheeky grin. Zoe made the mistake of cracking a smile, so Kyle gave Matt a whistle. 'Catch.'

Matt, who was now filming behind the bar, turned and caught the remote in his free hand. He played along with Kyle's game, holding the remote in front of the camera lens where he could view it more clearly. 'Some music might be nice.' He pressed the button that he thought activated the stereo system. When the wall of television screens were activated, their combined broadcasts melding into one loud crescendo of noise, Matt lowered the camera to take a closer look at the control panel in his hand and accidentally pressed a button in the process. 'Whoops!'

As the bar Matt was standing behind swung

back round into the wall, Zoe and Kyle rushed to his assistance.

'Press the red button, Matt,' Kyle shouted through the wall over the din of the television sets.

'It's all dark in here,' Matt yelled back. 'I can't see anything.'

Loud heavy metal music now began belting out from the radio. Zoe freaked, holding her hands over her ears to block it out. Kyle, on the other hand, nodded his head up and down in time with the music, rather well disposed towards the selection.

'Well, that's fixed up the music,' he commented loudly to Zoe, who glared at him in quiet disapproval. 'You'd better try another button.' Kyle raised his voice considerably to offer advice to Matt on the other side of the wall.

As Kyle awaited the next development, he strolled over to look at several glass display boxes containing models of various projects Nivok Industries had in development. One held a raw nugget of gold the size of a fist. Others contained shopping malls, hotels, resorts, casinos, and one even resembled a space station.

He moved to inspect the futuristic-looking model, when his attention was diverted to a picture hanging on the wall behind it.

The photograph was of a waterfall cascading into a large pool of brilliant blue water nestled amidst a lush forest. Kyle found it strangely familiar. 'Where is this?' he questioned Zoe, who was following him around to make sure he didn't touch anything else.

'Far north Queensland,' she shouted in his ear. The noise level in the room was now equivalent to a rock concert.

'I've never been there.' Kyle frowned, trying to figure out this odd affiliation he felt for the photograph's subject matter.

'Neither have I,' Zoe remarked. The song on the radio, although very loud, had a good vibe, which dulled her annoyance as it induced her to bop to the beat. 'I suppose I should go and check it out before I sell it,' she boasted casually.

'This is the five million dollar property?'

Kyle turned so abruptly, he startled Zoe. 'Well, yes . . .'

He took a step away from her, as if repulsed by Zoe's bragging. 'How could you sell a place of such beauty to Nivok Industries?'

The tone in Kyle's voice was meant to make Zoe feel ashamed, and it did. To her, Kyle's adverse reaction seemed to indicate an unexpected depth in his character; he had a soft spot for nature. This, coupled with Kyle's dark and distant demeanour, began to make him that much more interesting in Zoe's eyes.

She was not to know that this was a game Kyle played with anyone he decided deserved a kick up the arse. One of Kyle's useless talents was the ability to read people and push their buttons as required. This also made it twice as hard for anyone to get a rise out of him; but then in Kyle's eyes, he himself could do no wrong. 'So, what has Uncle Jim got planned for this piece of paradise ... a car park perhaps?' Kyle mocked her complacency. 'And how convenient, hey.' He motioned to the waterfall. 'A ready-made car wash.'

Zoe took offence at the cutting assumptions. Her uncle had given and given to her over the years, and had never once asked for anything in return. This land was her uncle's only stated desire that she could fulfil to repay some of what she felt she owed him.

'I have my reasons,' Zoe impressed on Kyle, 'and I don't feel the need to explain them to you.'

'Don't worry.' Kyle's mouth curved into a cocky grin. 'I don't expect you to be able to justify to me what you haven't fully justified to yourself yet.'

Zoe should have been furious, but the accuracy of his statement stunned her speechless.

Kyle, who had been expecting a slap in the face, was stoked to discover he had, in fact, amazed the young heiress.

'What in hell's name is going on in here?'

Kyle and Zoe turned to look at James Nivok as he stormed towards his desk to offload his briefcase and portable PC. Another man who, in Kyle's opinion, looked rather like a hired thug, accompanied Nivok into the room. 'Shut that racket off!' Nivok roared, making sure he made himself heard.

Zoe and Kyle looked at each other, unable to comply with Nivok's demand, when the room suddenly fell silent. As the problem resolved itself, Kyle smiled. Zoe, however, was not smiling.

She gave Kyle the foulest glare possible before approaching her uncle. 'I'm so sorry, uncle —'

'I don't want to hear it right now, thank you.'

Her uncle served her an 'I am most displeased' look. Zoe knew it was time to take her leave. 'Can I get either of you a coffee? Tea?'

'Nothing, thank you, Zoe.'

Zoe glanced at her uncle's rather large bodyguard, Ivan, who was still lingering by the door. He shook his head, and she was out of there.

Nivok was almost amused as he watched Kyle meander towards the office door after Zoe. With a glance in Ivan's direction, Nivok had Kyle hauled back by the overalls for a little chat.

Kyle saw the confrontation as fated, so he surrendered without a fight.

'Do you work for me?' Nivok took a seat in his soft leather desk chair.

'Yes, sir, I do,' Kyle replied in a loud cheery fashion.

'Good.' Nivok relaxed back into the chair's comfy confines. 'You're fired. Be out of the building in five minutes.'

'Thank you, sir.' Kyle slapped his hands together, very pleased by this turn of events, and moved quickly to make good his exit by the said time.

As Kyle had not given him the expected response, Nivok had to be suspicious. 'And I'd advise you to stay away from my niece in future ... or my associate here will make it his business to see that you do.'

'Hey,' Kyle delayed his departure to assure them both, 'no problem, what-so-ever.' He closed the door on his way out.

No sooner was Kyle out of Nivok's office, than he broke into a little victory dance. 'Yes! Yes, yes, yes, yes, yes!' He fell to his knees and looked to the ceiling. 'Thank you, God.' That's when he noticed Zoe standing over him, hands on hips.

'Did I miss something?'

'I got fired, and I wasn't even trying!' He sprang back to his feet.

'And this is surprising?' Zoe scoffed.

'Back on the dole, no eighteen percent non-payment period ... yes!' Kyle started up his little dance again, and Zoe rolled her eyes.

Well, ace, when you're done congratulating yourself, you might want to consider how much shit I'm going to be in tomorrow. And what about Matt? He's still stuck behind the bar, you realise?'

'Ah!' Kyle raised his eyebrows. 'Not for long.' He began stripping off his filthy overalls.

Zoe was a little taken aback until she realised Kyle wore a T-shirt and jeans underneath his uniform, both of which fitted his muscular physique rather well in her opinion.

Kyle discarded the overalls into the large rickety bin and motioned Zoe after him as he headed out into the corridor that led to the elevators.

More worried than curious, Zoe pursued him.

Never one to forego an opportunity, Matt saw his predicament as the perfect chance to do a bit of spying. He felt around underneath the underside of the bar top and found a switch. *I sure hope this is the bar light and not the alarm.* Matt closed his eyes in silent prayer as he flicked the switch on. When no loud siren was forthcoming, Matt ventured to open his eyes. A thin band of ultraviolet light trimmed the top, and although its glow was rather intense it gave off only a minimal amount of light. Still, it was enough to see by. Matt switched his camera's audio function to record and backed its in-built mike up against the wall.

'I don't care what happened.' Nivok sounded very annoyed. 'Burke could really make things difficult for us. Which is why I wanted him in our custody! In jail, he may as well be under police protection. Or worse, if the police bother to go back over their case files, they'll discover that he was wanted for questioning in regard to several incidents. If he talks to anyone, or gets anywhere near my niece, I'll have a real situation on my hands. I don't need that history disturbed right now.'

'What do you want me to do?'

Ear pressed hard to the wall, Matt was speculating as to who Nivok had in the office with him, when he noticed a miniature bottle of bourbon sitting on the shelf before him. *Don't mind if I do.* He cracked the cap as silently as possible and gulped down the contents in a couple of swigs.

'Find out if the policeman Burke hit is

pressing charges,' Nivok instructed, with a good serve of uneasiness in his voice. 'And if so, when they plan to release him. After twenty years be damned if —'

The fire alarm startled Matt and the empty bottle fell out of his hand and smashed all over the bar top. Matt bit his lip, sure that he'd be busted.

'Oh, for Christ's sake! What is going on here tonight?' Matt heard someone picking up the phone and dialling. 'Where's security, goddamn it? Come on.'

As Matt heard the office door slam closed, he breathed a sigh of relief and gave a thumbs up. 'Kyle, you total legend!' He took the remote in hand and pressed the red button. The bar swung around and Matt escaped into the office. He pressed the button, returning the bar to where it sat flush with the wall, and placed the remote back on the coffee table where they'd found it. He strode from the office with his camera, closing the door behind him.

'I can't believe you did that.' Zoe dragged hard on the cigarette Kyle had supplied her with in the wake of their little stunt.

'Settle, petal.' Kyle puffed away on a cigarette of his own. 'There's no harm done.' His focus shifted to the foyer as Matt emerged from the elevator and came dashing out the front doors and down the stairs to join them.

'I can't believe you did that!' Matt gave Kyle a high five. 'Legendary, man ... thanks.'

Zoe, thinking their behaviour childish, decided to put things in perspective. 'I fail to see what you're thanking him for, considering he's the one who got us into trouble in the first place.'

Matt, realising how much strife they had caused Zoe, moved to apologise, but Kyle butted in first.

'Oh, come on! You're not going to tell me you actually believed we had to clean your uncle's office?' Kyle argued. 'Admit it, you were bored and we seemed like mild entertainment value for a while. Your uncle isn't going to punish you for tonight's little episode. You don't even know the meaning of the word punishment.'

'All right,' Matt pulled Kyle back, 'that's enough soul searching for one evening. Why don't you go get the car?' He handed Kyle the car keys and sent him on his way.

Zoe stared at Kyle as he departed; he was, without doubt, the bitterest individual of her own age that she'd ever met.

'He had a rough childhood,' Matt explained.

Zoe half laughed, half scoffed as she considered her own youth. 'He's not the only one.'

'No, Zoe, I mean extraordinarily tough. The kind of upbringing that most of us couldn't conceive of, let alone live through.'

This was the first time Zoe had ever seen Matt being dead serious. 'So that gives him the right to treat everyone else like shit, does it?'

Matt conceded she had a fair point. 'Look, I'm not defending his behaviour, but it's easy to love and be compassionate and understanding once you've experienced those emotions yourself, but if abuse is all you've ever known …?' Matt shrugged, hoping she'd understand. 'He's a really good guy once you get to know him. Hey, why don't you come have a drink with us?'

Zoe backed up, a bit apprehensive of the idea. 'No, I —'

'Please.' Matt put on a pleading face. 'I want to ask you a few questions, anyhow. Like … who was the dude in the office with your uncle?'

'My uncle's bodyguard. Why?'

Matt was hesitant to be entirely open, and sidestepped the issue. 'You don't strike me as the kind of woman who'd rather bury her head in the sand than stir up trouble.'

Now Zoe was even more curious. 'And you'd be right. But I'm not one to jump to conclusions either.'

As Kyle drove up in Matt's wreck of a car, Matt turned to Zoe to beseech her: 'Please come for a drink. I really think we should talk.'

She looked at Kyle waiting in the car, then back to Matt. 'Do you have a leash for him?'

'You don't need protection from Kyle,' Matt assured her with a smile. 'He likes you, I can tell. Come on.' He beckoned her to follow.

'Jesus ... I'd sure hate to be in his bad books,' Zoe muttered under her breath. Every rational instinct she had told her not to go, yet her feet seemed to assume independent control as they descended the stairs after Matt. 'I'll follow you in my car,' she said, and Matt gave her a thumbs up and a wide smile of appreciation.

With a couple of drinks in hand, they found themselves a quiet corner in the beer garden and Matt set the camera up to replay his recording. It was a relief to find the tape of Nivok's conversation was audible, just.

'What?' said Kyle, once it was over. 'That's it?'

Matt nodded. 'Who's this Burke fellow, I wonder? What could he have on your uncle that would cause him so much concern?'

Zoe had gone kind of pale. 'Timothy Burke was the name of the man who tried to approach me at the Nivok seminar last night.'

'Approach you? Ha!' Kyle lit a smoke. 'The police are calling it assault, despite the fact he never got anywhere near you.'

'I don't have anything to do with that.' Zoe grew tired of having to justify herself. 'You heard the recording. Burke punched out the arresting officer. He's the one charging Burke with assault, not me.'

'So that's why your uncle instructed Ivan to find out when the police are going to release Burke,' Matt intervened.

'I suppose.' Zoe didn't know what to make of it. She felt uncomfortable snooping into her uncle's private affairs with a couple of complete strangers. Still, she had to admit that the malign tone of James Nivok's voice on Matt's recording revealed a side of her uncle that Zoe had never before encountered.

'Maybe,' Kyle sat forward to offer his viewpoint, 'Burke got himself arrested on purpose, to escape your uncle's crony.'

'A possibility.' Matt nodded. 'But just before the alarm goes off, Nivok says something about twenty years.' Matt rewound the tape to play the last bit, and they all hunched around the video camera to hear.

Find out if the policeman Burke hit is pressing charges. And if so, when they plan to release him. After twenty years be damned if —

As the alarm sounded, Matt switched off the tape. 'How long has this piece of land been tied up in your father's will?'

'Twenty years,' Kyle and Zoe responded in unison.

'Coincidence?' queried Matt. 'Would it be pushing the friendship to ask how your parents died?'

His big baby blues didn't appease Zoe this time — he was treading on hallowed ground.

'Yes, it would.' Zoe stood up. She really didn't want to go there. 'Look Matt, I know you're excited about your new camera and you've told me of your media aspirations —'

'You have?' Kyle looked at his friend, surprised that Matt hadn't mentioned it to him before today. Matt gave a vaguely apologetic shrug and Kyle realised that his friend's crush on the young heiress was more serious than previously imagined: *she* was at the root of this 'bettering himself' business.

'I know you're on the hunt for a big story, but my uncle is one of the most successful businessmen in the world, and his company's affairs are closely monitored. I'm sure he's not involved in anything that is as shady as you hope.'

Kyle smirked at her words, having another swig of his drink. 'I don't know why you're bothering to tell her any of this. How do you know she won't tell Uncle Jim what you've been up to?'

Zoe wasn't going to give Kyle the satisfaction of making her angry, and taking a deep breath, she managed to maintain her cool. 'I have no intention of mentioning this to him,' she assured Matt. 'Whose fault is it that you were in there in the first place?' Zoe raised her brow questioningly then turned to address Kyle. 'Chances are, we won't meet again, so let me say this . . .'

Kyle leaned back in his seat, amused that she would even waste her breath. 'Well, let's hear it,' he mumbled.

'If you persist in hauling that huge cross with you throughout life, sooner or later it's going to crush you. How do you expect to experience the future, if you're still living in the past?'

Kyle was a little disconcerted by her advice. He'd expected an ear bashing about how rude and conceited he was. He gave Matt an accusing glare, figuring he must have given her some insight.

'I didn't say anything,' Matt lied. He knew Kyle hated anyone knowing about his past. As it was, Kyle only ever confided in Matt during a drunken stupor or a bad trip.

Zoe threw her handbag strap over her shoulder. 'You're venting your anger on others,' she told Kyle. 'Me, in this instance, while I'm quite sure I'm not the one you're really mad at.'

'Well, thank you for that lovely diagnosis, doctor.' Kyle tipped his drink to her. 'If I need a shrink, I'll call you.'

'Please don't.' She forced a smile, which became more sincere as she turned to Matt. 'I'll be seeing you.' She kissed his cheek. 'Thanks for the drink ... and the entertainment.' Zoe glanced at Kyle, turned and departed.

'Well, aren't you the lucky one.' Kyle was being facetious.

'Kyle, my laddy ... I do believe I'm going to marry that girl.' Matt nodded to second his own decision.

'Oh goody.' Kyle raised himself to get them moving. 'Then I'll have the pleasure of her company all the time.'

They blew a joint on the way home in the car. Dope was in plentiful supply, because Kyle grew his own — hydroponics being yet another of his unusual skills. Matt was buzzing after they'd had the smoke, and he bopped along to the tune on the radio as he drove, singing the words he knew and humming those he didn't. Kyle was silently observing the storm that was lighting up the night sky in the west — the direction in which they were headed.

The way Kyle saw it, Matt had every right to be on top of the world. A beautiful, young millionairess had just kissed him. He'd discovered a vocation he was truly excited about, and if Matt's hunches proved correct, he'd have the chance to uncover a career-making story and save the heroine as well.

'What the hell is wrong with me?' Kyle shook his head at his own behaviour. 'Why do I always assume the worst of people?'

Matt snapped out of his joyous delirium when he realised how low Kyle felt. 'It's just a defence mechanism. You're afraid of people leaving you, so you block that fear by never allowing them to get close in the first place ... or some shit like that,' he explained. 'I read about it in one of the self-motivation books Zoe gave me to read.'

Again Kyle was surprised at, and even a little envious, of the extent of Matt's association with this girl. 'Is that a fact? So why am I still hanging around with you then?'

'Perhaps you don't see me as threatening enough.' Matt grinned his jester's grin.

Thinking back on the way in which they'd met, Kyle considered Matt's explanation to be true enough. Kyle had been hard up for cash at the time, and living on the streets of King's

Cross. He'd been of a mind to rob Matt when he'd encountered him in a dark backstreet alley, but Matt had played out his fear so much that he had Kyle in hysterics. Kyle couldn't bring himself to hurt such a clown. Kyle was always up for a good fight, yet had always felt compelled to defend any creature smaller or weaker than himself. Matt fell into this category.

'So you think Zoe's right about me living in the past.' When Matt gave a noncommittal shrug, Kyle considered the idea more seriously. 'I really don't know about that. There's so much of the past I don't know, or want to forget, that it doesn't really leave a whole lot of it to live in.'

'Living in the past is just a figure of speech,' said Matt. 'What Zoe really meant was that you keep all your emotions bottled up inside.'

'I express my emotions pretty well,' Kyle appealed.

'Yes, but not to the people responsible for invoking those feelings in you in the first place.'

'Well, every son-of-a-bitch foster father I ever had is either locked up or dead, so I can hardly take it out on them, can I?' Kyle justified. 'And God only knows where my real father is ... he's the worst of the lot for abandoning me in the first place.'

Matt never knew what to say when Kyle talked this way, having had a great upbringing himself and a solid family unit to fall back on. Should he be sympathetic, or was that only compounding the problem?

'Maybe I'm just a natural-born arsehole,' Kyle emerged out of his bitter contemplation to suggest. 'I could've inherited the trait from one of my parents ... but hey, how would I know?'

'How can you say that when your mother died giving birth to you,' Matt argued. 'You owe her your life.'

'Yeah, well she could have saved herself, and me, a lot of misery if she'd just opted for an abortion.'

It made Matt angry to hear such talk; now Kyle *was* just wallowing in self-pity. 'Then you never would have had the pleasure of my company,' he advised lightheartedly. 'And I would be short a best mate.' This was Matt's standard response when it came to Kyle's 'I wish I'd never been born' complaint. Matt just couldn't relate to it.

Matt had a great outlook on life and the

most uncanny luck that Kyle had ever encountered. This made Kyle feel all the more hard done by at times — times like now.

'So, how do I lose the cross?' Kyle asked, sincerely interested to know. 'How do I confront the past and be rid of it for good?'

'Counselling?' Matt suggested meekly, aware that Kyle wasn't going to like the solution. 'The book said there are people who specialise —'

'That just goes to show what books know.' Kyle threw his hands up in a disgruntled fashion. 'I've seen counsellors, Matt. I've *had* therapy, and I'm *still* like this!'

Out of ideas and energy, Matt shrugged. 'I don't know the answers, Kyle, I wish I did! Perhaps —' He paused before suggesting Zoe might be able to help, because (a) he didn't want Kyle moving in on his would-be wife, and (b) Matt didn't feel Kyle would be receptive to the idea right at this instant.

When Matt refrained from further comment, Kyle looked back to the spectacular electrical storm that was now almost directly above them.

'There must be another way,' he said quietly to himself, as the lightning flashed, the thunder boomed and the rain came bucketing down.

CHAPTER
THREE

BIRTH OF A HERO

Matt pulled the car into the curb in front of Kyle's rundown, single-storey terrace. The overgrown vegetation in the tiny front garden was beginning to envelop the house; Kyle had never cut it back because he liked the privacy it provided. The rent on the place was cheap, as the building should really have been condemned. In fact, it was probably only the weeds that held the structure together.

'I'll catch ya.' Kyle waved to Matt and closed

the car door behind him. Although the rain was pouring down, he didn't run for shelter. Kyle found the large, cool droplets beating down upon his body invigorating.

Overhead, a large dark cloud seemed to rumble and looking up, Kyle was amazed to see a bolt of lightning lash out and strike the ground somewhere in the vicinity of his porch.

'Awesome! Did you see that?' As he swung round quickly to catch Matt's reaction, the car took off up the road. 'I guess not.' Kyle opened the rusty old gate and fought his way through the jungle to investigate the spot where the lightning had hit.

At the top of the steps, on the small porch, Kyle could see a brown paper parcel and for the slightest moment he could have sworn that a small, brown, furry creature, no taller than ten centimetres, was seated atop the package — as if guarding it. A spear in one hand, it appeared to be not unlike a small bear. It stood erect and had horns protruding from the brow of its rather ugly, flat face. Upon discovery, however, it jumped down behind the parcel and out of sight.

Kyle dashed up the steps and grabbed the package, half expecting to expose the little beast.

'One of these days,' he mumbled, finding nothing.

From as far back as Kyle dared to remember, he'd been visited by these unearthly creatures. Over the course of several unsympathetic sets of foster parents, he'd been beaten or drugged into believing they were imaginary. He recalled conversing with some of them when he was very young. Most were tiny, but Kyle recalled one in particular that had seemed like an absolute giant to a three year old. Nevertheless, the monster hadn't intimidated Kyle; rather, he recalled having a fast friendship with the beast he called Ron. That is, until he'd been forced to take pills that made Ron and all the little monsters go away. These days Kyle's only interest in them was for their artistic value — they made great subject matter for sketching.

With the defining features of the creature committed to his memory, Kyle's attention turned to the parcel in his hands. There was no postage stamp attached, no mailing address or sender's details.

All that was written upon it was 'Kyle'.

* * *

After consuming half a microwave pizza and a couple of cans of bourbon and coke, Kyle took up the joint he'd made while waiting for the food to cook. It was a large Bob Marley number, which he sniffed and rolled in his fingers like a fine cigar, before he placed it between his lips and struck up a light. Kyle puffed away merrily for a few moments, then, finding his inspiration, he took up his pad and pencil and began to sketch.

After a while, Kyle became aware that he was frowning; his head had shrunk into his shoulders and he was feeling genuinely agitated. 'Rap music,' he shuddered, hitting the off button on the television remote. As he looked around for the stereo remote, his eyes fell upon the brown paper parcel that he'd dropped in the other armchair on his way inside. 'Oh, yeah.' In his rush to get bent and sketch the critter while it was still fresh in his mind, Kyle had forgotten all about the package.

He reached for it and stripped away the soggy paper to find an old leather bound book in beautiful condition. Kyle's eyes lit up as he ran his fingers across its cover, for worked into the green leather were images of strange creatures and beings the like of which had plagued him as a youth.

'Righteous, man, this is cool.' He smiled briefly before searching for a card or note, but there was none. 'Only Matt knows about my Otherworldly interests.'

Matt knew Kyle liked to sketch weird creatures; he just didn't know Kyle saw them on a regular basis. Kyle hadn't risked telling *anyone* about them since his childhood. 'Has to be from him.' Kyle tossed the wet paper aside.

The title page nearly took Kyle's breath away: *Book of Dreams* it read, in an iridescent lettering that made the words appear to sink to an infinite depth. Around the lettering were depictions of the creatures that Kyle had drawn all his life. In fact, they were exactly the sketches that currently lined the walls of his house.

'This is impossible,' Kyle mumbled, raising the book to compare it with the images on his wall. The pictures were identical, although the size and colour differed. 'No way ... Matt couldn't have done this without me finding out. *No way*.' He sank onto the lounge, excited and spooked. Such moments of mystery were what made life worth living in Kyle's opinion, as it was with the unexplainable that he'd always felt most at home.

Turning over the cover of the book he encountered a blank first page. Flicking through all the pages, Kyle found they were blank. 'Must be a sketchbook,' he deduced, and the thought of filling the pages with images made him smile. He ran his fingers over the embossed leather cover as his eyelids began to droop.

A loud pounding on the door startled Kyle awake, and he sat up too quickly for his hangover. 'Ouch.' He refrained from further movement, to soothe his splitting headache, but as the pounding on the door only amplified the pain in his brain, Kyle rose to answer it. 'This had better be important, Matt.' He opened the door to find his friend positively beaming with excitement. 'You finally got laid?' Kyle took a guess as to the reason for his mate's good cheer.

'Better!' Matt played up the suspense as he backed Kyle out of the way and headed inside. 'I got a break,' he informed Kyle, once granted entry. 'It was like a gift from God or something!

I'm driving home through the city when I come across all these police cars, television crews and shit ... there's this big siege going on! A couple of police had been shot, along with a Channel Nine cameraman who got too close to the action. Risking life and limb, I helped pull the injured from danger.' Matt ducked and weaved as he spoke and then stopped to scratch his head. 'Well, actually, I rescued the camera. I wanted to check it out before they had a chance to reclaim it. There was so much going on that no one even noticed until it was all over.'

Kyle lost interest in Matt's tale and flopped back onto the lounge. 'Wow, amazing ... you got to hold a real camera. Whoopee!'

'I'm not finished yet.' Matt sat on the coffee table in front of Kyle. 'I placed the camera on my shoulder, to get a feel for it. And at that precise moment, the gunman exited the building with his hostage in tow and attempted to flee. I aimed the camera at him and kept rolling.' Matt paused and grinned. 'I got the morning lead and two hundred bucks cash ... the producer loved me for it!'

Kyle was astonished for a moment, but then his jealousy took hold. '*I don't believe it!* Why is everything so *easy* for you?' He stood to vent his frustration. 'You decide you want to be a current affairs cameraman and the next day you're shooting the lead story.'

'Yeah. What are the chances, eh?' Matt couldn't wipe the smile off his face; even he couldn't believe his luck in this instance. 'What's the time?' He noted the hour on the video player. 'My story should be on soon.' He switched on the television and searched for the right channel.

'You really shit me, you know that?' Kyle wandered into the kitchenette to make coffee.

'Yeah, I know,' Matt retorted, unfazed by Kyle's mood. 'I work really hard at it, too.'

As Kyle poured the coffee, he remembered the book that Matt had left on his doorstep and decided that he really couldn't continue in this disgruntled state. 'Thanks for the present, by the way. I gather I'm supposed to use it for sketching?'

'What present?' came Matt's reply. 'I haven't bought you anything. I've been saving all my spare funds to buy my own camera.'

Coffees in hand, Kyle returned to the lounge and handed a mug to Matt. 'You didn't send me that book?' Kyle pointed at the floor, where the gift had dropped from his lap the night before.

'What book?' Matt replied, as clearly there was nothing there.

'Where the hell is it?' Placing his mug on the table, Kyle got down on all fours to hunt up the missing article, tossing aside rubbish, scraps of paper and articles of clothing in his search. 'It was right here! I'm sure it was.'

'Forget it.' Matt directed Kyle to the news report on the television screen. 'Check this out.' He pumped up the volume to hear the newsman at the desk saying, 'The siege lasted most of last night, with five people injured, including one of our own cameramen. The gunman attempted to shoot his way out of the building at around twelve-thirty at night.'

The broadcast ran Matt's footage. A little shaky at first, the camera steadied to show a gunman running from the building with a hostage, shooting at police in his attempt to flee. The camera zoomed in on the gunman as police officers overpowered him and the hostage escaped unharmed.

'This footage was shot by a brave young passerby,' the voice-over continued, 'who pulled the camera out of the firing line and filmed these events as they unfolded around him.'

A shot of an exhilarated Matt being interviewed after the event came to the screen. 'I've wanted to shoot news for a long time,' he explained.

'A long time!' Kyle scoffed at the lie.

'I didn't have time to think about what was happening really. It just seemed like the natural thing to do.'

'You look like a total dork,' commented Kyle, inwardly green with jealousy, as he took a roach from the ashtray and lit it up.

'Now there's a young man with a big future ahead of him,' commented the newsman before moving on to the next story of the day.

Matt hadn't even heard Kyle's dig. He punched his mate on the shoulder, impressed with himself. 'Hear that?'

'Yeah, I heard.' Kyle offered the half a joint to Matt, who screwed up his face. 'I can't ... gotta stay alert. Some of the guys offered to show me round the station this morning.'

'Your loss.' Kyle dragged hard on the roach to hide his envy.

Matt shrugged rather than voice disagreement, and didn't comment on Kyle's obvious lack of excitement. 'Well, I gotta motor. I want to grab a shower and get cleaned up before I head down to the station.' He rose, while Kyle wreathed himself in a cloud of smoke. 'Wish me luck.' Matt fished his car keys from his back pocket and made for the door.

'Why?' Kyle retorted, raising himself from the lounge to see Matt out. 'You obviously don't need any. It's you who should be wishing me luck … I'm the one who's got to face the dole office today.'

'Oh, yeah.' Matt recalled Kyle had been fired the day before. 'Well, good luck.' He attempted a little good cheer.

As soon as he closed the door, Kyle regretted putting a downer on his friend's good news. 'Why can't I just be happy for him? At least one of us is making something of his life.' Deep down, his lack of purpose haunted him.

Everyone likes to think they are special, different from everyone else, but Kyle knew that he *was* different. He kept expecting that one day his purpose would be made known, and then his luck would change. Perhaps he'd find out that his father was a millionaire who'd been searching for his long-lost son for twenty years, or a secret service agent who'd been trapped in a foreign country, which would be acceptable too. 'Yeah right.' Kyle mocked his own delusions, and wandered back to the lounge room. 'He was a devil worshipper more like, and that's why I am constantly being confronted by creatures from —' Kyle was startled to find the missing book on the lounge room table. '. . . hell.'

His eyes drifted back to the front door. Was Matt playing a trick — could he have put the book there when he wasn't looking?

As Kyle's attention returned to the book, he noted it was open at the introduction. What had been a blank page the night before was now filled with text. 'Impossible,' he mumbled, circling the mysterious item at a distance. 'Am I losing my mind?' He considered this thought momentarily. 'I know I've always hated reading, but this is ridiculous!' He planted himself in front of the book to admire the amazing text. It was a veritable rainbow of colourful calligraphy, so original in its formation that one would have thought it handwritten, but the way the text glimmered and continually changed colour Kyle knew it couldn't possibly have come from any pen he had ever encountered. 'How could I have missed this?' He flicked through the pages, now all inscribed with the colourful text. 'All of it! I must have been gone!' With a shake of his head, he began to read.

We bid you welcome, young Kyle.

Taken aback at being addressed directly, Kyle paused a second and then decided, 'Hey, nice touch.'

It has been brought to our attention that you seem to be completely lost. If you wish to come to know what it is that constantly eludes you in life ... I am your transport to seek within.

'Matt, you ham, this has to be you.' Kyle recalled their deep talk about the psyche the previous evening, and Matt had heard plenty of the same from Kyle on the numerous occasions they'd got totalled together. Perhaps Matt had pre-empted Kyle's need to read a book on psychological development?

Kyle reached for a warm, half empty bottle of Pepsi and took a swig before taking the book in hand to read on.

However, the journey in your case will not be an easy one and I think it only fair to warn you that there is no turning back. Once you have begun such a quest, to turn back, or QUIT, would forfeit any chance you will ever have of making something of yourself. Do you accept these terms?

Suddenly, the tone of the narrative was not really akin to Matt's style any more, Kyle considered, and with this observation the words, 'Do you accept these terms?', turned the colour of deepest violet and held Kyle's attention.

He was considering the question seriously, when a ripple travelled through the leather cover in his hands. 'What the —'

The movement prompted Kyle to cast the book on to the table. 'What's going on?' He wiped his hands down his shirt, deciding he must be imagining things.

Kyle did not take the book back in hand, instead he cautiously leant forward to read on.

You speak English, don't you? What is there not to understand? the text replied. *Either you don't feel you're up to the task, or you've decided it's time to make something of yourself. In which case, turn to the next page and start to read. Now, if your consciousness can cope with that, which is it? WE'RE WAITING!*

The book rose from the table as the rippling motion moved through the cover once more.

Kyle swallowed hard, stunned beyond rational thought. Nothing of such an extraordinary nature had happened to him in many a year and he was digging the intrigue. Yet, this extrasensory sight he'd always had was a curse: it set him apart from other people and often put him directly at odds with others. Was this instance going to prove any different?

'Hell, I don't think I can get in any more trouble than I have of late,' he reasoned with himself as he carefully took the book up and placed it in his lap. The words, WE'RE WAITING, undulated with great intensity as he followed the urge to reach out and turn the page.

There was a chilling movement in the cover once more and flipping the book over Kyle witnessed the creatures embossed in the leather turning to fur, feathers, scales and skin. Kyle sprang from the lounge and the book was tossed, cover up, onto the coffee table. The small beasts emerged and began to scamper, fly, crawl and slither about the room. But then Kyle noticed a much greater anomaly.

His own body was seated on the lounge engrossed in reading the book and appeared completely unaware of the commotion unfolding around him.

'I can't be dead,' Kyle reasoned from a standing position beside himself whilst he curiously eyed his seated body. 'Dead men don't read.' He looked down to discover that the body he was doing the observing from was slightly more transparent and colourless than his ignorant body-double on the lounge. 'This can't be good.'

The little creatures were making an awful racket as they explored the room, now interpenetrated by a vibrant ultra-green glow. On the coffee table sat the faintly illumed, plain leather copy of the book that the creatures had escaped from.

'You'll probably wish you were dead before Book gets through with you.' The little creature that had guarded the parcel the night before took up a position on the coffee table. It had a gruff voice and the other wee creatures all stopped still at its words. 'We are here to guide you in!'

'In?' Kyle found his voice.

With a nervous chuckle from all the creatures, the spokescritter pointed its spear towards the bathroom door. Slowly the door opened to disclose a dense red mist beyond.

Kyle's body was heard to laugh; he glanced at the bathroom door, and spying nothing out of the usual turned his attention back to the book he was reading.

The little creatures scampered for the door, urging Kyle after them.

'This is mad.' Kyle looked at the creature in charge, which had jumped from the table and was making for the door.

The wee beast halted, looking back at Kyle before directing him to the copy of the book on the table. 'Bring him,' it instructed.

'Him?' As he retrieved it Kyle wondered why the book had a gender. He would have asked the creature but it had disappeared into the red void that lay beyond Kyle's bathroom door. As keen for the adventure as he was, there was a forbidding vibe about the red haze that was now fast filling his lounge room and obscuring the ultra-green glow that interpenetrated all the physical world matter around him. 'I know.' Kyle smiled as the obvious solution came to mind. He opened the book to find his place. 'So, what's in the bathroom?' he mumbled as he scanned through the text.

Your unconscious soul.

Kyle's eyes parted wide with wonder as, in his mind, a male voice answered.

Everything that you ever wanted, or didn't want, to know about yourself!

'No need for a bookmark then.' Kyle closed the book, finding the telepathic communication strange but convenient. The threatening void beyond the bathroom doorway seemed to be gaining in intensity and a stormy atmosphere whipped around Kyle and drew him in. 'I'm dreaming, right?'

In a way. But just give the word and you can be back on the lounge with an empty book. Past this point, you must find what you seek. There is no other way back.

'Back from where?' Kyle appealed, struggling against the force. 'From inside myself, where I should be right now? This is insane!'

Make the commitment, or step back.

Put that way, Kyle swallowed his fear and inched forward to enter the red haze.

When the door slammed closed behind him, the floor ceased to be and Kyle found himself plummeting into a red abyss.

'Ahhhh!' Kyle yelled until he grew tired of it — the fall seemed to go on for an eternity. He could hear the chuckles and chattering of the little creatures which had led him into this peril, but they were nowhere to be seen. Not that Kyle was brave enough to open his eyes for very long — the tumbling fall was making him sick, and dislodged by the high spin the book slipped from his grasp.

'No!' Kyle was still yelling when he realised the falling sensation had ceased and he was standing safely on the ground. To hide how cowardly he felt, he dusted himself off and took a look around. He was in the middle of what could only be described as a dead zone.

Parched cracks in the red earth met to form large mounds on the surface. All the plants and trees within eyeshot were dead, charred or rotting. A nearby waterhole was filled with a colourful mix of red and green and black slimy algae, which bubbled now and then within the parched earth banks. The sky above was a mixture of red and grey smog, and an atmosphere of doom hung over the place, with a dark haze making visibility difficult.

Spying the book on the ground nearby, Kyle walked over and reclaimed it. 'Well, Book, I have to tell you ...' He brushed and blew away the excess red dust that had settled all over the cover, '... this is not what I expected my unconscious soul to look like.'

This is just a small part, coughed the book. *The highest sphere of your lower etheric world. That is ... the place in every human being where the lowest experiences gather.*

That's when Kyle noted the horrible odour and held his nose in an attempt to escape it. 'Sure smells bad.'

Human waste products — viruses, impurities and vices — merge to create the demonic entities that inhabit this place, feeding off their own excretions and the fear, guilt and hate built up over human history. It never used to be this bad, but it has become much worse lately.

The eerie groans and screeches of the inhabitants began to filter through to Kyle, and he lowered his voice to avoid attracting any unwanted attention. 'So why are we here?'

'Because you seem to like it here.'

Kyle was stunned by the comeback, as it was not the inner voice of the book that answered him, but a gruff, high-pitched voice that was external in origin.

'Take a look around you, young Kyle ... every negative thought, action and word that you draw from this wretched place returns here tenfold!'

Kyle was wondering about the unseen entity addressing him. Was it God? Was it the devil? Kyle didn't mind which as he didn't believe in either of them. And if it turned out that he was wrong about their existence, Kyle had a few bones to pick with both of them.

'Your bad habits and addictions feed the inhabitants here and your negative ego thrives on the stimuli of this place and its creatures.'

'So, scaring the shit out of me is going to somehow rectify this situation, is it?' Kyle clenched the book closer to his chest, but it seemed his guide had gone quiet.

Then a little green creature, with eyes that sparkled every colour of the rainbow, appeared. He was floating in midair, only inches from Kyle's face. 'You were never meant to be part of the problem!'

Kyle jumped back from the creature, which was reptilian in appearance. It had small, clawed hands and feet, and spikes that ran the length of its spine and continued down its long tail.

'You were to be the solution,' the strange floating creature concluded.

What Crystaleyes is trying to say is that what manifests here, just one stage behind your own world, will surely manifest there as well and has begun to already.

Kyle's attention did not shift from the floating green creature, which had slowly drifted backwards, and they were now eyeballing each other with interest.

'He's not at all what I expected.' Crystaleyes sounded rather disappointed. 'His subtle bodies are awash with the black haze of his addictions and fear. He has yet to even master his densest body, let alone the others.'

'What others?' Kyle wondered out loud. 'Just how many bodies do you think I have?'

This single manifestation of you has a physical body, which is the one you left behind, Book explained, *an etheric body, which is the vehicle you are functioning in at present, an astral or emotional body, a mental body, a causal being, a spiritual being, a monadic being and a universal consciousness.*

Kyle's mouth was left gaping. He had no idea what Book was on about. 'Intense.'

'And you have yet to master even the lowest of these,' Crystaleyes pointed out, shaking his head in concern. 'There's little of his parents in him.'

'My parents!' Kyle was taken aback by the mention of them.

More than you think, my good friend. Book ignored Kyle. *Although it took desperate measures to get his attention, I'm quite confident we can make something of him.*

Crystaleyes grunted, unconvinced. 'That would take a lot of work indeed, and more willpower than this one has.'

Kyle was beginning to lose patience with being ignored. 'Look, this is my subconscious experience, so don't speak like I'm not here.'

Upon Kyle venting his anger, the ground underfoot erupted, tipping over the few trees that had been left standing. The waterhole nearby bubbled as it was fed by the ill will, and the red mist thickened. After a moment the tremor passed away.

Now that Kyle had a clear fix on his situation, he decided against pursuing his protest. He looked at Crystaleyes apologetically as the creature floated closer to him, grinning.

'How right you are, Kyle. This,' Crystaleyes held his arms wide, 'is your subconscious experience ... and if you do not pay attention to what we are telling you, you will never transcend this hopeless consequence.'

Kyle was not keen on this arrangement and was about to voice his disapproval when a tremor built at his very thought.

Kyle, I must tell you that you are only denying yourself if you do not listen, Book advised kindly. *Air, Earth, Water and Fire are the four elements that make up your nature; all nature for that matter. Crystaleyes, for you, is all in your character that can be attributed to the element of Earth.*

Kyle's mind boggled at the news.

His Earth elemental, however, wore a smug, albeit grave, expression. 'You understand now that it has been *you* ignoring me ... since the day you were born, in fact! *Hard work, patience, good health, practicality* — none of my good traits have you shown.' Crystaleyes was now far more agitated than Kyle, but the ill will did not stir the surrounding area and Kyle thought this unfair. 'In spite of this, Book seems to have faith in you, so I will *try* to assist you one last time, and you can make of my guidance what you will.'

As the sound of the local inhabitants seemed to be approaching him, Kyle decided he really didn't have too much choice in the matter and so nodded to give Crystaleyes the go ahead.

'My advice to you is this ... although you are hopelessly lost and have seemingly little potential,' Crystaleyes floated down to the ground and picked up a charred piece of rock, holding it out for Kyle to view, 'if you can let go of your hate and fear, there is nothing in the universe that is not at your disposal here in the subconscious world.' The creature rubbed the rock with intense speed between his tiny claw-like hands, whereupon he produced a crystal ball. 'Here, willpower governs all. Anything is possible provided you are clear about what you want.' The Earth elemental tossed the crystal ball to Kyle and with a grin it disappeared.

'Thanks, but what if I don't know what I want?' Kyle looked about him, hoping the nasty little creature hadn't gone.

'This is your dream time,' Crystaleyes' voice called from beyond the mist. 'Use your imagination!'

CHAPTER
FOUR

CHAPTER

RAISING CONSCIOUSNESS

The crystal ball held Kyle's attention until the eerie chuckles and screeches of the local inhabitants snatched his focus; he was immediately very aware of being alone. His eyes darted about in search of company, but the red mist had grown too thick. 'So now what?' he said quietly to Book.

'Wanna smoke?' It was a puny, grey excuse for a devilish creature that strode forward out of the red haze. It stood just under a metre tall and was puffing madly on a huge joint. 'It's real good stuff.' It coughed to confirm its claim. 'Or perhaps a cone is more the order of the moment?' It pulled a large bong from midair. 'It's packed nice and tight, just the way you like it.'

'Book?' Kyle queried, but again his guide was out to lunch.

'Aw,' the creature waved off Kyle's concern, 'Book won't want any, the bloody goody-goody,' it advised, holding the joint out to Kyle in offering. 'But you ... *well*,' it emphasised, motioning to their surroundings, 'I know how you like a good smoke and, hey ... you don't have anything better to do now, do you?'

'Um?' Kyle frowned, for he could hear someone crying in the distance. 'Is someone in trouble?'

'How about a bourbon?' This demon was a deep shade of brown and had a great tyre of flab around its middle that wobbled as it staggered about. It popped onto Kyle's shoulder to offer a full bottle to him. 'It's well aged, the kind of drink you only dream about.'

Kyle shook the creature off and it landed on the ground beside the grey devil. 'Careful, you nearly spilt the booze!' It stumbled up to standing. 'What's the matter? Don't you want to party?' The demon attempted to do a little dance and fell over, which amused the grey demon no end.

'Party! Did I hear someone say party?' A third demon, red in colour and very overweight, entered the scene towing a cart piled high with junk food. It was munching on a burger and literally oozed grease through its pores. 'What's your pleasure, treasure? Pizza, burger? How about some fries?'

The crying was getting louder; it sounded like someone, or something, was in real torment. 'Who is that?'

'What the fuck do you care?' A green devil appeared on Kyle's shoulder. 'You got conned into this ridiculous quest with no idea what you were up against. So, fuck 'em!' This devil had wings and took to the air to flutter in front of Kyle's face before Kyle had the chance to shake it off. 'Nobody gives a toss about you, my friend, except us. You know it, I know it, they know it.' It motioned to its associates.

Kyle was starting to feel flustered, and the dope and pizza smelt really good.

'In times of trouble who was there for you? Not those fucking guides of yours, that's for sure! All they ever managed to do is land you in the shithouse ... remember?' The green cursing devil grabbed the bottle off its boozing mate.

'Hey,' the inebriated devil objected.

'Save some for the kid.' The winged demon held out the bottle to Kyle and served him a wink of encouragement. 'There's only one place you've ever felt good about yourself and that was right here with us. Go on, you know you want it.'

Kyle reached out to accept the bottle, but in his hand was the crystal ball that Crystaleyes had given him.

He has yet to even master his physical body, let alone the others,' Crystaleyes had said.

Kyle quickly withdrew his hand. 'Oh, I get it.'

'What is there to get?' The flying demon took to the air to be in Kyle's face again. 'Everything you've ever desired is right here.'

'I don't think so.' Kyle's resolve hardened and so did the attitude of his demons. 'I'm pretty sure that it will never be my dream to be sick, fat, bitter and twisted!'

'Look, you bloody ingrate ...' The flying devil lost his patience and the other three began to close in on Kyle. 'You can't just dump us. We are the very fabric of your existence. Where would you be without us? On medication or in a mental asylum, that's where!'

'What is there to look forward to in life without your next fix?' The grey elemental appeared on Kyle's shoulder to resume the debate by blowing the dope smoke in his face. 'I've seen you go cold turkey and it's not a pretty picture.'

'Did you say Wild Turkey?' The brown elemental appeared on Kyle's other shoulder, waving a hip flask in his face. 'Sure thing, we have everything here.'

'Get off me!' Kyle shook the demons from his person and the earth began to tremble deep and loud.

'Oh yeah, we love a bad temper,' chuckled the flying demon, as it increased in size and strength. 'It always makes you crave a little something to settle the nerves.'

It was true, Kyle did use his vices to control his angry streak. What else could do that?

Try the thought of something or someone you care about, suggested Book.

Matt's infectious laughter began echoing through Kyle's brain, and the recollection of his mate seized with laughter dispersed Kyle's bad mood. As he calmed, the surrounding environment stabilised too. 'Thanks, guys, for all the parties, but after seeing what it has done for you, I think I'll take my chances on the straight and narrow.' Kyle looked at the crystal ball, realising the crying was coming from within the ball.

'We're losing him.' The flying demon encouraged his mates to be more persuasive.

'Thai stick? Mowee-wowee?' offered the grey demon.

'No.' Kyle focused on the ball.

'Super supreme pizza? Large burger?' The greasy red demon brought forth his tray of goodies. 'How about some *chocolate*, or some potato chips?'

Inside the crystal ball, the distant vision of a beautiful beach became visible: the sand, the sea, the rocks, all sparkling blue, as if illumined by very bright moonlight.

'You don't want to go there.' The flying demon attempted to break Kyle's concentration. 'It will be hard work, tears, the purging of

emotions and facing the horrors of your past ...
you're not up to it. Not to mention education.
You know how you despise books!'

'I *used* to hate books,' Kyle corrected,
patting the book that was slung under his arm.

Kyle considered himself a great judge of
character, and although he hadn't been reading
this one for very long, it already felt like an old
friend.

The crystal ball became the focus of all
Kyle's attention and the world of red haze and
demons faded back into the depths of his
subconscious. A brief, disorientating, soaring
sensation ensued as the vision of the beach
seemed to bleed through Kyle's nightmare and
wash it away.

It was not moonlight that lit this place, but a
beautiful blue glow that radiated from within
the landscape: the sea, sand, trees, rocks and
vegetation were connected by each other's
light-filled energy emissions. This mystical
emanation then rose in a great mist towards
the heavens, which were shrouded from view
by the light-filled clouds.

Kyle looked down at himself and was

bemused to find that he didn't seem to be contributing to this great symphony of light, colour and energy. His etheric body was awash with dark, murky colours that dulled his illumination. Nature was extending Kyle its energy: from everywhere the light force extended towards his body, but once absorbed by his murky aura it seemed to vanish into a void. 'I'm sucking energy,' Kyle observed, a mite distraught about the fact, 'and I don't glow.'

Right on both counts, Book retorted in all seriousness. *Mother nature is used to being sucked dry by human beings, and yet she continues to replenish your energies, cleanse your spirit and nurture her spawn. She knew what she was taking on when she agreed to play parent to mankind. You'll start to feel her healing soon.*

The smells of the beach were far more potent suddenly, and there was no pollution to detract from the seaside scents. 'What is this place, Book?'

Your consciousness has taken a great leap up to an astral awareness. Book sounded rather wary. *And when I say a great leap, I mean vast! This is the part of you where deep-seated emotions and desires are stored.*

'Well, this is sure as hell going to be easier to cope with than where I was.' Kyle had decided that Book was being overly dramatic, when the sound of sobbing drew his attention to an uncomfortably large, fur-covered beast, which was seated on the sand not far down the beach. 'I could be wrong about that, of course,' whispered Kyle, ducking behind a rock.

There's no need for you to be afraid. Book sounded surprised. *Don't you recognise your own guardian?*

Kyle's eyes opened wide in astonishment at the news. Then, as the beast let loose a very loud howl, Kyle was forced to block his ears. 'Isn't a guardian supposed to be an angel or something?'

Not where you come from.

Kyle was struck by the comment. 'You know where I come from?'

Soon you will learn all that I know of you … all you have to do is keep your promise to me.

'Goddamn.' Kyle, unable to stand the wailing any longer, stepped out from behind his cover. 'What is wrong with him?' But with a second look at the enormous beast he thought twice about approaching it. 'Are you quite sure about this, Book?' Although he uttered his query softly, it seemed it wasn't soft enough. The monster stirred and its sobbing ceased.

It growled deeply, as, due to a neck that was virtually non-existent, the beast was forced to turn its large body around to view Kyle. The legs of the monster were longer than a human's; it rose up on its hind legs to stand about three metres tall. Long shaggy fur of a deep reddish-brown colour covered the entire body and its extraordinarily long arms hung all the way to mid-thigh; the nails of its four fingers were like the talons of a great bird of prey. The beast had a sloping forehead and a flat, black, wrinkled face inset with eyes like deep black bubbles. Saliva dripped from the fanged jaws of the animal as it released an almighty roar.

'Book?' Kyle backed up a few paces, holding Book in front of his face to protect himself from the force of flying sand and saliva. Then the monster fell silent. Kyle lowered his defences to find the monster had calmed down and was looking at him inquisitively.

The beast shuffled towards Kyle, who stayed perfectly still, figuring there was little point in trying to flee. 'Kyle? Is that you?' it queried, in a deep, heartfelt voice. 'Don't you know me?'

As the monster leaned his face close to Kyle, its tears welling anew, Kyle was astonished to find that he did recognise the creature. 'Ron?'

The beast nodded, tears of joy spurting from its eyes. 'That's what you used to call me when you were a little tyke,' it sniffled. 'You couldn't say Kyron.' The big woolly critter was overwhelmed with excitement and lifted Kyle into the air to swing him about as though he was still a young child.

Kyle was a bit alarmed by this, though he couldn't help but share the beast's excitement.

'I thought I'd lost you forever!' Kyron jumped for joy, crashing back to the ground with an almighty thud.

'My foster parents made me think I'd gone insane,' Kyle told Ron, and let out a relieved laugh, 'but finding you would seem to indicate that I was right all along … I am special.'

'Yes, you are,' said Kyron. 'It has been so sad watching you grow up unaware of your calling and thinking that you were all alone.'

'You know my calling?' Kyle nearly choked trying to get the question out.

'Sure.' The big beast shrugged. 'You're a warrior of the Great Spirit.'

'The Great Spirit?'

'The guardian of the land,' Kyron explained, as if this went without saying.

'The land?'

'The land of your people!' Kyron sounded distressed.

'My people?' Kyle's tone dripped with scepticism.

Kyron lowered Kyle to the ground and let him go. The big guy was in a state of shock. 'He doesn't remember anything I taught him.'

The medication did its work well, Kyron. It was not a failing on your behalf or Kyle's, Book reassured the creature, hoping to prevent another sobbing fit. *We've no time to waste on regrets as we must teach him again from scratch ... we shall make him remember everything and more.*

Kyle's heart went out to the beast, but he didn't know what to say. 'I remember little bits.'

Kyron planted his big furry butt on the ground, overwhelmed by the task ahead.

You need a good challenge, Kyron, Book encouraged. *You see, Kyle, one of the reasons*

Kyron is your guardian is that he has a great fear of the first plane, your present home. So while he protects you, he must also learn from you, but when you feel worthless and weak, so does he.

Kyle placed a hand on the great beast's shoulder, empathising with him. 'Look, Kyron ... I need you, buddy. If only to figure out what the hell you're both on about.'

Kyron raised his miserable sights to look at Kyle, a glimmer of hope in his eyes. 'Buddy?'

Kyle smiled. 'You betcha. We —'

At that moment, a great bubbling sound erupted, which Kyle pinpointed as coming from one of the larger rock pools in front of the huge cliff that towered over one end of the beach.

A strange blue man rose out of the bubbling, turbulent water. His skinny little body was almost non-existent compared to his oversized hands, feet and head. His round face reflected the look of some of the Indigenous people of Australia, with wide dark eyes and a mass of dark curly hair.

'You wanna know more about where you're at? Then talk to me.' The man's voice had a strong Aboriginal accent as he stood on the water to address them. 'This is the home of your emotional body. Love, desire, your deepest emotions and aspirations are all around you here ... do you feel it flowing through you?'

In a gesture of sarcasm Kyle looked down at himself ... and noted that the murky patches that had been stifling his illumination were fading, and he had started to emit the same blue glow as everything around him. 'Will you look at that!'

'We are one.' Blue gazed mysteriously around him before looking at Kyle once more. 'You cannot hide anything from us.'

Curious, Kyle wanted to approach the blue being, but Kyron held him back.

'He is an undine, a water spirit,' the huge beast warned.

What Kyron means to say, Book added, *is don't take anything Blue has to say too lightly ... it's easy to drown in your own emotions.*

'It's cool.' Kyle passed Book to Kyron. 'I've never been a very emotional kind of person.' Kyle confidently strode towards Blue, until the being motioned with his hand for Kyle to halt and Kyle obliged the little fellow. Blue held out his large webbed fingers towards Kyle and concentrated very intently upon him. 'So what is on your mind, young warrior?'

Kyle wondered what the being was playing at, but was not given time to ask.

'Aahh ...!' Blue announced, enlightened, whereupon he turned his focus from Kyle to an area beside the young man.

Kyle looked where Blue directed, to see a glowing white image manifesting. Soon the vision took a female form and the spirit of Zoe stood silently beside him wearing a welcoming smile. Kyle was confused and perturbed by the appearance.

'Ooh! It's her.' Kyron, sounding lovestruck, ventured closer. 'We like her.'

'No, we don't!' Kyle protested strongly, looking to Blue for an explanation. 'What's she doing here? Little Miss Privileged has nothing to do with me.'

Blue folded his arms, appearing smug, and somewhat insulted. 'Shows what you know. Think you know everything, do you? Well, I could show you a truth or two ... *young* warrior. Come and look into my pool.' Blue stepped off the water on to the rocks. He bowed to Kyle and motioned him towards the pool with a large cheesy smile. 'If you dare.'

Kyle was apprehensive, but with all this talk of him being a warrior, he was not about to turn down the challenge. He gazed back at Kyron, who looked worried, then to Zoe, who only smiled, and then to Blue still grinning broadly in invitation.

Kyle stepped up to the edge of the pool and gazed into it. 'So what's in here?'

'I told you — the truth,' Blue replied. 'But you must stand in the middle of the pool if you wish to see it.'

Kyle did not trust this character. Still, if Blue was his water elemental, as Crystaleyes was his earth aspect, then not trusting Blue was the same as not trusting his own emotions. Kyle thrust his hand into the pocket containing the crystal ball his earth element had given him and recalled the counsel of Crystaleyes. 'Anything is possible here, right? No fear.'

Kyle stepped slowly on to the water, and shifted his weight gradually to discover that his feet did not break the surface. 'Wow,' he exclaimed, completely stoked with himself as he took another step towards the middle. 'Hey, check this out, I'm doing it,' he commented to the others, before looking down into the water below his feet. As his gaze fixed on the glowing surface of the pool, it gave beneath him and with a yell Kyle was swallowed up by the watery hole.

Blue slapped his knee and burst into hysterical laughter. '*Humans*, they're so gullible.'

Kyron was not amused and let out a growl of objection.

'He's okay.' Blue attempted to catch his breath, and he motioned for the huge beast to relax. 'I'm not going to drown him ... not physically anyway. He'll be back presently.'

Kyron, still disenchanted by the trick, backed down when Zoe laid a hand on his shoulder in quiet reassurance and they sat together to await Kyle's return.

Despite trying hard to surface, Kyle just sank deeper and deeper into the undine's underwater realm. He was panicking; although he'd always been a strong swimmer, he knew that he was soon going to run out of breath. When at last he was forced to release the stale air in his lungs, fully expecting them to fill with water with his next inhalation, Kyle was shocked to find they did not. He had no difficulty breathing, yet there were no bubbles as he did. He did not even feel wet, although he was definitely underwater.

Could it be that the body I left behind on the lounge is doing the breathing for me? And that these experiences are more or less a dream? The title of the book he'd left himself reading suddenly took on a new meaning.

Kyle stopped fighting his predicament and began to float calmly, enjoying the weightlessness of his descent. The pool had widened into a vast space and Kyle heard distant voices united in a chant.

As it was above the water, everything below the surface radiated a blue energy that enhanced the natural colour of the fish, coral and rocks to the point of luminescence.

Watching several schools of brightly coloured fish swim by him, Kyle realised this was the most blissful experience he'd ever had, until he noticed that a dolphin, a shark, a stingray and a killer whale were coming straight towards him from the glowing blue depths. The four of them were swimming in a perfect diamond formation.

Fear besieged Kyle's being, even though common sense told him that there could be no such creatures in the pool he'd fallen into, and that this particular selection of sea creatures did not usually engage together in formation swimming.

He had to be dreaming; this whole adventure was a dream.

As the sea creatures came close enough to be threatening, they began to transform into four breathtakingly beautiful mermaids, who swam around blowing him kisses as they admired his form.

Kyle couldn't help but smile broadly at this development. *It's confirmed. I'm definitely dreaming!*

The mermaids spun Kyle around to face the shark nymph with her long ash-blonde hair and eyes like dead, dark pools. Of the four, she had the smallest breasts, for nurture was not her first calling. She drew Kyle's body in close to her and kissed him hard and long.

Naturally, Kyle was not about to complain,

but the attack on his senses was suffocating him. His head started spinning and he felt that he might black out. He struggled to free himself from the shark spirit, but she held him fast and seemed to be tearing along through the water with him. He couldn't open his eyes as the speed prevented it.

Suddenly the pressure ebbed. Kyle opened his eyes to find he was flying — soaring beneath a clear night sky filled with stars. His focus drifted downward to a large and very grand house. Two people, a man and a woman, were exiting the front door, and Kyle swooped down to gain a closer perspective.

They looked like nice people ... and rich! The kind of parents Kyle had always dreamed of having. They were dressed up for a formal engagement and were in good cheer.

His perspective drifted backwards and upwards for a broader perspective of the couple as they strolled arm in arm into the separate dwelling that housed their cars.

Soon, the automatic door on the garage opened. The luxury car within exploded upon ignition, blowing the garage door halfway across the property, ahead of much flying debris and a fireball that engulfed Kyle's consciousness.

Kyle was only momentarily alarmed at being consumed by fire; the only heat he felt was the flush in his cheeks as he was released by the shark spirit and spun around to face the sandy-blonde, blue-eyed dolphin nymph.

After his last experience of being kissed, Kyle attempted to back away, but the other three nymphs had a good hold on him.

The dolphin spirit's smile was very enchanting, however. Ever so gently she took his face in both her hands and drew his mouth to hers.

Her kiss felt like cruising through the water and diving over waves on a warm sunny day. His heart was doing backflips as his mind and senses were drawn into her dreaming, and his sight became shrouded by darkness for a time. The chant that Kyle had been hearing from afar since he'd fallen in the pool, suddenly became much louder.

Sight restored, Kyle found himself soaring through a clear night sky, full moon glowing. Below was a bonfire, around which a gathering of Indigenous Australian people danced and chanted. The moon's reflection glimmered brightly in a large body of water, fed by a waterfall, in close proximity to where the ritual was being held.

One young couple standing on the outskirts of the gathering captured Kyle's interest. The woman might have been part-Indigenous and was heavy with child. The man with his arms around her swollen belly was the only white person present, so the pair seemed out of place. Just like the couple Kyle had seen during his shark dreaming, they appeared to be young and in love, and he hoped that he wasn't about to witness another grisly disaster.

This fear made Kyle turn away to look over the whole gathering. He felt strangely aroused by the chant and the music of the rhythm sticks and the didgeridoo. He'd never met an Indigenous Australian in his life, nor wondered about their beliefs. *Your people,* Kyron had said. Had he been referring to the Indigenous people of Australia?

From within the huge bonfire a strange mist began to rise and dance over the gathering. Like a snake being charmed it wound its way across the gathering until it came to hover over the pregnant woman.

Two helicopters rose above a nearby hill and headed towards the gathering, searchlights blazing, and a voice on loudspeaker warned the crowd to disperse, because they were trespassing on private property. On the ground, police began to emerge from the bush surrounding the clearing to converge on the crowd.

When Kyle's attention was drawn back to the anomalous mist, it was gone. The young woman was gripping her belly in pain and as she pushed her partner away, Kyle willed himself closer.

'Go,' she urged. 'If they get their hands on you, they will lock you up and throw away the key ... never mind if you're guilty or not.'

'Not like this, Alex. Not now!' he argued, referring to her contractions. 'You need me at the birth. I'm getting you to a hospital.'

Alex, suppressing her own pain, grabbed hold of his shirt to insist. 'We need you free! You're no good to anyone rotting in jail.' She kissed him and thrust him away. 'Now go!'

A couple of the men grabbed the reluctant male and hurried him off towards the water, gagging the fellow to silence his protests.

Others of the group gathered around the pregnant woman to comfort and aid her, until they were all overpowered by the police and carted away.

'What the hell are you doing here?' the policeman wondered of the heavily pregnant woman, who did not really look as though she belonged to the clan. 'A woman in your condition would be far better off at home.'

'This *is* my home,' she told him defiantly.

'Well, Nivok Industries disagrees with you.' He dragged her to her feet. 'Save it for the judge.'

Kyle had never, in living memory, so strongly wanted to accompany someone, and yet he felt himself being drawn back to his dream weavers. He resisted their summons, straining with all his will, but it was no use: Kyle was forced to turn.

It was a beautiful black-haired, dark-skinned nymph in front of Kyle now. Her blazing green eyes glared at him sternly as she gripped his jaw firmly in one hand. What sea creature had this mermaid been associated with? He couldn't recall.

Her kiss was paralysing, and Kyle completely lost control over his body. Darkness descended as he drifted to the sea floor and buried himself in the sand.

The stingray, Kyle concluded, as he warily awaited her vision. *What kind of tragedy can she conjure up for my viewing horror?*

James Nivok's office was not exactly where Kyle had expected to find himself.

He was alarmed to see Zoe being confronted by her uncle, who was very angry with her.

'Why was he in here?' Nivok demanded to know. 'You've got an apartment if you want to play with your boyfriends.' He cocked an eyebrow in suspicion. 'Are you covering for him?'

'Please, uncle … I told you,' she appealed to him, obviously unaccustomed to seeing her uncle so riled. 'He said he had to clean —'

Nivok's patience snapped. He cut her explanation short with a sharp slap to her cheek, which was hard enough to tip Zoe off balance.

Kyle wanted to intervene, but he was rooted to the spot, forced to witness the consequences of the trouble he'd caused. *Your uncle isn't going to punish you for tonight's little episode.*

You don't even know the meaning of the word punishment. His cruel words to Zoe came back to haunt him and his heart began to ache. He'd never before felt deep remorse for his actions, and it hurt ... a lot.

Zoe held her hand to her face, shocked. She turned her eyes, now full of contempt, back to her uncle and regarded him as if he were a stranger.

It seemed that even James Nivok was surprised by his harsh reaction and apparently stricken with guilt. His anger fled and he moved to reassure his niece. 'I've been under so much stress and now I'm taking it out on you.' He placed an arm about her shoulder and gave her a squeeze. 'I've never before struck you. Please forgive me.'

Zoe was in shock for a moment. The only person she had ever really trusted, the one mainstay in her life, had just turned on her. Now she'd seen a side of her uncle that she'd never imagined existed and that lifetime of trust had been shattered. 'I never wanted this job.' Zoe pulled away from her uncle.

'I had to know for sure if you were interested in the business,' Nivok explained.

'After all, your parents have left you two-thirds of it and I don't want you to sell unless you're sure —'

'Nothing you could say or do is going to keep me in this place.' Zoe walked over to the lounge to retrieve her handbag. 'I've got my own plans.'

As Zoe stormed from the office, Nivok smiled broadly.

The feeling returned to his limbs and the heavy, buried sensation lifted, but Kyle felt as if he'd been battered to a pulp, emotionally. Guilt, confusion, distress and many questions warred in his mind, not the least of which was: What's next?

Please ... I don't think I can take any more. His body was still being supported in the water by the nymphs and when he felt his chin being raised, Kyle opened his eyes.

A milky-white-skinned beauty with long black hair, streaked with white, and deep brown eyes, was confronting him and she had the largest breasts Kyle had ever seen.

Aware of his exhaustion, the whale nymph brought Kyle's head to rest on her bosom and gently stroked his hair as she lulled him into a false sense of security.

The next thing Kyle knew, she had rolled on top of him and proceeded to plough through the water with him. He felt like the attacker and the attacked, the victim and the hero, the wise man and the fool.

Night had fallen since his last visit, but Kyle was back in Nivok's office.

Does my entire life revolve around this room? he protested, praying he hadn't gotten Zoe into any more trouble.

But it was Matt and not Zoe who greeted him this time.

Where have you been? In his mind, Kyle heard Matt's voice, but the presence of Matt he was viewing did not speak.

He was standing in the doorway of Nivok's office, raising a camera to his shoulder.

What are you up to now? Kyle turned to see what Matt was filming, but the room was filled with smoke; water began teeming from the ceiling, and Kyle could not see if anyone else was present.

Then his perception shifted into slow motion. A bullet shot forth out of the haze and water. It flew past Kyle to hit Matt in the stomach, sending him hurtling to the ground.

'*No!*' Kyle yelled into the ensuing darkness, his heart thumping ten to the dozen in his chest.

'Kyle, you're back,' Kyron spoke to make his charge aware of his surroundings. 'Are you all right?'

When Kyle saw that he was standing on the surface of the pool, he moved to the sand; he didn't want to risk falling victim to the Pool of Truths again. 'Physically, I'm fine. Emotionally ...' Kyle glanced at Blue, 'I don't think I'm doing so well.' He did feel calmer now that he'd been released by the water nymphs, but, rattled by all that they had revealed to him, Kyle took a seat on the sand to collect his thoughts.

Kyron, and Zoe's astral form, were very concerned for him, but it was Blue who spoke first. 'So ... what did you make of your dreaming, young warrior?'

'That was more than a dream,' Kyle insisted.

'And what are dreams but subconscious realities?' Blue posed.

It had been a very long time since Kyle had

had to deal with that mysterious, buried side of his personality that felt and questioned and wondered. He barely knew where to begin with his dream analysis. 'You spoke of my people earlier.' He looked at his big, furry guardian. 'Are they Indigenous Australians?'

Kyron nodded, unsure of how Kyle would react to the news.

This explained a lot and Kyle bowed his head to shed a tear, for he knew he had glimpsed his parents in the dream of the dolphin nymph. 'I have a whole extended family in far north Queensland somewhere?' He tried to breathe through all the mixed feelings, each fighting for precedence. 'Is my father still alive?'

'Yes,' replied Blue surely.

'Then why has he never come for me?' Kyle's tears were flowing freely now.

Blue merely shrugged, indifferent to the question. 'Why ask me ... you're the one who thinks he knows everything.'

Kyle was really sick of having every smart aleck thing he'd ever said or done come back to haunt him. 'Aren't you supposed to be helping me?'

'Not if I don't wanna,' Blue enlightened him. 'We elementals don't have to be disposed towards you, but if I wasn't, you'd dehydrate, mate. Or I could drown you in your own bodily fluids,' he suggested, winningly. 'So, I wouldn't go givin' me too much cheek. I've helped you plenty already.'

'I really appreciate that, Blue.' Kyle attempted to be humble, anxious to know more about his father, but a more urgent concern sprang to mind. 'Matt!' he exclaimed in a mad panic. 'He's been shot!'

'No, no, no. He hasn't,' Blue insisted, to prevent the lad rushing off. 'That instance is in the future of your reality.'

'Then I must get back to my reality and prevent it.' Kyle raised himself and went marching off down the beach.

Do you think movement has anything to do with travel in and out of this realm? There is only one way back for you, Kyle, Book finally broke his silence to inform his charge, *and that is through me ... you promised to finish reading.*

Kyle stopped dead in his tracks, realising he had no idea where he was going or how to get back to Matt in the physical world. 'If you were the only way back to reality, Book, then why did you feel the need to make me promise to keep reading?' He did an about-face, and found Zoe's spirit walking forward to meet him. Recalling what he'd learnt of her during his 'ray dreaming, he really did feel he'd had his head buried in the sand in regard to this girl. 'Aw, Zoe, I was so completely wrong about you. I'm sorry I got you in trouble and I'm sorry that —'

Her fingers pressing against his lips silenced his apology. 'It doesn't matter now.'

She leant forward to kiss him and Kyle found himself spellbound by her lovely gaze. His eyes closed as their lips met.

After a few moments, when nothing had happened, Kyle opened his eyes to find Zoe had vanished. 'Where did she go?'

Kyron, Blue and Book were all laughing, and after a moment of disappointment and annoyance, Kyle cracked a wry smile to concede that Blue's prediction about romance seemed to be right on track.

'She was just dreaming,' Blue informed his deflated charge, 'and now she's waking up.'

The undine sniggered, making a mockery of Kyle's prior claims about the girl. 'I can see that you don't like her at all! Yes, it's plain to see she's nothing to you.'

Kyle could feel his cheeks flushing. 'So, she's cooler than I thought,' he admitted.

There's no need to be embarrassed. Everyone falls in love —

'Steady on there, Book, let's not get too excited. I don't even know what lo— ... that word, means!' he stated in his own defence, most uncomfortable with the suggestion.

Blue smiled now. 'You cannot hide anything from us,' he reminded Kyle.

Was love the uncomfortable feeling in his gut that was twisting it in knots every time Zoe was around, or even mentioned? Was that why he was so intrigued by this girl and so jealous of how chummy Matt was with her? As Kyle thought, he dug both of his hands deep into his jacket pockets and finding the crystal ball in one of them, he retrieved it to look within.

Kyle saw a vision of Zoe asleep in her bed and the discomfort he was feeling intensified. 'She is certainly all that dreams are made of.'

Kyle felt himself drawn to her, wanting to know her better.

'Bye bye,' bid Blue, 'sucker!'

The vision in the crystal ball bled through to the astral beach, obscuring Kyle's sight as his being shifted location.

When the particles of his reality stabilised and hardened into physical form, Kyle found himself gazing down at Zoe when she woke from their dream.

She was wearing a huge smile on her face as she stretched to assist her return to a waking state. Then, as her faculties kicked in, her expression changed to one of shock. 'No!' She sat bolt upright. 'Not that *self-righteous bastard* ... no way.' Zoe shook her head violently, trying to rid herself of the memory.

Kyle ventured to step forward to give her a wave, and was delighted when she clambered out of bed without paying him any heed.

'She can't see us,' he commented back to Kyron, who was huddled in the corner, horrified to be in the physical realm that he feared — he was cuddling Book for comfort.

'I think it's for the best,' said the creature.

'So do I,' agreed Kyle as he watched Zoe flit about her room in a panic, wearing nothing but a little white camisole top and matching knickers.

'It was so real!' Zoe was disgusted by her recollection. 'How could my subconscious have mistaken Kyle for some warrior hero to be admired? I can still feel the anticipation of his impending kiss ...' Her anger ebbed as she dwelt on this. When she caught herself grinning, however, her anger returned. 'Oooh! Stop it!'

Kyle was smiling. He'd never imagined he could affect a woman this way — especially this woman. It was delightful. He looked back at Kyron trembling in the corner. 'Will you be all right here? I'm just going to ...' Kyle pointed in the direction Zoe had gone.

'Go right ahead,' the beast stammered. 'I'll be fine.'

'Good ... um ...' Kyle almost said, man. 'What are you anyway, Kyron?'

'Your people have many different names for my kind,' Kyron answered, 'but the most popular term lately is yowie.'

Kyle frowned, for he was familiar with that term. 'Like a yeti, or a sasquatch?' He was stoked. 'I have my own "big foot" as a guardian? Awesome!' Then Kyle frowned. 'I thought you guys were supposed to be ferocious and fearless?'

'Supposed to be,' mumbled Kyron, ashamed of himself.

As Kyle could clearly see the premise was upsetting for the beast, he commented lightly, 'We must discuss your history when I get a moment.'

Kyron nodded, like a reprimanded child.

'Hey, don't sweat, my friend.' Kyle gave him a chug on the shoulder. 'You're helping me sort out my problems. I'm sure that between the two of us we'll be able to sort out whatever your problem is too.'

Kyle's promise made the yowie attempt a smile.

'But first things first.' Kyle went looking for Zoe.

He found her in the bathroom, splashing water onto her face. 'Wow, she's peakin'. She must have really felt something to get all riled up like this. Don't you think, Kyron?' he called to the beast in the bedroom, but there came no response.

Kyle thought he should check up on his guardian, but Zoe unknowingly turned to face him and pulled her hair away from her face with both her hands. The view through the white silk and lace that Zoe was wearing was just too mesmerising for Kyle to walk away from.

'It's okay.' Zoe turned back to the mirror to reassure herself. 'You're awake now ... just calm down.'

Kyle was not fast enough to get out of the way as Zoe exited the bathroom and passed right through him. Shocked by the event, he gasped, having been filled with a sensual, warm delight that melted his horror into a delirious grin. Kyle did a quick about-face to catch Zoe's reaction. Had she felt that same magical feeling?

She paused and closed her eyes in apparent bliss. Then, waking up to herself, she was panicked again. 'Stop this!' she demanded of herself. 'Why are you feeling this way about a guy you truly *despise*?'

Kyle, rather impressed by his power to charm, approached Zoe to whisper. 'Truly?'

Zoe closed her eyes and unable to shake her

strange enchantment, she resolved, 'I need to meditate.' She immediately returned to her bed and fished a remote from the bedside table. She switched on some relaxing music and assumed the lotus position.

Kyle was tickled by the apparent lengths Zoe was forced to go to in order to put him from her mind. He circled the bed, watching over her fondly as she drew in deep, relaxing breaths. 'You're really not at all what I expected.' He stopped still in front of her and reached out to place a hand against her cheek, and although he could make no physical contact, Zoe's head leant into his palm ever so slightly, and her exhalation sounded suspiciously like a sigh. As Zoe continued to breathe deeply, Kyle became spellbound, for he began to see the recent past through Zoe's eyes.

'How could you sell a place of such beauty to Nivok Industries?'

Kyle saw himself posing the question in Nivok's office, and he felt the doubt and guilt his taunting invoked.

'Your uncle isn't going to punish you for tonight's little episode. You don't know the meaning of the word punishment.'

The ignorant assumption made him so angry!

A sharp slap to the cheek rocked Kyle, with the kind of life-shattering fear that he'd not let himself experience since he was a child. He looked back at his attacker, James Nivok, feeling abandoned and betrayed.

He withdrew his hand from Zoe's cheek, heart pounding and tears of remorse filling his eyes. 'I need to get myself a new role model … I am turning into one of my god-damn foster fathers!' Seeing himself through another's eyes made this obvious to Kyle for the first time.

Zoe opened her eyes, appearing disappointed. 'This isn't helping.' She arose and wandered over to the window that afforded a panoramic view of Sydney. 'How could I be attracted to an abusive man, who makes me feel this bad about myself? He's destroyed my trust in the one family member I have left, and forced me to quit my job! Not that I was that excited about the position, but I certainly would have liked to depart on better terms.'

'*Okay*,' Kyle appealed in desperation, 'I admit that I have been a total arsehole! But, you're perceptive.' Kyle joined her at the window. 'Maybe you see beyond my bullshit, and recognise the scared, directionless, orphan who's just like you?' The money factor had prevented Kyle drawing any parallel between Zoe's life and his own, and he suddenly realised how similar their situation was. 'Kindred spirits perhaps?'

Zoe's depression suddenly lifted. She smiled as if she'd had a nice thought, although she said nothing to indicate what that thought might have been.

The morning sunlight played upon her dark hair and fair skin, highlighting the emerald sparkle in her eyes, still glazed by the dreams of sleep. Her freshness and serenity was enchanting. Kyle's gaze became transfixed on her and he knew this moment would stay etched on his memory forever, for he had never seen such a vision of bemusing loveliness. 'Could I be falling —'

A knock on the door prevented Kyle from considering the premise, and Zoe broke from her silent contemplation to get the door. Kyle delayed to close his eyes and hold the moment captive, and when he was sure Zoe's image was clearly imbedded in his mind, he opened his eyes to view the cityscape. 'I must have been insane to imagine that such a goddess could ever love a scumbag like me ... or that a scumbag like me could love!'

'So,' Kyron didn't venture from his corner, 'you're a fool.' He shrugged in conclusion.

'Is that supposed to be encouraging?' Kyle turned to the beast, considering that perhaps his guide needed a brush-up course on guidance.

Kyron nodded. 'Well, yeah ... many a fool has found true love despite his delusions.'

'Point taken.' Kyle smiled and nodded to concede. 'Thanks buddy.'

CHAPTER
FIVE

BROKEN DREAMS

Zoe looked through the peephole of her apartment door. 'Matt!' she panicked, opening the door and quickly pulling him inside.

At the sound of his best friend's name, Kyle wandered into the lounge room to be sure that he'd heard correctly. 'What's he doing here?' He directed the query at the couple, but of course neither of them perceived it. Kyle had never had cause to be jealous before, but when Zoe took up both Matt's hands in her own, Kyle's heart began to ache like never before.

'How did you go?' She sounded concerned for him.

Matt smiled broadly as he pulled a large bunch of keys out of his jacket pocket and placed them in Zoe's hand. 'I got copies of all of them. Do you know how hard it is to find a locksmith, after hours, who'll take on a job like this?'

Kyle folded his arms, observing them both suspiciously. 'What are you two up to?'

'Thanks, Matt, you're a champion. How did you go at the television station?' Zoe skipped to more cheery subject matter.

Matt burst into a grin. 'They gave me a job,' he said, very proud of himself as he held out his arms to be congratulated.

When Zoe responded by giving Matt a friendly hug, Kyle took a step forward, not liking it one bit.

'Matty, that's great! I'm so proud of you.' She released Matt and for a moment they gazed at each other affectionately.

'Hey! What gives?' Kyle looked on, disconcerted. 'I didn't think you were serious about marrying her.' Kyle ignored the thought that this was a convenient lie.

Matt covered his desire by adopting his happy-go-lucky demeanour once more. 'I'm only a shit-kicker, of course, but it's a step in the right direction.'

'Oh, you seem to know how to get what you want fast enough,' Zoe assured him, her tone a little too sultry for Kyle's comfort. 'Tea?' she offered and when Matt smiled, Zoe moved to the kitchen to put the kettle on.

'I figure I'll still keep up the cleaning for a couple of days, so I can have a snoop around while the place is empty.' Matt made himself comfortable on the lounge.

'Good idea,' Zoe commented. 'I'm going to clean out my things today, so I'll put the keys back before he misses them.'

Matt opened his bag up, pulling out bits and pieces and placing them on the coffee table. 'I brought the tape for you to listen to, and I looked into this Burke bloke that your uncle is so concerned about.'

'You're going after Nivok. Are you crazy?' Kyle came to squat in front of Matt, concerned for his wellbeing now that the plot was somewhat clearer. 'You'll be shot!' The vision from the Pool of Truths came to mind. 'Literally. I'm not kidding, Matt, you can't do this. I won't let you!'

'I couldn't find a damn thing on the internet, so the case is probably before its time. Either that or it's been deliberately suppressed,' Matt confessed, disappointed, and Kyle breathed a sigh of relief. 'I plan to visit a library as soon as I get a free moment and check out the newspaper archives.'

Zoe smiled broadly as she appeared at the kitchen door with Matt's cup. 'No need.' En route to Matt she retrieved a couple of files from her kitchen bench and handed them to him, setting his tea down on the table. 'It would seem that Mr Burke was once in the employ of Nivok Industries, more than twenty years ago, which was even before my parents died.' A sorrowful expression flashed across her face and was gone. 'I wonder if he knew them?'

Matt was both stunned and delighted by Zoe's revelations.

Kyle was thrown into panic all over again, while Matt excitedly opened the file to read through it. Kyle leant over his mate's shoulder, interested in Zoe's findings and was thunderstruck to recognise the person pictured in the file as being from one of his visions. 'Hey, that's him!' The white man Kyle had seen at the ritual during his dolphin dreaming was readily recognisable in the old picture. 'Timothy Burke is my father!' Kyle nearly choked on the realisation and staggered about dazed.

Matt stopped reading and gazed into space as he pondered what he'd learnt. 'A geologist, huh. Now why do you think your uncle would want to keep this man away from you?'

'A geologist,' Kyle echoed, impressed by his father's qualifications.

Zoe merely shrugged at the question.

'We need to talk to this guy,' Matt decided.

'Well, that could prove a little difficult. He's still in prison as far as I know,' Zoe informed him, and was startled by another knock on the door. Concerned, she rushed to the peephole. After a quick glance she turned back to Matt with a look of utter horror on her face. 'Jesus, it's my uncle,' she whispered, flying over to the table to aid Matt to pile the incriminating evidence back into his bag.

Matt raised himself to standing and with bag in hand he turned this way and that, not knowing what to do with himself.

Kyle, arms folded, watched the scene play out in front of him and couldn't help but find it amusing. 'Busted, Matty ... way to go.'

Zoe quickly escorted Matt to the bathroom. 'In here.' She pushed him inside and closed the door. Back in the lounge, Zoe spotted his teacup on the table and quickly took it to the kitchen and dropped it in the sink. She collected herself as the knocking was repeated. 'Coming.' She took a deep breath and opened the door to find a large bunch of flowers in her face.

Her uncle popped his head out from behind the floral arrangement, sporting a large smile. 'What were you doing ... hiding a man in here?'

Kyle chuckled. 'A couple, in fact.' He approached Nivok to observe him at close range, enjoying his advantage immensely.

Zoe, accepting the flowers and kissing her uncle's cheek, stepped back to allow him to enter. 'No, I was meditating. And you can't come out of a trance too quickly or you spin out.'

'You learn something every day,' he replied, obviously having no knowledge of such things.

On her way to the kitchen to put her flowers into some water, Zoe noticed her uncle's keys sitting in full view on the bench top — Kyle noticed them too.

'A distraction … coming right up.' Kyle rushed to the mantel on the opposite side of the room and was surprised to recognise the couple featured in the ornately framed photograph. 'It was Zoe's parents, the couple who died in the car explosion.' His memories of the shark dreaming confirmed this. Kyle looked at James Nivok. 'Let's see what kind of a reaction this fetches.' Kyle attempted to push the picture off the mantel but his hand passed right through it. *Here willpower governs all,* Crystaleyes had said. Focusing, Kyle willed it to fall, which didn't work either. Then, as a last resort, he envisioned his wish, and the picture fell off the shelf.

As Nivok glanced over at the disturbance, Zoe clutched the keys and deposited them quietly in a drawer, breathing a silent sigh of relief.

'How impressive was that?' Kyle stood

staring at his achievement, stunned by his newfound capability.

Nivok retrieved the picture of his deceased brother and sister-in-law from the floor and replaced it on the mantel. He seemed spooked as he viewed the picture, and then cast his eyes around the small apartment with a look of apprehension on his face.

'Would that be a look of guilt I see?' Kyle moved in close to the magnate to observe him. 'What's wrong, Nivok, are you afraid the past is coming back to haunt you?' Kyle didn't know what his assumed father had on James Nivok, but it must have been pretty nasty to have made them enemies. 'I do believe Matt is right about you ... I've learnt to spot treachery from a mile away.'

'Would you like a cup of coffee?' Zoe called out from the kitchen.

Nivok relaxed to respond, 'No, thank you, sweetheart, I can't stay.' He took a seat, unaware of the lad standing right beside him, peering down on him with arms folded in mistrust.

'What a shame.' Zoe was hard pressed to hide the relief in her voice. 'Why not?' She re-entered the room, and after placing the flowers on the mantelpiece next to the photo of her parents, she took a seat on the lounge opposite him.

'I just came to make sure all was forgiven for the other day.' He forced a smile to reassure her. 'I didn't mean for you to leave the company, you know.'

'Look ... I wasn't interested anyway. It's for the best,' she insisted. 'Please just forget it ever happened.'

Nivok smiled and there was a slight pause before he added, 'And I need to ask you a favour.'

Kyle's eyes widened. 'Here we go.'

'Seeing as you are going to sell me this land in less than a week or so, I wanted to get your permission to have a couple of my people go up there and start surveying it for me.'

A brief image of the hunk of rock in Nivok's office came to mind. 'If Tim was a geologist ...' Kyle's eyes narrowed as he looked at Nivok accusingly, '... then I think I've got a real good idea why he was forced into hiding.' Kyle immediately moved to stand by Zoe. 'Don't allow it, Zoe. Say no.'

Zoe hesitated to answer — almost as if she was considering Kyle's plea. Nivok waited patiently for a response. 'To tell you the truth, uncle, I'd really like to see it before you start blowing it up ... or whatever you intend to do with it. After all, my parents must have felt something for it to have kept it pristine and undeveloped this long.'

'That's my girl,' Kyle stated proudly.

Nivok was concerned by her reluctance to fall into line. 'It's not like they bought the property, honey. They inherited it, just like our grandfather did.'

For the first time Zoe wondered why her grandparents had passed the land on to her father, the younger of the two sons. Maybe they hadn't wanted James to get his hands on it?

'You're not thinking of backing out of our deal? Five million is a lot of money.'

'Of course not.' Zoe laid on the girlish charm to comfort her uncle and get her own way. 'It's only a week for heaven's sake. Surely it can't make that much of a difference to your schedule?' She came to sit beside him, taking hold of his hand. 'I'll try and get up there before we exchange contracts. Just out of respect ... I think I owe it to my parents to at least see this piece of land.'

Nivok smiled, outwardly resigned to her pleading. Kyle was impressed. 'Damn, this girl is a better bullshitter than I am.'

'I want to go now.' Kyron had left his sheltered spot in the bedroom.

Kyle turned to see the yowie appearing even more terrified than usual. 'What is it?' The beast was backing away up the hall, its fearful eyes focused on Nivok. 'Do you recognise this man, Kyron?'

The beast shook its head. 'I want to go!' it repeated, threatening to burst into nervous tears if the request was not met.

'Okay.' Kyle moved over to the huge creature to reassure it. 'We'll go somewhere else.'

'Anywhere,' the beast encouraged him. 'Just will us out of here.' Kyron grabbed hold of Kyle to be transported to the desired destination.

To Kyle's mind, the first place to flee during a confused moment was home; when Kyron made contact with him that was exactly where they went.

When equilibrium was restored, Kyle found himself standing in his own lounge room.

Kyron was still with him, rather anxious about the situation, clutching Book tightly. Kyle's physical body was seated on his lounge seemingly as perturbed as Kyle felt. Dwelling on all that had unfolded in Zoe's apartment, he was more than a little disturbed. '*Nivok*!' Kyle's liberated form muttered with a good serve of malice.

'Matt was right about that guy.' Kyle was stunned as his physical self echoed his conclusion.

Kyron stopped his nervous fidgeting and looked from one Kyle to the other, amazed. 'What's happening?' he quietly asked the book in his hands.

A miracle ... I do believe Kyle is actually in tune with himself, which could be dangerous at this early stage of his re-education. We should not have come here; it was not my intent. Kyle's will is growing in strength ... we should move on and quickly.

Kyle lost his wonder abruptly and looked at Book to protest: 'I need my body back. I have to help Matt.'

'I have to help Matt.' His physical self echoed his sentiment, and stood up with the book, reading on as he moved towards the door.

Too much emotional knowledge too soon. I was afraid this would happen. You must listen to me, Kyle, and put all physical world affairs to the back of your mind. Although you have learnt well so far, there is still much you don't know. You are nowhere near prepared for what you must do here ... we haven't even started work on your mental body yet.

Kyron, finding himself more fearful for his charge than himself, stepped forward and placed a hand on Kyle's shoulder. 'Listen to Book, Kyle. Book is all-wise, all-knowing. Don't leave us again so soon.'

His promise to finish reading pained Kyle now, and he would not listen to reason. He took hold of the book, not to be swayed. 'I'll have to take my chances. Matt will be shot if I don't. He has no idea what he is getting himself into —'

Neither do you ... and I will no longer have the power to advise you, once you have quit.

Kyle was annoyed by the suggestion that he was giving up, but was resigned to the cause of saving his best friend. 'I'm not quitting! We're just experiencing a slight delay.' He moved towards his physical self with the book; Kyle's physical self turned from his path to the door to confront his unconscious form. 'I'll be back.'

No Kyle, don't, there is no way back ... this is a mistake!

Kyle ignored Book's plea, fighting with his better judgement to do so. He placed his book into the *Book of Dreams* that his physical form was still holding.

I should have taught you patience first.

Kyle heard Book's last regretful thought as the two books merged to become one. 'Whoa!' He felt suddenly dizzy and the floor rushed up to meet him with a heavy thud.

Wakefulness brought Kyle's attention to a throbbing on one side of his head and he immediately wanted to retreat back into dreamland. His eyelids parted and he saw the view across the timber floor in his tiny entrance hall. He sat up, still clutching the book. Kyron was gone and Kyle was alone in the room. 'I'm back! Ouch!' His excitement was cut short by his physical ailments — headache, hunger, thirst. That was one of the nice things about an etheric form, no physical pain. It was a relief to be back in control of his own person, however, and he wriggled his body parts to get a feel for wielding his denser body.

'I won't let us down,' he swore to Book, feeling a wee tinge of remorse now that telepathic communication between them was broken.

Kyle grabbed an old sports bag that was amongst the mess on his lounge room floor and placed Book carefully inside it. 'Sorry about the smell.'

Putting on a jacket, Kyle checked his watch and was surprised at the time. 'Shit!' He tossed the bag over his shoulder and bolted out the front door.

Kyle strode in through the glass double doors of the Nivok Industries building and straight up to the night watchman at the security desk. He held no fear of being reprimanded, as he had made friends as well as enemies in this place. 'Hey, Charlie. How's it goin'?'

'Kyle. What are you doing here?' Charlie gave him a large smile as he came out from behind his desk to frisk Kyle and check his bag.

'I heard you got the flick ... the boss's niece, huh?' Old Charlie gave him a wink, having a chuckle at his young friend's misfortune.

'Yeah ... seems you were right about her.' Kyle retrieved his bag. 'Nivok kicked me out so quick that I left some of my stuff behind. Do you mind if I go get it?'

'No worries, son.' Charlie waved Kyle through to the elevator and went back to his newspaper, shaking his head and smiling with amusement. 'Oh, to be twenty again.'

The elevator doors opened on level ten and Kyle stuck his head out to glance around before proceeding. All was as usual for this time of night — no soul was about. But when he moved out into the corridor, he was startled by a harsh whisper.

'What are you doing here?' Zoe came rushing from the darkened shadows up the hall and she sounded rather perturbed.

Kyle, knowing of the impending danger, was not pleased to see her. 'I'd ask you the same question. You don't need any more trouble with your uncle. I'll help Matt.' He turned Zoe to face the elevator and pressed the down button. 'You, go home.' Not waiting for an argument he strode off up the corridor.

Although Zoe wondered how Kyle even knew what Matt was up to, she was more perturbed about being ordered about. 'You didn't seem to care so much for my wellbeing when you were getting me into all that trouble with my uncle ... I've quit, you know?'

Kyle halted, realising how blunt his address must have sounded just now, so he turned back to apologise. 'Aw, Zoe, I was so completely wrong about you.' He walked back towards her, suspecting that Zoe's memory might be jogged by a recollection of their dream. 'I got you in trouble and I'm sorry for that.' Kyle, noting Zoe's wonderstruck expression, smiled. 'Then you say —'

'It doesn't matter now,' Zoe whispered along with him, awed by the fact they were having this conversation.

Kyle's smile broadened upon realising that she did indeed remember. 'And then you kissed me.'

'I never,' she insisted, unable to wipe the curious smile from her face.

'You wanted to.' Kyle pushed his luck.

Zoe chose to ignore the comment, although deep inside she knew it was the truth. 'How could you know my dream?'

'It was my dream too,' he claimed playfully. He loved this man of mystery guise that he now held in her eyes. 'It came to me while I was meditating.'

Zoe caught her breath at the comment.

'Now please,' Kyle became more serious, 'go home.' He turned and kept going.

Zoe was stunned beyond rational thought as she watched Kyle disappear into the Nivok offices. 'No, it's not possible.' Could they have had the same dream? *While he was meditating?* Kyle certainly hadn't struck Zoe as the kind of guy who meditated. She both hated and loved that she couldn't wipe the silly smirk off her face. 'This can't be happening.' Her whisper held far less resistance to the idea of their attraction.

The elevator doors opened in front of her.

Nivok's office would have been in darkness, if not for the moonlight streaming in through the windows and one small light source at the far end of the room.

'Matt?' Kyle entered cautiously.

Startled from his rummaging through cabinets, Matt dropped the files in his hands and shone his torch onto Kyle, who squinted as the harsh light annoyed his eyes. '*Jesus*, Kyle .. . you scared the shit out of me! Where have you been?'

Kyle reached out and encouraged Matt to lower the torch. 'Are you crazy bringing Zoe back here? Why didn't you tell me what you were up to? I've been at home reading a book since you left me. All you had —'

'You didn't answer the phone.' Matt was confused. 'I called and called. I even went round and nearly bashed your door down. But you never answered, and I figured you weren't there.'

Now Kyle was dumbfounded.

'Hold on.' Matt backtracked a little. 'Did you say you were reading a *book*? *You*?' He placed a hand to Kyle's forehead. 'Have you caught something?'

'Stop it.' Kyle slapped Matt's hand away. 'This is serious shit, so be swift. I'll keep watch for Nivok.'

Matt knelt down and collected the files he'd

dropped. 'How did you even know I was here?' He was suddenly concerned that he'd not been cautious enough with his investigation.

'Does this matter right now?' Kyle stressed, heading off towards the door, but his pace slowed as he thought to give Matt his due. 'You're right about Nivok being up to something. He's got plans for Zoe's piece of land that are not in the land's best interest, I'll warrant.'

Matt smiled, thinking that was the closest thing to praise he'd ever got from Kyle. 'Nivok's been a lot more anxious about things since a tremor hit that other resort of his which is close by Zoe's land.' He returned to his rummaging.

'When? What tremor?' Kyle had a scary feeling that his little tantrum whilst in the realm of demons hadn't only shaken the otherworld. *Could my ill will be so strong?*

Matt looked back at Kyle, surprised. 'A couple of days ago. Jesus, Kyle, where have you been? Don't you ever watch the news?'

What manifests here, just one stage behind your own world, will surely manifest there too, Book had cautioned.

Nah. Kyle decided he must be misinterpreting the information and opened his mouth to comment, when Zoe came charging into the room.

'He's coming!' She was clearly flustered as she closed and locked the door. 'Should I try and stall him?'

'No. Better that he doesn't see you if possible.' Kyle spotted the remote control sitting on the moonlit coffee table. 'The bar.' He grabbed the control and they made haste in the direction of the revolving bar.

Matt didn't bother replacing the files he held. He just closed the filing cabinet and ran for the bar emerging from its hiding place in the wall.

Zoe snatched Matt's camera from her uncle's desk and joined the lads as the bar revolved back into its hiding place.

The door unlocked and opened. The office light was heard to switch on and the door closed.

Matt turned on the bar light and handed Zoe the files in exchange for his camera.

'I'd rather not take any chances,' Nivok informed his company.

The sound of a lighter was heard and Kyle guessed Nivok was lighting a cigar; the magnate had an expensive box of them sitting on his desk.

'If they're releasing him tomorrow, then we may have to arrange a little accident,' Nivok concluded.

Zoe gasped, but Kyle clamped a hand over her mouth in time to smother the sound. He looked at Matt, who patted his camera and smiled to assure him that he was recording.

'No worries, Mr Nivok,' came the reply. 'Just like before?'

Zoe's eyes opened even wider.

'Just,' Nivok confirmed. 'I'll drink to that.'

Before they had fully realised what had been said, the bar was swinging around into the bright light of the office. Nivok was close by them, so Kyle grabbed a full bottle of grog and cracked the tycoon over the head with it. This sent the cigar in Nivok's hand flying into a nearby rubbish bin full of paper as he hit the floor.

Upon witnessing her uncle's unconscious form on the floor, Zoe felt a twinge of doubt and remorse. Ivan, the bodyguard, moved to block their path to the door; he'd seen Zoe and

Kyle together before and she knew he would advise her uncle of her involvement in this affair. She had never seriously considered how a falling out with her uncle could affect her future, but considering the side of her uncle that had surfaced of late, the prospect scared her.

Ivan was reaching inside his jacket when Matt, on impulse, went charging at him and cracked the muscle-bound fellow in the temple with his camera. The heavyweight was knocked unconscious.

'My poor baby, are you all right?' Matt hugged his camera, immediately remorseful.

'He's just using you to get to the land.' Kyle grabbed Zoe's arm and dragged her towards the door to make good their escape, but the sound of a gunshot brought both of them to a grinding halt short of the door. Kyle looked at Matt and was relieved to find that he had not been the target.

James Nivok kept the gun in his hand aimed at them as he slid up the wall to his feet, using his free hand to mop at the gash on his head with a handkerchief. Angered by the sight of his own blood, Nivok glared at Kyle. 'I remember you.' He then looked at Zoe. 'Have you lost your mind? I could have you arrested, along with your mates, for tonight's little piece of work.' He pointed to the files she held. 'I'll take those, if you don't mind.'

The voice of her guardian compelled Zoe to follow his order and yet her intuition demanded the opposite. 'And if I refuse?'

'Why would you wish to refuse?' he appealed. 'What on earth have these boys been telling you?'

'Nothing that isn't fairly obvious to me now,' she replied.

Nivok's expression cooled somewhat. 'Careful, princess. I want to do right by you, but I wouldn't try my patience.'

Zoe was flabbergasted. Was that a threat?

Kyle eased himself sideways to stand between Zoe and her uncle's gun. 'That's a fine way to speak to the woman who owns two-thirds of your company.'

'Only if I'm alive,' Zoe stated accusingly from behind Kyle. 'If I die, he inherits ...' She nearly choked on the realisation.

'This is true,' her uncle conceded cheerily.

Kyle's blood chilled at the implication. Kyle glanced around to see Matt raise his camera onto his shoulder in order to draw Nivok's fire. This was the vision from Kyle's whale dreaming and, just as foreseen, the world seemed to slip into slow motion.

The smoke from the fire in the rubbish bin triggered the alarm and water started to spurt from the jets in the roof.

Kyle dropped his bag to dive at Nivok and as they collided the gun fired.

The falling water hit the unconscious Ivan's face and when he showed signs of coming to, Zoe grabbed a large vase and dropped it on his head.

Kyle managed to knock the gun from Nivok's hand and it went flying off in Matt's direction. James Nivok packed a hell of a punch for a pretty-boy businessman, Kyle decided as he copped a couple of jabs in the jaw.

Matt was preoccupied, shoving his camera in Kyle's bag to save it from the water, so Zoe grabbed a huge decanter from the bar. As the heavy crystal bottle met with her uncle's head, he relinquished his conscious state.

Kyle was very grateful to see the bastard fall. There was blood all over Nivok and himself. He'd felt the gun go off between them and raising his shirt he discovered a long bloodied wound on his left side. 'Bummer.' His knees gave beneath him and he collapsed in a heap on the floor.

'God, no!' Zoe fell down beside him. She began ripping fabric from her skirt to place over the wound, and applying a little pressure, she tried to ease the bleeding.

'We have to get him out of here ... give me a hand,' she implored Matt. He threw the bag strap over his shoulder and took hold of Kyle under one arm, motioning Zoe to do the same.

'Aw!' Kyle regained consciousness as they lifted him, pained by his wound. He rolled his head round to rest on Zoe's shoulder. 'You look great, all wet like that.'

Zoe smiled at him affectionately, unable to believe he could find humour in this moment. 'I think he's delirious,' she commented to Matt, as she gently wiped the wet hair from Kyle's face.

Zoe, as friendly as she'd been to Matt, had never bestowed on him the ardent gaze with which she now regarded Kyle. 'What's your excuse then?' Matt posed to Zoe.

The look of disappointment on Matt's face was heartbreaking. Zoe immediately removed her hand from Kyle's face, and knowing they had no time to discuss this unexpected development in their relationship, Matt headed them all towards the door.

This late in the evening there weren't many people in the foyer, although a couple of fire officers were supervising the search for the emergency. The alarms had been shut off, and Charlie was chatting to the fireman in charge when the doors of one of the elevators opened.

Matt, carrying the bag, bounded out through the foyer, waving to Charlie on his way past. 'See ya, Charlie. I've got a big story to shoot, no time, got to run.'

'Did you see anything of this fire on your rounds?' Charlie's question pulled Matt up mid-flight.

'Are you kidding?' Matt responded. 'I thought it was another false alarm.' He looked perplexed. 'Otherwise I'd still be up there shooting it for the evening news. Is there a fire?' he asked eagerly, whereupon the fireman nearby signalled Charlie to let the lad go and tell him nothing.

'No story here.' Charlie dismissed Matt, who bounded off on his merry way.

Charlie looked back to the elevators as the second set of doors opened and Kyle and Zoe stepped out.

Zoe had her arm wrapped around Kyle's waist, and her jacket was hung over her arm to hide the wound in his side. Kyle had his arm over her shoulder for support and they made it appear as if they were engrossed in intimate conversation. As Zoe spied Charlie approaching she kissed Kyle, and then whispered, loud enough for the security man to hear, 'We could go to my place … get out of these wet clothes?'

As Kyle smiled broadly at the suggestion and Zoe's unexpected defence tactic, he glanced past her to see Charlie change his course and head back to the fireman.

'Should we question them?' Charlie inquired of the fireman, who smiled and shook his head.

'They might be aware of a fire,' the chief commented, 'but it ain't the kind we're looking for.'

'G'night Charlie,' Kyle yelled across to his friend and gave him a wave with his free hand.

'You kids okay?' Charlie asked now that he had their attention.

'Just a little wet, that's all,' Kyle assured him.

'No kidding.' Charlie chuckled and returned the wave.

'I think that fire alarm is faulty, hey? You should have it looked at,' Kyle suggested. 'That's the second false alarm this week.'

'Yeah, we know.' Charlie sounded exasperated. 'Will do.'

Kyle was feeling considerably woozy as they exited onto the front steps. 'You stayed?'

Zoe smiled at him to hide her concern for his wellbeing, as he was getting heavy and difficult for her to support. 'I rarely do as I'm told.'

'Then we have something in common,' Kyle said softly, his large brown eyes seeking her affection. 'Nice kiss, by the way,' he ventured to say, figuring that she was hardly going to hit him in his present condition.

'That wasn't a kiss,' she scoffed, pretending not to have been deeply moved by the experience. '*This* is a kiss.'

Her lips touched his so tenderly, and with such heartfelt longing, Kyle's senses went into overdrive.

'Extraordinary,' he mumbled, smiling deliriously in the wake of her attention. 'How can something so wonderful leave me so cold?'

Kyle's smile fell from his face as his sight blurred. 'It's so cold.'

Just then, Matt came rushing up the stairs to help his mate to Zoe's waiting car. Kyle's eyes rolled back into his head. 'Kyle!'

Far off in the distance, Kyle heard his name being called, but he could not shake the cold darkness now besieging his body.

A hospital was out of the question. If Nivok reported the night's events, Kyle would end up in the slammer; or there was the possibility that Nivok wouldn't report the incident to the police and opt to let his own security force take care of the matter. Either way, Kyle would be a sitting duck in a hospital room.

'I'll take him to my Uncle Max. He's a GP.' Matt informed Zoe of his intended destination, as he drove through the quiet city streets.

'A GP!' Zoe panicked. 'Matt, I think Kyle needs a surgeon. There's blood everywhere back here. We have to get him to a hospital.'

'If we do, then we may as well take him straight to jail.' Matt tried not to sound frustrated with her argument. 'And believe me, Kyle would rather die than be institutionalised again.' He knew that much for certain.

Zoe gasped as the full realisation of their tragic circumstances hit home. 'This is all my fault,' she mumbled, dissolving into tears. 'How could I have been so blind —?'

'Hey,' Matt cautioned her gently, 'let's just focus on one drama at a time. Okay? I really need you with me on this one.'

With a deep inhalation, Zoe swallowed her grief and nodded in agreement.

'Besides, if anyone is to blame it's me.' The car skidded as Matt turned a sharp bend in the road. 'My big story could cost me my best mate's life!'

'No, it won't,' Zoe insisted, realising that Matt was more distressed by Kyle's injury than she was and that it was up to her to keep him focused and positive. 'It's a good plan, Matt. How long until we get there?'

The turning of the car into the driveway of a covered gatehouse answered her question. In the headlights of the car a large set of double gates blocked their passage to the house.

Matt wound down his window to speak into the intercom.

'Surgery is closed,' a sleepy male voice advised them through a speaker in the wall of the gatehouse on the driver's side. 'I will be available for consultation from nine o'clock Tuesday morning,' he yawned, before saying, 'This is a recording.'

Matt slammed a finger down on the intercom button. 'Uncle Max! It's me, Matthew. I know it's late, but I've just come from covering a big story. One of my workmates has been injured pretty badly and I was kind of hopin' you might patch him up for me?' Matt paused and took his finger off the button to give his uncle a chance to respond. When silence followed, Matt pressed the button once more. 'Uncle Max, please! I know you're there.' Matt held his breath, praying his uncle *was* still there and that he wasn't wasting time pleading with a recording.

'Matty, it's like this ...'

Matthew breathed easy again, when he heard his uncle's voice.

'... I have a beautiful woman in my bed and we're leaving to go away for the weekend in less than two hours ... a hospital is what you need, my lad, and there's a perfectly good one just around the corner.'

'The crooks who shot my friend are still at large and he's the only one who got a good look at them,' Matt explained. 'I'm afraid if I take him to a hospital, they'll try and finish him off.'

Silence.

'Uncle Max? I'm begging here. He's my *best* friend ...' Matt's voice faltered in desperation, but before he could summon the words to beg again, the gates parted before them. 'Thanks, Uncle Max.'

They drove up the drive and parked at the front door, where a handsome middle-aged doctor stood waiting for them in his bathrobe and slippers.

'Book?' Kyle stirred momentarily and called out as he was lifted from the car by Zoe and Matt.

'Now that's the last item on earth I thought Kyle would be calling for in a delirium,' Matt commented to Zoe, who was very pale and upset. 'Well, he's still with us, so he's going to be okay.' He conjured a smile of reassurance.

'Holy shit, Matthew!' His uncle observed the patient, while relieving Zoe of Kyle's weight. 'Your friend needs a surgeon.'

Matt looked at his uncle with a knowing and desperate expression on his face.

Max didn't have any children of his own. Matthew was his favourite relative because of his happy-go-lucky attitude to life, and he couldn't bear to see his nephew so distraught. He served Matt a wink of encouragement. 'Luckily for you and your friend, the finest surgeon at that hospital around the corner is currently in my bed.'

'You're kidding?' Matt's spirits soared. 'And Kyle thinks I'm a lucky son-of-a-bitch!'

'But ... this is a hell of a situation you're putting us in.' He felt he had to warn Matt against taking his lady friend's involvement for granted. 'If your friend here doesn't pull through to sign a release form, we could both be in a lot of shit!'

'Then let's get moving,' suggested the beautiful brunette who had appeared in the doorway and was now holding the door open for them with a concerned look on her face.

'Quickly,' she urged. 'If your clothes are anything to go by, he's lost a lot of blood.'

CHAPTER
SIX

WORTH LIVING FOR

Time began slipping into the past for Kyle.

Zoe's kiss filled his senses, as it was the only instance of true tenderness that his soul-mind could recall; this moment of pure bliss preceded a great release and then a short uncomfortable, excited period as their lips parted. 'This is a kiss,' Zoe said invitingly.

The fear of love that lodged in Kyle's throat grew in intensity. The ardent look in Zoe's eyes shocked this fear back down to his heart, where it had been at home so long.

Zoe scoffed and smiled once more. 'That wasn't a kiss.'

She cares for me, he thought as his consciousness was ripped away from Zoe and catapulted back through his friendship with Matthew, which had brought a little of joy and hope into his life.

Back beyond the day they'd met was a long, dark stretch of life that Kyle had suppressed from living memory. Yelling foster parents and siblings mingled with the lectures of doctors and social workers into a noisy, unpleasant montage that sped rapidly by, and so Kyle was spared reliving every beating, and every long period of dulled pain from the heavy drugs fed to him to subdue his angry outbursts and suppress his fantasies.

From the harrowing halls of foster homes and orphanages his being travelled outdoors. There, in a large rolling field, way back in his early youth, Kyle sat chuckling at the antics of the unique otherworldly creatures surrounding him. 'Ron, Ron,' he cheered, as Kyron demonstrated how a boomerang was thrown.

When the weapon was returned to the creature, it was presented to Kyle as a gift: 'From your people.'

The boomerang. This had been something so sacred to Kyle as a youngster that he'd kept it a secret, locking the item in a metal box and throwing away the key to ensure that no one could destroy, steal or otherwise take it from him. He'd carted the box around with him for so long that he'd forgotten why, or even what it contained. He still had the box somewhere, hidden amongst the relics of his long-suffered past.

All visual perception faded; the sound of a beating heart and the chant of a ritual gathering became the centre of his focus. He felt powerful beyond measure in this darkness, and filled with higher purpose, until a bright, persistent flash of light lulled him into a state of feeling nothing more than warm and content.

A deep red mist inflamed the darkness and a familiar foul odour caused a cold dread to besiege Kyle's being.

'Game over.' The green winged devil appeared before him. 'You lose!' The other demons echoed the ringleader's laughter as they manifested around their ex-patron. 'We'd offer you a drink in condolence, but …' the demon gestured at Kyle with both its hands, '… *no body*.'

Kyle's consciousness drifted down and did a full three hundred and sixty degree turn in search of himself. *I'm nothing more than a ball of consciousness.*

'Afraid so.' The demon raised both of its hairless eyebrows. 'Your subtle bodies probably burnt up during descent,' it theorised and shrugged. 'Well, that's death for you.'

Death! Kyle objected. *I can't be dead. There's too much going on in my life! I'm finally starting to piece it all together … I can't die now!*

'Don't complain to us.' The green devil folded his arms. 'If you'd listened to me you'd still be living. But no … you had to go put your faith in those *natural* elementals. Who, just for the record, have all *abandoned* you.' It grinned. 'And as we are now forced to find ourselves a new source of sustenance, we're also going to piss off and leave you.'

Do you know if there's a way back? Just answer me that. The appeal sparked a round of laughter.

'We don't owe you anything.' The fat, greasy demon protected the huge burger it was stuffing into its mouth.

'Can't help you, kid,' said the grey demon, casually blowing smoke rings out its ears.

'Dead is dead, dude,' the staggering drunk belched in conclusion.

'And as you never dragged your consciousness out of the rubbish dump, you can now stew in the marvel of your accomplishments.' The demon held wide its green-winged arms admiring the vast wasteland. 'Enjoy the fruits of your labour.' The demon vanished with a wave, as did the others, one by one.

Did my selflessness in death count for nothing? The thought had great volume, though only in his mind. The atmosphere around his being remained undisturbed, which seemed to confirm the demons' claim that he no longer held any sway in the outcome of creation, for better or worse.

'*There is no way back.*'

In retrospect, Book's parting words seemed more like prophecy. Kyle realised how much he'd been enjoying Book's wise tutelage, but felt that the unexplainable gift from the cosmos had been wasted on him. He'd never fully appreciated or believed in the magic that had been his to wield since birth. He'd beheld and befriended an entire world of beings that no one else seemed to know existed. Others had made his otherworldly talent seem like a curse because they feared or envied him, and he'd been stupid enough to surrender his own judgement and believe that the majority must be right.

Just as I am doing now, he noted, when from within himself came a mournful howl, which yet seemed worlds away. It was Kyron and the beast sounded restrained and panicked — like he wanted to come to Kyle's aid, but was unable to do so, and thus howled out a plea for help.

I don't believe it. This thought had a defeated overtone, but as it echoed through his consciousness Kyle realised what a profoundly powerful statement it was. *And why would I believe a pack of life-sucking killjoys? They've been hacking away at my self-esteem for most of my life, encouraging me to be less than I am. Well, I don't believe I am powerless to decide what is to become of me.*

A mild tremor rumbled forth from Kyle's present location and, despite the disquiet that it caused him, Kyle was relieved to discover that he was not without influence after all. Still, anger wasn't going to get him where he desired to be. If anything would pave the road back to the land of the living it would be the will to love and nurture.

A curious idea began to play with his consciousness and Kyle became preoccupied with this premise: Did he possess the will to create, just as he possessed the will to destroy? Could he heal this place with his good intentions, just as he had damaged it with his outbursts and detrimental desires?

Kyle focused on a small crack in the parched ground, imagining a green stalk sprouting forth. When this did not eventuate he entertained the notion that there was a certain due process in nature that needed to be adhered to; that it was simply unrealistic to believe that lush vegetation could grow in such a situation. *Due process,* he resolved. He then imagined a small cloud growing and that the cloud was his spirit filled to overflowing with the desire to honour and protect all life.

This desire rained down to feed the seed of his mortal self and grow it anew. After this storm had flooded the landscape and dispersed the red haze, rays of sunlight burst through the cloud, shining love and strength upon the seedling of himself.

A green stalk sprouted from the moistened ground, and around it green stalks reared their heads in all directions. So clearly did he see this happening that Kyle could not define the event as real or imagined. A great forest grew from his one tiny seed, and the enormity of the vision caused an explosion of pride and joy in his being. All trace of any hellish existence had been smothered and Kyle now beheld a landscape of rare beauty.

'You *can* make it happen.' A woman stood beside him, one whose face was now familiar.

Mother.

She smiled fondly, although her expression reflected regret: 'You must go back and see to it.'

With this encouragement his mother vanished in a wash of white light, submerging Kyle in the awareness of having form once again.

Pain! The throbbing ache in his side was so intense that it caused Kyle to stir; it felt like his whole upper body was bruised and pinning him down. He was very stiff and very cold. The blinding white light of his vision didn't disappear as he parted his eyelids, but then a shadow appeared and slowly sharpened into an image.

Zoe's weary expression lifted as she noted his eyes upon her. 'He's awake,' she whispered, but her gaze and broad smile did not waver from the patient. 'It's about time ... you had us worried.'

Matt, who'd been dozing in a nearby chair, snapped to life and came to stand beside Zoe. 'Hey there, 007, how're you feeling?' Matt smiled, but the dark rings around his sunken eyes betrayed his anguish.

'I died, didn't I?' Kyle knew without question that he had — he remembered everything.

The smile slipped from both Zoe and Matt's faces, and Matt nodded as his uncle stepped forward. 'This is my Uncle Max ... he's a doctor, remember? You're at his place and no one else knows you're here.'

'Except for this lovely lady.' Max referred Kyle to the surgeon. 'Dr Frederica Urov, whom you have to thank for reviving you and patching you up.'

'You can call me Fred,' the surgeon advised, as Max stepped in to give Kyle a quick check.

'How long was I dead?' Kyle inquired calmly.

Matt was discomforted by this seemingly morbid question, but he was straight with his friend. 'The longest five minutes of my life.'

'Mine too.' Kyle realised that it had seemed longer.

'How do you feel?' Frederica asked. 'You lost a lot of blood, but lucky for you the bullet passed right through you without hitting any bone or major organs.'

Kyle felt great, despite his injuries. Reborn even. 'I'm good,' he replied, 'although my chest is a bit sore.'

'I gave you a transfusion; that would have done wonders.' The surgeon confirmed that he was doing as well as could be expected. 'Your chest is probably a little bruised from the resuscitation. You'll be fine in a few days, but no strenuous exercise for a while, or you might split those stitches.'

His friends did not appear to be faring as well as Kyle was in the wake of the ordeal. 'I'm really sorry for whatever I put you guys through last night.'

'No problem,' Matt's mood lightened. 'Just don't do it again.'

'If you'll just put your autograph on these release forms, which state that you won't sue us for helping you, Fred and I will be happy about our part in your misadventure.' Max handed Kyle a pen.

'Well, considering I was dead, I can hardly complain!' Kyle would have laughed if it wasn't agony just thinking of it, and he was happy to sign his name on the forms.

'Right, then.' The doc took his lady friend by the hand to lead her from the room. 'We'll be back to check on you a bit later.'

'Sorry about your weekend away, Uncle Max.' Matt trailed them to the door.

'Not to worry,' said Max, 'there will be other weekends. But you can stop calling me Uncle Max. It makes me sound like a senior citizen.'

'Fair enough, but ... I haven't told you the whole truth about what happened last night.' Matt felt he should come clean with Max, after all his uncle had done for them.

'Oh, really,' Max exaggerated. 'Matty, I don't want to know.'

'But the police —'

'The police?' Max inhaled deeply and then waved off the warning. 'If anyone comes here looking for your friend, I'm pleading ignorant. I was just doing a favour for my nephew,' he emphasised. 'It's up to you to explain to the police, and your parents, what happened. Fair enough?'

Matt nodded solemnly.

'Your friend will be all right to move in a day or so . . . so see to it.'

Yes, Unc— I mean, Max . . . I will.'

'Then all's well,' Max concluded. 'But you owe me one.'

'I know it,' Matt assured him. 'I owe you big time.'

Max and Frederica departed, and Matt returned to watch over Kyle.

Zoe was biting down on her lip to restrain her tears as she gazed down at Kyle, yet she needed to satisfy her curiosity. 'You remember dying, Kyle?'

'Every second.' Kyle looked up at her, and as raising his left arm obviously pained him, Zoe gently took his hand in both of her own. 'You were the first thing I saw in the afterlife.'

The comment made her laugh and cry at once. 'Perhaps that's because I was holding you when you passed out.' She raised his hand to her face and caressed it against her cheek.

'Or perhaps it was because I needed a good reason to come back,' Kyle retorted and wanted to cringe when he considered how confused Matt would be by the sudden attraction of his best mate to his would-be girlfriend.

Zoe strained to smile through her tears. Matt was clearly feeling uncomfortable, so Kyle quickly switched subjects to one more pressing. 'We have to warn Burke.' The realisation ripped through him like a bullet. 'Get me up.' As he moved to raise himself, the pain made it impossible. 'Ouch!'

'You're not in shock any more and the drugs are wearing off.' Zoe readjusted Kyle's bedclothes like a fussy nurse, when she noticed he was shivering. 'The ordeal your body went through to shock your being back into your body is going to take some time to heal.'

'I'll warn Burke,' Matt impressed on him. 'You've done enough.'

Kyle frowned, shaking his head in protest. 'Not as much as I should have.' He wasn't going to risk losing his father before he ever got the chance to meet him.

'*Rubbish*,' Matt objected. 'That bullet was aimed at me and don't think I don't know it. Me and my big ideas. I'll handle this investigation from here on in. It should never have become your problem.'

As Matt gathered his things, Kyle resigned himself to his lot, not yet ready to explain his own reasons for being so involved. Although he strongly suspected that Timothy Burke was his long-lost father, the *Book of Dreams* had yet to confirm this for sure. *Book!* Kyle was gripped by another fear. 'My bag. Do you still have it?'

Matt, who was loading his camera, placed it aside and reached for the item in question. 'Yeah, it's right here.' After removing the stolen files from it, he was puzzled. 'But, besides these, there's nothing in here.'

'What?' barked Kyle, alarmed. 'Let me see.'

Matt held the bag open in front of Kyle, so that he could view the inside for himself.

The book resided in the bottom of the bag, right where he'd left it, and Kyle smiled broadly in relief. 'Incredible … here.' He wiggled all ten of his fingers, eager to take possession of his property.

Matt became a little concerned for the mental wellbeing of their patient when Kyle cuddled the empty bag to his person like it was a teddy bear. 'Well, if you don't need me for anything else, I'd better get down to the jail.' Camera loaded, Matt packed it away in its carry case.

Zoe put the files into Matt's bag and then refrained from handing it over to him. 'I'll walk you out,' she suggested, a little awkwardly.

To Kyle, Matt seemed reluctant to agree, and he pretended not to notice how jealous Matt was that Kyle was being left in Zoe's care. The bullet might have been aimed at Matt, but it had been meant for Zoe; Kyle had ultimately saved her life. Had this simple twist of fate been the deciding factor in who won her heart?

Kyle gave Matt the thumbs up in parting. 'Be a legend, Matthew. There's a real big story out there with your name on it.'

Matt returned the gesture, somewhat shocked by Kyle's encouragement.

'And be careful,' Kyle added as Matt gathered his luggage and Zoe moved to escort him out of the room. 'Nivok might have reported us to the police … although I suspect he is the kind of man who likes to take care of problems himself.'

'I won't get shot, if that's what you mean.' Matt mocked the predicament Kyle had landed himself in. 'I know what I'm doing,' he assured his friend in a cocky fashion.

'Yes, you do,' Kyle admitted in all seriousness. Matt was again stunned at the change in his friend's attitude.

Silently, Matt's bags were packed in the back of Zoe's car. Matt had left his vehicle back at the Nivok building and it was too risky to go back and retrieve it.

Zoe hadn't imagined that she'd ever see her easygoing friend this sombre and it was heartbreaking to think that she was partly responsible. 'Matt, I feel like I've led you on, or —'

'Hey …' He held up a hand to end her confession. 'He's my best friend. I can't blame you for liking him, and I sure as hell can't blame him for liking you. You're the closest thing to heaven Kyle's ever encountered, that's for certain.' He forced a smile of gracious acceptance.

His words just made Zoe feel worse. She could hardly believe she was passing up the chance to be with a man this understanding and considerate. She thought she'd cried all the tears she possessed last night, but they welled in a second coming.

'Truly, Zoe, it's not your fault. Don't feel bad.' Matt stepped in to comfort her with a hug.

'It just seems so unfair.' Zoe hated that Matt was comforting her when she was breaking his heart.

'No,' Matt corrected. 'It would be unfair of me to protest about you loving a man whose need and want are *far* greater than my own.'

Zoe pulled away to look Matt in the eyes, loving his perceptive and generous nature — she'd never met anyone like him. 'Your parents really did good with you,' she sniffled.

Matt nodded to confirm that he agreed. 'I shall recover,' he told her. 'Kyle never would.' As Zoe was clearly amazed and beyond words, he added, 'But I'm warning you ... he's a bit rough around the edges, and difficult to handle when the mood takes him.'

Zoe had calmed down and was gazing at Matt, her astonishment reflected in the warm smile on her face. 'I think you must be some kind of angel sent to Earth to show us orphans and social outcasts what friendship really means.'

Her theory amused him for many reasons. 'You're hardly a social outcast, Zoe. Women like you are the very essence of high society.'

'That's where you'd be wrong.' Her good mood ebbed a little. 'I never related well to my peers at school. We weren't on the same wavelength, as the material world has never interested me very much. I was labelled "weird" because of my interest in new-age concepts. In fact, I could safely say that I never knew anyone I considered to be a good friend before I met you.' The confession choked her with emotion and she cleared her throat, wanting to continue before Matt had a chance to speak. 'That's why this whole situation with Kyle is so distressing to me. I'm afraid of losing my only true friend.'

'I'm not going anywhere,' Matt emphasised, then realising he was holding the car keys, he conceded, 'Well, I am … but I'll be back. Believe me, if you're serious about Kyle, you're going to need a friend who even vaguely understands what goes on in that head of his.'

Zoe laughed at this, for Kyle's mysterious ways were already perplexing her. 'I'm not too sure what I feel about Kyle,' she admitted. 'It's not really an attraction. It's more like a haunting.'

'He's a spooky lad to be sure,' Matt backed her up on this, 'but you gotta love him.' He gave a cheeky wink of encouragement and opened the door of the luxury vehicle. After briefly admiring his ride, Matt climbed into the driver's seat.

No sooner had Matt and Zoe left the room than Kyle was lifting Book onto his lap. He regarded the treasure like an old familiar friend that he was very glad to see; the regrets he'd had in death were still fresh in his mind and Kyle was now eager to put his magical gift to its best use. He opened Book at the dog-eared page, scarcely believing his own lack of respect for damaging the treasure in such a fashion. 'I must get a bookmark,' he noted out loud, to let Book know it wouldn't happen again.

Upon finding his place Kyle was alarmed to find only one sentence beyond what he'd read.

You are not alone.

The rest of the book was entirely blank; the text had simply disappeared.

'No, don't lock me out,' Kyle quietly pleaded, although Book's parting prophecy, that there would be no return to the story after his little sidetrack, was preying on his mind. 'I've been to hell and back to resume this quest. Please give me one more crack at it.' Kyle stared into the blankness below Book's final statement, but when the text did not appear, his sight drifted upward. 'What is that supposed to mean, anyway ... You are not alone?'

Kyle was startled when Zoe came through the door and her presence seemed to explain Book's conundrum. He dropped his hands onto the bed and the book fell open on his lap. Kyle was, by now, confident that no one else could see Book, so he didn't bother trying to hide it. Zoe wore a warm smile on her face, a nurturing look that Kyle had seen in the movies but never in his personal life. He loved that her attention was intent upon him, but with Tim being released from prison and probably being on the police *Wanted* list himself, Kyle felt that reading Book was more pressing than romance at present. How was he going to persuade Zoe to leave him alone, without hurting her feelings?

'You must have things you'd rather be doing than babysitting me ... I'll be fine here on my own if you want to go.' Again Kyle had to refrain from cringing, not really happy with the way the offer sounded.

Zoe wasn't sure how to interpret his opening statement. 'I'm currently in hiding, just like you. And I really don't think you'll be fine on your own when you can't even raise your arms without assistance.' She served him a sensible look. 'However, if you are too tired to deal with us at present, I can leave you to rest.'

Kyle felt he must be looking grateful for the offer, but as she'd been wonderful enough to award him an easy way out he didn't have the heart to take it. 'I hope I am never too tired to deal with us,' he replied with a smile. 'What's on your mind?'

Zoe was gratified by his interest and came to sit beside him on the bed. 'Our dream, and the morning after it ... you were there when I woke, while I meditated, when Matt and my uncle were there ... yes, you were,' she challenged him, as Kyle had begun shaking his head! Then Zoe gasped in understanding. 'It was you distracting my uncle with the falling picture so I could hide the keys, wasn't it?'

Kyle cracked a cheeky smile. 'How could I have been there?'

'It could have been connected with your recent NDE.'

'My what?' Kyle laughed, and it hurt.

'Near Death Experience,' Zoe added, excited by her theory. 'You said you'd seen me in the afterlife. Was it that morning?'

Kyle had a think about what she was suggesting and was rather impressed by her reasoning. 'Good theory, but ... no.'

Zoe regarded him with a wary but playful expression. 'You see, I spoke with Matt last night and I know for a fact that he didn't tell you about our plans for my uncle. Apparently you'd just disappeared? And we both know *I* didn't tell you.' She smiled as the smug grin slipped from Kyle's face. 'So, explain how you knew and where you were.' She paused only a moment as she leaned in close to her hostage. 'You can't, can you?'

Kyle had no explanation, but since he thought Zoe was about to kiss him, he decided to play dumb and yield.

'*So*, are you going to tell me how you got into my dreams, how your spirit got into my apartment?'

Zoe's intimate but pressing tone was a little unnerving for Kyle. He hadn't had a whole lot of success with women, and his experience for handling such moments was limited.

'I know how you feel, Kyle. I literally recognise your energy.' She surprised him by this sudden turn in the conversation. 'That's how I know you were there that morning. I believe you have psychic ability that you're either denying or hiding from the world ... so, which is it?'

'Are you a witch?' He was only half joking with the inquiry.

'Which is it?' she repeated, folding her arms, determined to get an answer.

Kyle rubbed his face with his hands, trying to think. 'When you said coming back could be disastrous, I thought you meant the bullet,' he mumbled to himself, before deciding to confide in Zoe. 'All right ... I'm in denial and have been for most of my life.'

Zoe saw some promise in his answer. 'But not lately.'

'No,' he confirmed. 'Lately ... I've really woken up to myself.'

'And do you like what you see?' Zoe leaned in close again.

'At present, I *love* what I see.' Kyle could barely believe he'd said the 'L' word, but his horror was dispersed during a long and luscious kiss. When they parted, Kyle found himself staring straight down Zoe's shirt. The view was stimulating to say the least. *Well, at least I know the lower half of me still works.*

'What's your talent?' Zoe lifted his chin with an outstretched finger so that Kyle was looking her in the eyes. 'Besides telepathy.'

'I can't read the minds of others.' Kyle was flattered by her assumption.

'No, you read their emotions,' Zoe informed him. 'I've witnessed you do it many times. But there's something else, isn't there?'

Kyle nodded, his trust strengthened by speaking with an obvious believer, a person who had some idea what they were talking about when it came to psychic phenomena. 'I don't know if there is a name for my talent,' he began rather awkwardly. 'I've always been told it was a delusion induced by my want of family.'

'You see ghosts?' she said with a gasp.

'Not until my recent death,' he clarified. 'No, I see otherworldly creatures.'

'Creatures?' Zoe's eyes opened wide in awe. 'Sylphs, salamanders, gnomes, undines?'

'Yep,' Kyle confirmed, 'and more besides.'

Zoe was smiling so broadly her face was aching from the stress. 'I've seen them too.'

The statement was such a shock, and so exciting to Kyle, that he sat bolt upright. 'You have?' The movement was agony, but the news was ecstasy. It was confirmation that he wasn't insane.

'Not here in the physical world, you understand,' Zoe clarified, 'but in the astral world I have seen them. You see, one of my psychic talents is OBEs —'

'Out of Body Experiences.' Kyle knew about them well enough. 'I've just started doing that, but I need elemental assistance. Wow, you can do that by yourself?'

Zoe nodded, over the moon to finally find a like-talented soul. 'I can teach you some time, if you like?'

Kyle was enthusiastic about that idea. Maybe he wouldn't need the book, after all. Maybe he never did? 'Teach me now.'

'After an NDE, I don't know if an OBE would be the best idea,' Zoe reasoned, 'but there is a name for your talent. The ability to see etheric world intelligences is part and parcel of being clairvoyant.'

'Clairvoyant?' Kyle wasn't sure he liked the sound of that.

'It's from the French, meaning "clear vision",' Zoe explained. 'Do you hear your little creatures as well as see them?'

'They're not all little,' Kyle corrected her misconception, 'but, yes, I do.'

'Then you're clairaudient as well.'

'No shit.' Kyle was amazed by her knowledge.

'From the French, meaning "clear audio". If you perceive sounds or words, when no person or physical world entity is present, and they are inaudible to normal hearing *that* is clairaudience. These sounds can appear to come from within the head or from out in the atmosphere.'

'All of the above.' Kyle was dumbfounded by Zoe's depth of knowledge and, clearly, he was a pleasant surprise for her.

'Tell me more about your creatures,' Zoe begged, like an excited child waiting for a good bedtime story.

She was the first person who had ever truly believed him; how could he possibly resist the opportunity to tell her a lifetime of stored-up tales.

Matt leant on one of the pillars holding up the huge building that housed the jail, keeping himself out of sight. Amongst the general movement in the street out front, he noticed a man sliding out from underneath a vehicle. Not even looking back to the car, the fellow strolled off up the road, brushing his hands clean. Matt had to empathise with the stranger, as car troubles always put a total downer on anyone's day. He returned his sights to the large double doors of the jail in time to see Timothy Burke being escorted out of the building by an Indigenous fellow. The pair appeared in good spirits as they bounced down the stairs, and Matt made haste to catch them up. 'Timothy Burke?' he called, and managed to secure Burke's attention. Matt held out his hand and shook Timothy's firmly. 'I'm Matthew Ryan. I need to speak with you urgently. In fact, your life might depend on it.'

Not knowing what to make of Matt, Timothy looked at his friend, who shrugged and gave Tim a slap on the shoulder. 'I'll warm up the car.'

His companion took off down the stairs, whereupon Tim looked back to Matt and was a little put out when he noticed the large bag slung over the lad's shoulder. 'Is that a camera bag, perchance? If you're a reporter, forget it, I have nothing to say.' Tim had hoped to make a quick getaway.

Matt gripped Tim's shirt to keep him in place. 'Before my very short — we're talking a week here — but eventful career as a cameraman,' Matt smiled and released Tim, who was obviously perturbed at being held — he seemed a fairly virile fellow, so Matt wasn't game to push his luck, 'I was in the employ of Nivok Industries.'

The mention of the company captured Tim's interest.

'And I have good reason to believe — *proof*, in fact — that James Nivok is planning to kill you.'

Tim was not at all surprised by the news. 'Can you tell me something I don't know?'

Matt grinned in response, when, out of the corner of his eye, he noticed Tim's companion getting into the same car he had earlier watched the man crawl out from underneath.

'What proof?' Tim pursued the conversation, even though he seemed to have lost the young cameraman's attention.

'Is that *your* car?' Matt queried anxiously, as he ran off down the stairs. 'No!' he yelled out to Tim's friend, who didn't hear him over the street noise. 'No! Don't start the —'

The car exploded in front of Matt and the force of the blast threw him off his feet and back on to the steps. He rolled over to catch Tim's reaction and saw him running towards the car that was now a furnace. Matt leapt up and bounded across the steps to intercept Timothy.

'Harry!' Tim, in a fit of rage, thrust Matt aside and continued his rush down the steps.

Matt was not to be deterred so easily. He sprang on to Tim's back and wrestled him to a standstill. 'Whoever set that bomb is likely to be still around here, making sure you got snuffed,' Matt uttered into the irate man's ear. 'You can't do anything for your friend. I have to get you out of here.'

Timothy growled in protest, trying to release himself from Matt's restraining grip, but Matt only tightened his hold. The headlock started to make Tim lightheaded.

'I'm going to do this one way,' Matt tightened his headlock again, 'or the other.'

Tim relented, collapsing on to the steps, and Matt let him go, flopping down beside Tim to catch his breath. Tim looked at the stranger, confused. 'What is your problem?'

'I'm sorry, I really am,' Matt assured him, panting as his heart raced in his chest, 'but we've got to go now. You see, Nivok is after my arse too.' Matt glanced up to notice police flooding from the building, and moved fast to grab his camera case before they got too close.

'So what's Nivok pissed at you for?' Tim queried as Matt raced back up the stairs.

'Oy, you!' A policeman targeted Matt with his finger. 'That's one of the men wanted for kidnapping James Nivok's niece.' He sent his men chasing after the suspect as he fled with Timothy Burke.

'You kidnapped Nivok's niece!' Tim yelled as they ran.

'No.' Matt was just as startled by the charge. 'Zoe's a friend of mine.' Matt sighted the Saab and unlocked the doors with the remote as they ran.

'Impressive wheels.' Tim was most relieved at the fact.

'Thanks, it's Zoe's.' Matt realised that this information made him seem guilty of the charge against him.

'Shit! I'll drive.' Tim snatched the keys from Matt, who had no time to argue.

The luxury car was tearing out on to the street before Matt had even got his door closed.

'Jesus!' Matt dragged on his seatbelt. He could feel himself going pale. 'I'm in so much shit.'

'Don't worry, kid. I'm real good at this,' Tim advised him while remaining intent on escape. 'We'll be in the next suburb before they even get out of the car park.'

'But won't they be looking for this car?' Matt reasoned.

Tim smiled and, around the next bend, drove

into the huge multi-level car park of a shopping mall. Ascending a few floors, Tim parked the car in a nice dark corner and tossed Matt the keys. 'We should be able to find a more suitable vehicle around here somewhere, don't you think?'

Matt had been imagining a long high-speed chase that ended in disaster or arrest. The speed and ease of their escape amazed him. 'That was legendary.'

'We're not in the woods yet.' Tim climbed out of the car to speed Matt along.

'Don't you mean out?' Matt retrieved his bags and locked up the vehicle.

'Nope.' Tim made a beeline for the stairs that led to the lower levels.

The excitement of the conversation had worn Zoe out. Try as she might to keep her weary eyes open, she'd finally succumbed to her exhaustion and was sleeping soundly on the bed alongside Kyle.

He'd told her about Crystaleyes, Blue and Kyron, and the different creatures he'd been perceiving and drawing since early youth. He hadn't mentioned Book, because Kyle was not entirely sure what manner of entity Book was. However, he had told Zoe that if she found him in a trance at any time to leave him be, as he would be conversing with his elementals — which wasn't a lie.

It was very awkward trying to lift up the book at his side to read and not disturb the much needed warmth of the blanket around him, so Kyle merely placed his hand on Book and closed his eyes to visualise the vanished text returned to the page.

The cover of the book began wriggling under his fingers, and the wee occupants emerged into Kyle's world and scattered all over the bed. A couple of the creatures took an interest in Zoe, admiring her face at close range. The ugly beast that was their chieftain had taken a stand on top of the book and, pointing his spear at Kyle, said in a husky, deep voice: 'Your destiny is being assigned to someone more capable. We must take back the book ... the matter is out of our hands.'

As the creatures converged on his treasure, Kyle shook the little beasts off. They squawked, growled and chattered in objection. 'It's a bit rude to give away my destiny when I'm not yet dead, don't you think?'

You should be deceased and reality is still catching up with the unexpected change in events.

Kyle heard Book's response in his mind. '*Should be's* don't count,' he argued.

'It is the perfect description of you though: "should be". He who should be and never is.'

Kyle recognised the voice, and looked around the room in search of Crystaleyes.

From the dirt in a large pot plant, the strange green creature burrowed his way out. He shook off the soil and floated up into clear view. 'We abandoned you last night because we were obliged to do so.'

'Obliged by whom?' Kyle inquired with great interest.

The water in the fish tank against the far wall of the room began to bubble and the undine, Blue, rose to stand on the surface. 'By the laws of creation and a great governing Spirit, whose name I will not utter in your presence for fear of attracting his attention to the fact that you are still alive.'

Crystaleyes nodded to second Blue's reasoning, as he obviously shared his concern.

'Well, I don't see the point in being alive if my destiny has been reassigned. You all either support me or you don't,' Kyle stressed. 'Can't I lodge an appeal or something with this governing Spirit?'

'We are taking care of that,' Crystaleyes whispered in a harsh tone, deeply offended, 'even though you are nowhere near ready to address him ... all great spirits reside in planes far from your present reach.' The small green creature floated down beside Kyle to fix his colourful, hypnotic eyes upon those of his charge. 'We,' Crystaleyes motioned to Blue, 'have put ourselves at risk. We could end up demoted to being servants of vegetable kingdom consciousness ... the great architects of creation don't appreciate it when we mere worker beings take physical world matters into our own hands. If we get caught supporting you before we can activate your full potential for planetary service, well ... need I say it would mean de-evolution for us all, and not all of your elemental guardians believe you are worth that risk. They are only sustaining you for long enough to observe you in person and to decide what your fate will be. In order to win their full support, you're going to have to start proving your worth ... in that you can dedicate yourself to a task and see it to completion.'

'I won't be disturbed this time. Zoe will see to that,' Kyle promised, comprehending the severity of their situation and honoured by their faith in him. 'I am very grateful for your aid and I am entirely at your disposal.'

Crystaleyes nodded. 'How right you are. Bring him out.' The being raised his arms into the air, and set Kyle's world into a spin.

CHAPTER
SEVEN

BREATH OF LIFE

When his exterior perception stabilised, Kyle was standing before a huge white castle. Bursts of iridescent colour passed through the walls of the round structure.

In the gardens, dynamic flowers grew, like tiny firecrackers in constant motion, blooming and changing colour in a never-ending stream of combinations. Soft mists constantly billowed out and fell from the fountains and waterfalls, their hues changing in periodic bursts. The sky and sun above were a vibrant shade of mauve, in stunning contrast to the iridescent white of the mammoth fortress and the white mist that cloaked the ground between the flowerbeds and the billowing colour-filled garden features.

Turning in circles to admire the breathtaking gardens, Kyle was thrilled to spy Kyron nearby. The beast was snuggling into the soft mist that covered the ground and seemed to be in a state of complete bliss. 'Ron!'

The huge creature ceased trying to scratch its back against the ground and flipped quickly onto its hands and knees. 'Kyle!' It scrambled along on all fours eager to greet its charge, but then stood up to take Kyle in hand and toss him in the air. 'They told me they'd bring you back to me ... and here you are, safe and sound.' He cuddled Kyle to his big furry chest.

'Thanks, buddy.' Kyle pushed himself away from the animal to avoid getting fur in his mouth. 'How did you manage to persuade them?'

'I howled in a few favours.' Kyron took the hint and put Kyle down. 'If you die, so does my means to make amends with your world.'

Kyle was intrigued. 'Amends?' he queried. The huge creature was so sweet and timid in nature Kyle couldn't imagine what he could possibly have done to atone for. 'Are you talking about overcoming your shyness of the physical world?'

'I was not always the placid being I am today,' Kyron confessed with a guilt-ridden expression. 'When pushed, I abused the strength given me by the Great Spirit, and so it was taken from me and will remain absent from my character for as long as the rift I created in your world remains unhealed.'

'What did you do?' Kyle had to ask, although Kyron appeared to be wary of the topic.

Now is not the time, Kyron, Book interrupted, and the creature bowed, quietly relieved by Book's intervention. *I have brought you forth to the mental realm, Kyle. We have exercised and cleansed your emotional body to some degree. Here is where your mental body can be whipped into shape.*

'A bit of a brainwash, hey?' Kyle figured his mind probably had a few cobwebs that needed removing. 'I'm up for it.'

The castle behind you is of the air.

Kyle and Kyron turned to face the glittering, white construction.

Inside you will find Adreana, who is the very breath you breathe. For obvious reasons, to hold her favour is all-important. Wipe all negative thoughts from your mind, or you will surely offend. If she finds you worthy, then you have only one more element to persuade to your cause in order to gain an audience with the Great Spirit.

'Yes ... Fire.' Kyle sounded daunted at the prospect of meeting this last elemental. Meanwhile, he approached the air elemental's castle, which had neither gates nor door, and certainly no knocker or doorbell. The sparkling substance of the walls appeared as solid as cement and as he stood before the stronghold wondering how he would gain entry, Kyle's shivering became more obvious. 'Is that why I still feel so cold ... because my fire element is not disposed towards me?' Book gave no comment. 'Well, are you going to tell me how I get into this fortress?'

Does your mind not know the meaning of the word 'exercise'?

Kyron, seeing Kyle's dilemma, strode towards the large wall, his hands held out in front of him. 'I shall get it open for you.' The huge beast charged towards the wall and disappeared into it.

'Kyron?' Kyle hugged Book to his chest, seeking extra warmth for his freezing form, but the book failed to assuage his need.

A moment later Kyron stuck his head through the wall. 'There's nothing to it, come through.' The creature disappeared behind the wall once more.

Kyle ventured to stick a hand into the solid-looking substance; it felt slightly denser than the air itself. 'Here goes.' He walked on through, momentarily blinded by the illusion of the structure's substance.

Beyond was a room of cathedral-like appearance and proportions. Wispy curtains hung down the walls in shades of purple, mauve, lavender and lilac. The fabric lent a dramatic atmosphere as it fluttered in the breeze: there were no windows in the walls, hence no breeze to blow the sheer drapes. There was no furniture to speak of, but huge columns were set in a circle to support the ceiling and the transparent dome in the centre of it. These were no ordinary columns as they were not solid, but were composed of a cloud-like substance that moved in a slow tornado-like motion as they stood in place. Beautiful music wafted through the dwelling: no voices or instruments, only melodious tones that seemed to stem from everything and from every direction.

On a round, stepped platform in the middle of the room, Kyle spied Zoe's subtle form in the company of an astoundingly beautiful spirit.

The spirit was unlike any human female that Kyle had ever seen, for her features were elf-like. This entity was Adreana, Kyle assumed. Her long hair was streaked with brilliant blue and violet, and her skin was a pale shade of mauve. All the colours of her environment — purples, pinks, blues and silver — were reflected in her flowing, glittering attire.

The two women were lying opposite each other on lush lounges of deep purple velvet, sipping drinks from silver goblets as they quietly conversed. Upon sighting Kyle, Zoe sprang to her feet, delighted to see him.

'Here you are! We've been waiting for you.' Her goblet vanished as she rushed down the stairs to greet him.

'Have you?' Kyle was uneasy at being the topic of girl-talk.

Zoe's mental being was positively glowing with an ultraviolet light; Adreana and her palace emitted the same radiant colour. Glancing down upon himself, Kyle realised he was still illumed in the blue glow of the astral world.

'Is my violet body at the cleaners?' he queried Zoe, who shook her head ahead of hugging him.

'It would be truer to say that your mental body needs to go to the cleaners.'

The majestic female spirit began to rise into the air. As Adreana rose, her image began to expand and fill the huge space inside the room. Her unusually large, round eyes of deepest violet became the focus of attention when light appeared to radiate from them.

Kyron backed away, overawed by the power of her manifestation. Kyle wanted to, but overcame his fear to hold his ground. Upon seeing this, Kyron followed the example of his charge, stopping still and standing tall.

In a voice as soft and sweet as a gentle breeze, Adreana spoke: 'The rainbow serpent has arisen in you.'

How perplexing Kyle found this statement must have shown in his expression for Zoe offered him understanding.

'In ancient Sanskrit the Kundalini was also known as the rainbow serpent ... the invisible, coiled life force conductor that begins at the base of your spine and fuels your subtle bodies.' Zoe moved around in front of Kyle to will the exposure of the whirling flower-like centres of her own subtle bodies. 'The serpent is fed by these centres, known as the chakras.'

Kyle was astounded to view a rainbow array of spinning light centres in her body which were fairly evenly spaced from the base of her spine to the tip of her head.

'As you evolve physically, emotionally, mentally and spiritually, higher chakra are activated,' Zoe continued. 'And from the primeval instincts of your root chakra,' Zoe motioned to the spinning red centre that was the lowest of the seven and located in line with her coccyx, 'your consciousness rises through the creativity of your spleen,' she raised her hands to motion to each centre accordingly, 'the gut instinct of your solar plexus, the unconditional love of your heart, the communication of your throat, the divine sight of your third eye and, eventually, to your crown chakra. As your centre of conscious function rises, so too does the coiled Kundalini rise. When the Kundalini reaches the crown chakra, it unites with the silver cord that allows the spirit to evolve to a higher plane of awareness, whereby physical world incarnation is no longer necessary.'

'The rainbow serpent is a spirit of the water, rain and floods, for without these the earth would become parched and life would cease to exist ...' Adreana took over the lesson. 'So too would life cease to be if the soul was starved of vital life force. Blue's emotional trials allowed your consciousness to punch a hole through the lifelong blockage in your heart centre, young warrior. However, the serpent has now hit a block in your throat, and communication is my department. Will you be of violet hue when you leave my presence and a step closer to reclaiming your destiny? We shall see.' There was a friendly challenge in her tone, and

Adreana smiled. 'Zoe, Kyron, please leave us now.'

Zoe gave Kyle a smile of reassurance as she took Kyron by the hand.

'Kyle?' The creature double-checked with his charge.

'It's okay, buddy, I'll be fine,' said Kyle most unconvincingly, as he was not game to argue with the majestic presence.

Reassured, and seemingly oblivious to Kyle's apprehension, Kyron was perfectly happy to escort Zoe out through the wall and into the garden.

The giant manifestation turned her attention to Kyle and frowned as she studied him. 'So you are the one who is causing so much concern?'

Kyle bowed his head slightly as the entity circled him, aware that she was scrutinising his every movement and possibly his every thought. *Stay positive*, Kyle warned himself, deciding to remain silent and hopefully out of trouble.

Upon completing her circuit, Adreana became stationary. 'Do you realise the very awkward position you have put us in? It is not at all wise to contradict creation. It was only due to Kyron's plight that I considered sustaining you long enough for this audience.'

'We are sincerely grateful.' Kyle had begun to bounce up and down, rubbing the tops of his arms in an attempt to dispel his shivers.

'The reason you feel so cold is that your fire elemental is still undecided about sustaining you.'

'I figured.' Kyle was rather disturbed at such confirmation of his plight, and decided the best way to be rid of the cold was to get on with this quest. 'So, what does my air elemental have to speak with Zoe about?'

Adreana smiled, seeming pleased that he'd raised the subject.

Kyle, you'd better know your mind in this affair ... see the truth by heeding your instinct.

'Yes, thank you, Book.' Adreana was most displeased, having overlooked dismissing Book with the others.

Zoe unexpectedly emerged through the wall to join them, looking at Adreana as if the entity had requested her presence.

'I regret I must bid you to leave us also, Book.' Adreana's glare of disapproval disappeared immediately and she motioned to Zoe to come forward and take possession of the item in Kyle's hands.

Adreana placed her hands on her hips, but smiled amiably as Zoe carried Book back through the wall, then turned her sights on Kyle to answer his query. 'I had to consult with Zoe on this issue ... after all her future did lie alongside yours —'

'What do you mean, did?' Kyle objected.

'Well, unofficially you're dead, my sweet,' she explained rationally, although there was the hint of a tease in her manner. 'And in light of what's happened ...'

Kyle observed Adreana cautiously as she floated around him, pondering how she could reassign his future.

'I suppose Zoe's future could just as easily lie with Matthew ... Zoe is quite fond of him, as you know.'

Kyle placed his hands on his hips, irked by the suggestion. 'Did Zoe tell you that?'

'Perhaps.' Adreana playfully avoided answering him. 'What do you think?'

All his better instincts knew that this was a test, and as he didn't wish to fail it, Kyle decided not to say anything before first carefully considering his response.

Adreana, therefore, took the opportunity to expand her theory. 'After all, why shouldn't Zoe like Matthew? He is a sweet boy, who would surely take good care of her. A girl could depend on him and trust him to do the right thing by her no matter what circumstances might arise. And Matthew did, if you remember, find her first.' Adreana paused to study Kyle, who had slowly begun to pace, assembling a response in his mind. This made Adreana briefly smile, but she hid the reaction as Kyle looked at her to see if she was quite finished. 'I also recall that the means by which you won Zoe's affection was not entirely sportsmanlike. You knew how Matt felt about her. Why shouldn't he get the girl? It would seem perfect karma to me.'

Kyle ceased his pacing, suddenly understanding Book's warning. 'What I really feel about this situation is not what you would have me believe.' Kyle looked at Adreana, wising up to her game and very confident of his own mind.

'Really?' Adreana smiled at his apparent

certainty. 'Then, young warrior, pray express yourself.'

'We're not just talking about some girl I romanced out from under my best friend.' Kyle decided to speak frankly, hoping he would not offend. 'And it's not that Zoe's rich, beautiful, intelligent and caring. What I find most alluring about Zoe is that she's the only person who has ever truly believed in the real me. Our attraction is due to our otherworldly interests. We connect on a higher level.' Kyle had to smile, realising that Zoe's discussion with Adreana before his arrival was evidence of this. 'The true dispute underlying my current situation is that I broke my word to Book, and to you all, to go and prevent my best friend from being shot. And if you think Matt would have done any different in my place, then you underestimate our friendship. If I've mucked up some higher schedule, I am sincerely sorry, but I wasn't prepared to sacrifice my best and only friend just to keep bettering myself.' Kyle found it difficult not to sound frustrated by the coldness he couldn't dispel.

Adreana chuckled, amused. 'Is that what you think this little adventure is all about, bettering yourself? There is so much more at stake than just you.' However, satisfied with his answer, the air spirit assumed a normal size and floated down to Kyle, coming to rest a short distance away.

Kyle hoped he had her favour as he launched into his final appeal. 'I realise I have forced you all to make a difficult compromise, but I have a mystery to sort out downstairs. The most exciting thing that's ever happened in my life is going on right now, and I'm missing it. My best friend will probably get his head shot off if I'm not around to prevent it, and I've finally got a really amazing woman interested in me and my weird pastimes!'

'Breathe easy.' Adreana smiled, finding his concerns and determination most appealing. 'I shall not detain you much longer. You do possess great insight, and you express yourself beautifully. Now, if you would only use these skills for good and not to cause mischief in your life, all would be well.'

Kyle took a moment to digest her criticism, before vowing sincerely, 'All will be well, I promise you.'

'Then, I forgive you for the inconvenience

and worry you have caused,' she announced finally. 'I believe you are still our best hope for the quest at hand, and thus I support your plea for life.'

'That is a great relief. I thank you.' Kyle gave a slight bow of gratitude. 'Now about this "quest at hand" you mentioned ... you all speak as if there is an event in my future that is a foregone conclusion?' All the secrecy and innuendo was beginning to bug him.

'Trust that you have everything you need to discover that answer yourself. Every decision you make will be the right decision; every path you take is the one that leads to your destiny. Your inner story is fast racing towards a climax, and beyond this place in your lower mental realm resides the formless worlds where the Great Spirits of this evolutionary chain reside. You need only the blessing of your fire aspect, and the rainbow serpent will fully arise in you. Once you are in direct contact with the architects of your creation there will never be a question you cannot obtain the answer to. All shall be clear.' Adreana floated around behind Kyle, and placed one palm over Kyle's throat centre and her other palm over his third eye. 'I bestow on you the blessing of the Sylphs. May our virtues of intellect, speed, communication, detachment, adaptability, learning, travel and fast thought flow freely through your form to the aid of all there is.'

A great rush of awareness passed through Kyle's being, and the vibrational frequency of his subtle form rose and changed in colour from ultra-blue to ultraviolet. 'Whoa!' he mumbled, feeling lighter and somehow freer than before.

'I give you leave to move on to the next scene in your story,' Adreana let Kyle go, 'and I trust that Burn-a-debt will find you as full of promise as I do.'

'Bernadette?' Kyle opened his eyes, finding the name disconcerting. 'My fire elemental?'

Adreana nodded. 'During the trials and quest ahead, remember that Will creates intelligently, Desire, blindly and unconsciously. Desire is Will discrowned — the captive, the slave of matter.'

Kyle was surprised to understand her meaning. 'I believe I now see the difference.' He contemplated the advice long and hard. 'I have been such an idiot,' he concluded. 'I have blamed everyone else for my misfortune, using my plight as an excuse to be a failure and good for nothing. I've even blamed my mother for dying on me, and even for giving birth to me in the first place, when she died to give me life … the life I am now fighting for.' Kyle looked at Adreana, his eyes wide with revelation. 'I brought about my own death,' he stated surely. 'I had such little regard for my life that I actually willed to take that bullet. Whereas Matt, with his great regard for life, probably wouldn't have died even if he had been shot.'

Adreana nodded in agreement. 'Matt has developed a very strong will. His subconscious instructions to the universe are very clear.'

'That's why he always gets what he wants,' Kyle realised, and then raised a finger, having figured something else. 'However, in regard to Zoe, my will to be with her must have been stronger than his?' he supposed.

'You are more deeply connected to Zoe than you can possibly realise at this stage of the story, but there are karmic factors at play as well as your personal will,' Adreana told him.

Kyle noted that she had not really confirmed his theory, but then he *was* getting a little off the track. 'So,' he rubbed his hands together, to aid concentration, 'the more I appreciate the life I was given, the better my chances are of keeping it.'

Adreana melted into a warm smile as she gave a slight nod. 'And I have a little gift that is sure to help you with that.'

The beautiful Sylph blew Kyle a kiss, and as the gentle breeze of her breath made contact with his face, his eyes closed to fully appreciate the heavenly scent of spring in the wilderness.

In the wilderness was exactly where Kyle was when he opened his eyes. A beautiful waterfall cascaded down the mountain before him into a pool of sparkling spring water. *I know this place.* It was the land pictured on the wall of Nivok's office.

'Home.' Kyron stood a short distance away, gazing up at the mountain with pride and awe.

'This is where you live?' Kyle was interested to learn as much. Perhaps this was why he thought he had recognised the mountain from the beginning; maybe he was picking up on his guide's love of the place?

'This mountain was named after me,' the beast advised Kyle proudly, 'or rather, my howl. The locals call it Turrammelin, which means "makes big noise".'

'As you do when provoked,' Kyle concluded with good cheer. However, Kyron seemed concerned at Kyle's words and merely nodded as he wandered towards the water.

Massive trees surrounded the large waterhole, all of which Kyron was attempting to hug in turn. 'Friends,' said the creature as he embraced the trunk of an old white gum, 'it's so good to see you after all this time.'

Huge ferns and native wildflowers were abundant around the water's edge where the sunlight managed to penetrate the canopy.

The critters which had sent Kyle insane as a youth were everywhere: tending flora, enjoying the water, whistling through the trees and flying on the breeze.

Kyle had never even been camping, let alone in a rainforest, and that was probably a good thing. In the city, at least, Kyle only saw a critter every now and again. If he'd been raised in the bush, he would have gone completely nuts pretending not to see them; they were everywhere.

All life here was exchanging ultraviolet energy with Kyle's being and with every other being, just as all-that-was on Blue's beach had exchanged energies. Only this time Kyle wasn't sucking the life force out of everything in his immediate area — he was clear, he was light.

His body was still possessed by a deep chill, however, and the warmth of the sun on his face was very welcome. The sun overhead was ultraviolet, as it had been when Kyle last saw it. This seemed to indicate that he was still in Adreana's realm. It was also apparent that just as he had many different bodies on many different levels of awareness, so did the Earth, for this place was clearly the virgin version of the forest he'd seen pictured on Nivok's wall. 'Please don't tell me Nivok is planning to destroy this place.'

'I'm afraid the Nivoks destroyed much of this place a long time ago.'

Kyle turned quickly towards the female voice.

She was a young woman, with long dark hair and a coppery complexion. She was all suited up for trekking; a large backpack sat on her back with a net stuck though it.

Kyle's eyes opened wide as he realised who this shapely, beautiful woman was. 'You're my m—' Startled by the revelation, Kyle lost his footing on the rocks and came to land on his behind in the shallow water. '—other!'

She nodded with a grin of amusement.

'But you're so ...' He implied 'shapely' with his hands. '... young!'

She laughed, offering him a hand up. Kyle, still overwhelmed by this development, accepted her aid. 'Well, I wasn't that much older than you are now when I died —' She shied away from finishing her sentence.

Kyle anticipated her words and felt a sudden twinge of guilt as he came to stand on his own two feet once again. 'Giving birth to me.' Alex gave an awkward nod and Kyle had to wonder if, in all those times he'd cursed her for giving him life, she'd heard him. 'I know I must seem like an awful ingrate —'

'No, you don't,' Alex insisted, discarding her backpack to hug Kyle, wanting to quell his anxiety. 'My death wasn't a possibility your father and I had considered, and you must believe that we did have a much better life planned for you.'

Having never known a mother's embrace, Kyle felt a deep security in her arms, and the foreign sensation of love without desire was all-consuming. 'I do believe that now.' Kyle was suddenly overcome by another realisation. 'And if you are my mother, then Timothy Burke *is* my father.' Kyle stepped away from the embrace, suddenly defensive. 'He's been in hiding all these years ... why? Is there a reason why he never tried to find me?'

'If he'd come out in the open to get you, he would have been killed, Kyle. And he feared placing you in danger. He had no choice but to stay away from you.'

'But why is he in hiding? What did he do?' Kyle wanted to know.

'Your father's only crime was in trying to save this place.' Alex motioned to the paradise around them. 'Those who want to develop it have been trying to frame Tim for the murder of the owner of the property since before my death.'

'Nivok.' Kyle's eyes narrowed, remembering the magnate's expression when he'd viewed the picture of Zoe's parents in her apartment that fateful morning. 'That was guilt I saw in his face.'

'But you'll have a hard time proving he was to blame,' Alex advised him, 'or at least Tim has had a fine time trying to clear himself of the charges.'

'So Dad has had a few quests keeping him busy.' Kyle finally had to concede that he'd been sorely mistaken about both his parents and he still didn't know the half of it. 'I understand Tim wanting to prove that Nivok is framing him, but what is his attachment to this place?'

'You,' Alex explained.

'Me?' Kyle's frown begged for more information.

'Shall we?' Alex suggested they take a seat on the sun-speckled rocks by the water's edge and, removing their shoes, they dangled their feet in the water. 'My family believe that for a child to be born, a spirit must first enter the mother's womb to give the child life. This spirit derives from a particular piece of land, depending upon the child's ancestry. The place is the source of that person's life force and he or she is inseparably connected with the piece of earth and bound to protect it.'

'What happens if you don't?' Kyle queried, curious.

'Well, when you die the spirit returns to the site from which it came. However, which level of the earth's consciousness you shall occupy will depend on the effort you devoted to the earth in your lifetime. If you made this world a more beautiful place, with your respect and nourishment, then you will rejoice in paradise.' Alex smiled, motioning to the forest surrounding them. 'But if you neglect your duty to creation,' her tone became more sombre, 'you shall live out your days in the desolation created by your laziness and disregard.'

Kyle's Near Death Experience had taught him enough about the hell in which his next otherworldly stay would be spent if he didn't do something to mend his connection with creation soon. He also had the horrid realisation that that decrepit location in Density would be this beautiful place, should mankind be allowed to do its worst. Kyle also suspected that the reason he was the only person he'd seen during his stay in Density was that he was the main person who, by his idleness, could bring about the destruction of this paradise.

'If you have striven to aid the Great Spirits

of the land,' Alex continued, 'your afterlife will be spent in the peace and enlightenment of the planes that lie beyond the astral and mental realms.'

'So why are you still here in the mental realm?' Kyle glanced up at the sun overhead.

'Because when I died, I, like the rest of my forefathers, could not rest in peace. The piece of land to which I am connected is still under threat, and we have chosen to frequent this realm in the hope of averting that threat.'

He nodded, accepting this. 'And I connect Tim to this land how?'

'Because you were conceived here.' Alex's statement so stunned Kyle, he grinned. 'Your parents were engaged and married here, and the night I went into labour with you, I was attending a summoning ritual right here.'

Kyle's jaw gaped open a moment, having seen this himself on one of his journeys with Book. 'So, what do you think the chances are that my spirit might be derived from this piece of land,' he joked, and Alex laughed. Then Kyle became serious once again. 'Tim never came for me because he's been fighting to save our eternal resting place.'

'Coupled with the slight matter of a suspected murder charge.' Alex shrugged.

Kyle couldn't help but cringe as he thought about breaking the news to Zoe. Should he even suggest to her that her uncle was in some way responsible for the death of her parents? 'What has Nivok got planned for this place?'

Kyle. Kyle. Kyle!

Kyle straightened up — he thought he heard Zoe calling him.

Kyron, who had finished hugging the trees and was now paddling happily at the water's edge with Book under his arm, suddenly came racing towards Kyle, holding Book out in front of him. 'No,' he cried in warning, 'you must stay. You're not finished!'

I'm so sorry. Zoe sounded like she was crying. *Please wake up. Please!*

'Oh, no.' Kyle reached for his mother, who had already begun to fade into a bright light. 'No!'

CHAPTER
EIGHT

PLAYING WITH FIRE

'I'm so sorry,' Zoe repeated as she shook Kyle out of his deep trance. Lifting his eyelids she could only see the whites of his eyes. She knew he was way out of his body and that it was dangerous to drag him back to reality this abruptly, but what choice did she have? 'Come on, Kyle.' She rocked his whole upper body and the intense pain shocked him awake.

'Ahhh!' he roared, angered by the torture and at being forced to break his vow yet again.

When he came to focus on Zoe, Kyle found an outlet for his anger. 'You promised me!'

'I'm so sorry.' Zoe struggled to stop her tears as she cowered away from Kyle, startled by his fury.

'It's not her fault,' Max said. 'I told her to wake you. The police are on their way down the driveway. I don't know why they're here and the less I know the better.'

The news was a rude slap in the face for Kyle; he'd never solve this mystery from a jail cell. 'My mistake.' He apologised as he rolled out of bed, keeping his subsequent moaning to a whisper.

'We've packed all your belongings in your bag, along with some extra bandages and painkillers,' Max advised him. 'You can get out the back. Zoe knows the way.'

'Wait a minute.' Kyle searched the covers on the bed for his book, and then, although causing himself pain, got down to look underneath the bed, but it was not there either.

'Kyle, we have no time!' Zoe insisted, frustrated by the delay. 'The rest of your clothes are in the bag.'

The doorbell rang and startled them all.

'I won't be able to hold them long,' the doctor advised.

'Damn it.' Kyle was forced to give up the hunt. *Every decision you make will be the right decision; every path you take is the one that leads to your destiny.* Adreana's wisdom lessened his frustration.

'Please, Kyle,' Zoe begged, as she gently took hold of his arm. He allowed her to lead him away.

'Good luck, kids.' Max waved as they parted company in his hallway.

Through the back door, Kyle and Zoe stumbled down the path to the gate. When he grabbed the handle to open it, Kyle discovered that it was locked. 'Christ!'

'Yes, my child.' Zoe reached into the ivy-covered wall and produced a key.

'Good old Uncle Max.' Kyle smiled as they passed through the gate and Zoe locked it behind them.

'I'll post him the key.' She placed the key in her bag and headed off down the road with Kyle.

'Stop! Police,' yelled an officer from behind the gate.

Fortunately, the doctor's walls were designed to keep people out and due to the long spikes along the top of the fence, the police officers would be forced to go around the block to get to them. Nevertheless, Zoe and Kyle knew they only had a small window of opportunity to make good their escape.

'We need a miracle.' Zoe panicked; she'd never been in trouble with the law before.

'No.' Kyle calmly considered what might be of aid. 'What we need is a cab.' He looked up the street, hoping to will his solution into being.

When a 'Vacant' cab appeared at the crossroads and turned down the street towards them, Zoe squealed happily, tears of relief flooding her eyes as she hugged and kissed Kyle while waving down the cab.

Kyle could only laugh at the coincidence. Or had he willed it into being? It didn't matter; all that mattered was that they were in luck. Still, speed, travel and communication were all gifts of the air. Maybe Adreana had had something to do with this happy twist of fate?

A couple of blocks away, they ceased peering over the back seat and relaxed.

'So now what?' Kyle pondered aloud.

'Well, the first thing we need is a bank.' Zoe exposed a secret compartment in the bottom of her handbag which revealed a keycard and a passport.

'Your uncle has probably frozen all your accounts and he'll trace us if you use that thing,' Kyle warned.

'Not this little treasure.' Zoe smiled. 'Money can buy anything, even a fake ID.' She handed him the passport, showing a totally different name. 'No one has total control of my life, not even a man as powerful as my uncle.'

'You are a woman with unexpected foresight ... Lisa Roberts.' Kyle read the name on the ID and grinned at his love interest's devious and clever thinking. 'How much is in here?'

'More than enough to get us to north Queensland in comfort,' she assured him with a wink, and Kyle realised that Zoe was way ahead of him in planning their next move.

'There's something I need to get from home first,' he told her, knowing it would throw a spanner in the works.

'You can't go home, Kyle. The police will be watching it for sure,' Zoe whispered. She didn't want her voice to carry over the cab driver's football broadcast.

'You know I wouldn't ask if I didn't think it was important.' He tried to plead with her. 'We'll have to figure something out.'

When Kyle got that puppy-dog look on his face, Zoe just couldn't argue. 'Well, first things first. Let's get some transport, some new clothes and some supplies.'

'You're the brains of this operation,' Kyle conceded happily, 'I'm just the muscle.' He moaned as he straightened up. 'At least, I think I am.'

'How is your bod doing?' Zoe asked sympathetically. She took a peep at the wound inside his shirt and noticed the blood seeping through.

'Actually, I feel better to be on the move,' Kyle lied. Mentally, he did feel good, but his body was cold and weak. Now that he'd lost Book and the chance to meet his fire element, perhaps his chances of staying alive were still in doubt.

Kyle wasn't surprised that Zoe was a long time in the bank; large cash withdrawals were no doubt checked and double-checked. She had been very confident when departing to deal with the financial side of their operation, and Kyle, having a fear of large institutions, was more than happy to sit and eat a full breakfast inside the cafe across the road.

'Kyle?'

Kyle nearly jumped out of his skin. He looked up to find the old security guard from the Nivok building standing over him, looking very displeased. 'Jeez, Charlie, you scared the life out of me.'

'Not any wonder, with the trouble you're in,' he grouched, albeit quietly.

'Do you want to sit down?' Kyle asked. The old bloke was obviously dark on him, and wasn't going anywhere. He had something on his mind.

Wary of being seen with Kyle, Charlie scanned the area in a glance and reluctantly pulled up a chair. 'What have you done with Nivok's niece?' He leaned over the table to quietly discuss the matter.

'Well, nothing yet.' Kyle assumed he was referring to their romance. 'I've only just met the girl.'

'Kidnapping is no joke,' Charlie whispered harshly. 'I lost my job because of you, and if I'm to have any chance of ever working again, you'll tell me what you've done with her.' The guard grabbed hold of Kyle's shirt and yanked Kyle towards him, battering Kyle's wound against the table in the process.

Kyle released a quiet groan. Then Zoe arrived and pried Kyle's shirt from the security guard's fingers. 'I'm right here,' she said, stating the obvious as she placed a comforting arm around Kyle. 'What gave you the insane idea that Kyle had kidnapped me? You saw us leave together the other day,' Zoe pressed on with her attack. 'Did it look like I was under duress?'

'Well, no.' Charlie was gratified by this turn of events, because he had felt the charge was a little fishy in the first place. 'Your uncle told the police that you'd been kidnapped by Kyle and Matt. I must confess I didn't believe it ... but when I was fired for letting Kyle in and out of the building after he'd been dismissed, well ...' The old bloke shrugged, bemused. It seemed he was not the only one who was being used as a scapegoat by James Nivok.

'That seems to explain why the police are so keen to find us.' Kyle regained the ability of speech, the pain of the knock ebbing away.

'Oh, Jesus!' Zoe's eyes widened in shock. 'Matthew's got my car!'

'Not good,' Kyle conceded. 'Please god, don't let him return to the doc's house.'

'He promised me he would,' Zoe fretted.

'It's way too dangerous for us to go back there.' Kyle had learnt his lesson — a soul as wilful as Matt could take care of himself. Zoe agreed. 'We have to stick to our own plan now.'

'So what is going on?' Charlie inquired. 'I mean, as I've been done out of my retirement fund and a means to earn a living, I would like to know why.'

'We're still trying to figure the answer to that question ourselves.' Kyle felt sorry that he couldn't help the old guy.

'Please don't be concerned.' Zoe placed a hand on Charlie's shoulder. 'I actually own two-thirds of the company that just fired you ... you won't be out of a job for long, I swear it.'

Kyle read so much more into this statement than just words of comfort for their hard-done-by friend: 'Is that a business tone I hear in your voice?' Kyle teased, knowing how much Zoe detested the world of big business. 'If I didn't know better I would think that you were planning to challenge your uncle.'

Zoe merely smiled, and made no comment.

'Is there anything I can do to help?' Charlie offered his services.

The couple were shaking their heads to decline the offer, when Kyle suddenly thought more of it. 'Actually, there is something you can do.'

Charlie made it past the gate at Kyle's place, but by the time he reached the front porch there was a plain clothes policeman crossing the road to question him.

'The occupant of this house is being sought for questioning.' The man flashed a police badge at Charlie. 'Do you know anything of his whereabouts?'

'I wish I did,' Charlie said angrily. 'The little bastard just got me fired!' His hands implied that he'd like to wring the suspect's neck. 'And since we've had this falling out, I'm here to pick up an old chest Kyle was storing for me.

It's just here.' Charlie reached in under the house and pulled out a slim, reinforced metal case, that was padlocked twice.

'What's in there?' The policeman didn't really suspect anything underhand was going on, but he was curious. 'Why the padlocks?'

'Just some old junk really,' he explained. 'I used to have a key for the padlocks, but my kids lost them ages ago. You'd be doing me a favour if you bust them off and check inside,' Charlie said.

'Thanks. I'll mind not to hurt the chest.' The policeman thought it best to know what he was allowing to leave an area that was under surveillance.

Charlie smiled as he watched the policeman return to his car for some tools. Everything was going to plan.

'You got it?' Kyle pounced on Charlie the minute he got home. 'And you got them to bust the locks off, you total legend!' Kyle hurried to place the chest on a table and open it up.

'Yep.' The old fellow grinned. 'The policeman was rather bemused by the contents. And so was I,' Charlie confessed.

Zoe moved closer to see what had been so important it had delayed their escape.

Inside was a faded blue baby blanket.

'Was that yours?' Zoe went all gooey and sentimental.

'I guess,' Kyle shrugged, pretending not to remember how he'd once dragged the piece of cloth everywhere. He unwrapped the blanket to expose a boomerang. Seeing the depictions of a large ape-like creature on the weapon, Kyle felt an immediate affinity with the object; memories of learning how to hunt with the tool came flooding back.

His young feet were running over a field in pursuit of a target; entering the bushland, he stalked his prey, his heart pounding in his chest as he took aim at the feral cat that had scampered up a tree and let his weapon fly. The death screech of the animal rang in his ears.

'Kyle?' Zoe gestured at the item, wanting him to explain his connection to it and its importance.

'I don't know,' he confessed. 'I just know it will be crucial to our success.' He knew he wasn't making sense, but he also knew he had no hope of doing so at present. 'We should go.'

'Yes, we should,' Zoe wholeheartedly agreed.

'Thanks for this, Charlie.' Kyle wrapped the boomerang and placed it in his bag for safe cartage. 'And thank your missus for the cake.' Kyle motioned to the kitchen he'd raided.

'Can I give you kids a lift somewhere?' Charlie offered, not having anything better to do.

'We're going to an airstrip out of town.' Zoe thought their destination was probably further afoot than Charlie cared to go.

'We are?' Kyle was surprised and excited to learn this fact.

Zoe nodded and grinned, pleased to surprise him yet again. 'I have friends there.'

'I thought you said you didn't have any close friends?' Kyle queried.

'These are the paid kind,' she advised him, and Kyle looked perplexed. 'They taught me how to fly,' she enlightened further.

'You have a pilot's licence?' Now Kyle was definitely in love.

Zoe shrugged as if it were nothing. 'Part of my well-spent youth alone.' She was gratified to finally find a silver lining to her life. 'And flying is just one of the numerous solo pursuits of the disgustingly rich and shameless.'

'Well, how about I take you out of the city and you can get a cab the rest of the way?' Charlie suggested. 'That way I'm home for supper and I don't know your final destination.'

'Thanks, Charlie.' Kyle accepted, filled with emotion by Charlie's gracious offer. 'I'm real sorry I got you fired, but I'm going to make it up to you.' Zoe nodded to show that she agreed. 'I count you among the only three true friends I've ever had … human friends that is.' The comment made Zoe smile, and although Charlie wasn't sure what to make of it, he was warmed by Kyle's apology.

'You didn't get me fired, son. It was my own mistake that got me fired,' Charlie acknowledged. 'I've always had a good feeling about you, Kyle. I know you and this lass here well enough to trust you. If you say there's something fishy going on, then I believe there is. I've worked security at the Nivok building since it was built. Your grandfather,' Charlie motioned to Zoe, 'Halifax Nivok, hired me himself. The Nivoks have always been good to me and I'd hate to see the company that your grandfather built, and that your good father poured his all into, fall into disrepute.'

'You knew my father and my grandfather?' Zoe was overwhelmed at the opportunity to have some questions answered.

'Do you remember a guy named Timothy Burke?' Kyle jumped in, also excited by this unforeseen source of information.

'Why of course I do,' Charlie stated. 'He was the one James Nivok was trying to frame for the murder of Miss Nivok's parents.'

Zoe gasped. 'I was never told that murder was suspected. I was told my parents died in a car accident.'

'*Trying* to frame, you say?' Kyle queried. 'You didn't believe the charge against Burke then?'

Charlie thought back. 'Tim was a really nice fellow. He was smart. He had a beautiful wife, a promising career and a kid on the way ... now why would a man like that suddenly become a murderer?' Charlie asked, and there was quiet for a moment while they pondered the answer.

'We should talk en route,' Charlie suggested. 'If I'm not home by the time the missus gets back from bowls, I'll be in strife.'

* * *

'Now we're in the woods,' Tim told Matthew as he paid the cab driver.

Matt gazed at the parched fields, with forest and mountains beyond, raising both eyebrows to concede Tim was right. It had taken a bus, a couple of trains, another bus and a cab to finally get them here, so Matt was mighty pleased to be in the woods.

'Are you sure you want to be left here?' The cab driver thought he'd best warn them. 'Most of this land is privately owned, but blackfellas still frequent the area, especially at night, so it pays to keep a gun handy.'

Matt couldn't quite believe what he was hearing, and Tim certainly didn't take kindly to the implication.

'Those blackfellas are my family,' Tim crouched low to enlighten the driver inside the cab, 'and it's your kind I keep a gun for.' Tim reached inside his bag, which compelled the cab driver to put his foot down and the car tore off up the road. 'Some things never change.' He turned to Matt. 'I don't really have a gun.'

'I do,' Matt grinned, patting his bag. 'It's Nivok's.'

This boast amused Tim. 'You and I really do have to have a long chat, Mr Ryan.'

To avoid being identified by association, Tim and Matt had travelled the same route, but had mostly kept their distance from each other. That way, if one of them was spotted, the other might still have a chance to avoid capture.

'You have no idea how happy I —' Matt was suddenly dragged off to the side of the road into some bushes. 'What?'

Tim pointed to the four-wheel drive vehicle headed along the road towards them.

'No one could possibly have followed our trail, Tim.' Matt thought him paranoid. '*I* don't even know where we were half the time!'

'Sh,' Tim requested. The vehicle pulled into the same rest area the cab had used to drop them off, and the driver's door opened.

'So that's it. Mount Turrammelin.' Zoe climbed out of the car to admire the mountain in the distance and stretch her legs.

'Zoe!' Matt stood and when Zoe turned around, he released a howl of laughter and triumph. 'How the hell did you do that?'

'Matt!' She ran and pounced to hug him. 'I

was so worried!' She laughed and cried at once. 'My uncle has you up on kidnapping charges!'

'So we discovered when I picked Tim up,' Matt informed her, 'but he got us away without even scratching your car. It's in the shopping mall car park not far from the jail, if you're looking for it.'

'The police already found it,' Zoe told him. 'I heard on the radio.' Zoe looked at Tim who, despite his rugged informal attire and his greying, shoulder length, straggly dark hair, seemed to be a rather distinguished and fit fellow. He had a handsome face, and a small beard and moustache which only added to his air of integrity. No matter how she tried, Zoe could not see this man as the murderer of her parents. 'We sure had to go to a lot of trouble to finally meet.' Zoe held her hand out to Tim.

'That which is destined cannot be prevented by mortal man,' he announced and shook her hand gladly.

'Where's our hero?' Matt looked back to find Kyle had slid himself out of the car and was now leaning against it for support.

'Champion!' Kyle gave Matt the thumbs up for not getting caught, and although he was glad to see his friend he couldn't take his eyes off Timothy Burke. *This is my father.* The words were resounding in his mind. *Will he know me? I think not.*

'Kyle, this is Tim,' Matt introduced them, having noticed Kyle's interest in their new companion.

'Pleased to meet you.' Tim moved to shake Kyle's hand. 'Any enemy of Nivok's is a friend of mine.' But as Tim got closer his pace slowed; Kyle almost heard the penny as it dropped in the man's mind.

'How's it going?' He shook Tim's hand, pretending not to notice the stunned look on his face. *Maybe he does know me?* The notion that his father might have been watching him from afar warmed him inside, for it was clear that something was going down in Tim's mind. 'We were hoping you might be able to tell us what Nivok has got planned for this land.'

'I can,' Tim seemed to snap out of his daze, 'but the side of the road is not really the place.'

'Is there a road that way?' Zoe pointed to the mountain.

'This is as close as it gets,' Tim said. 'We used to four-wheel drive it many years ago, but there are wire fences further afoot and the gates are kept locked these days — your uncle's attempt to keep the locals from their sacred waterhole on the far side of the mountain.'

'Not a problem. We'll just go through the fences,' Zoe shrugged, as she headed for the car. 'After all, they are mine.'

'Yeehah!' Matt cheered her on, and proceeded to haul his gear over to the vehicle. 'Break down the walls ... I like the sound of that!' Matt unpacked his camera and threw the rest of his belongings in the back. 'That ought to be worth shooting.'

'I'm beginning to suspect our girl is some sort of undercover superhero,' Kyle advised his mate. 'Zoe flew us most of the way up here. That's how we got here so quick.'

Matt was a little amazed and then grinned. 'Sounds like you had an infinitely better travel agent than we did.'

'And an infinitely bigger budget,' Tim added from the back seat. 'Did you use cash to get here?'

'Yep.' Zoe planted herself in the driver's seat.

'And fake ID,' Kyle added.

'My, my, you are organised.' Tim looked at Zoe, impressed. 'Did you already suspect your uncle of foul play?'

'Not until this week,' she admitted. 'I've just learnt to listen to my inner voice, which doesn't seem to trust my uncle as much as the conscious me does. Better safe than sorry.'

Kyle, intrigued by her answer, had wandered around to the open passenger-side door. 'Perhaps your parents are still watching out for you?'

'No perhaps about it,' Tim responded and Kyle felt that there was a subtle message in that statement for him too.

Zoe turned in her seat to view Tim. 'You knew my parents well?'

'Well enough to get them killed.' Remorse was evident on his face as memories flooded his mind. 'I was the unsuspecting cause of their death, but I was not their murderer.'

'I didn't think that you were.' Zoe forced a smile as she put on her sunglasses to hide her tears. Once Matt was settled in the back, Kyle managed to drag his damaged body into the front passenger seat and Zoe started the engine. 'Let's explore!' The car accelerated over an embankment and flew onto the flat land that led to Mount Turrammelin.

They managed to arrive at the sacred waterhole of Turrammelin mountain in one piece, surprisingly.

'Wow!' Zoe bounded out of the car. 'That was so liberating.' She was on a high after ramming her vehicle through the wire fence, and was jumping up and down in an attempt to expel some of the adrenaline rush.

'For some, maybe.' Kyle stumbled out of the car, nursing his wound.

'Oh, you poor chook.' Zoe galloped over to see if she could make him feel better, but Kyle held up a hand to defend himself.

'I'll be fine until you mellow,' he reassured her. His eyes came to settle on her breasts. 'Feel free to continue jumping about though.'

'Yep, off you go,' Matt encouraged, coming to stand beside Kyle with his camera rolling, at which point Zoe acted coy.

'Dammit, can't a girl have any fun without being perved at?' As both lads shook their heads, Zoe rolled her eyes and strolled off to take in the scenery. 'Typical.'

Tim followed her towards the waterhole. 'You want to see why Nivok wants this place so badly?' He glanced back to see Kyle and Matt both nod in the affirmative. 'Then follow.'

'He's rather intense, isn't he?' Kyle whispered to Matt, interested to hear his impression of Tim.

'A bit like someone else I know,' commented Matt, as he obediently fell in behind his travelling companion.

Matt's comparison was heartwarming to Kyle. He *was* like his father.

At the pool, Tim stripped to his trousers and dived straight in.

Zoe squealed as she was suddenly sprayed with cold water. Still, it brought cool relief from the humid heat of the day and she was tempted to dive in herself.

Kyle looked about at the trees ... infinitely smaller and less abundant than what he recalled from seeing this same place on the mental realm of awareness. *I'm afraid the Nivoks destroyed much of this place a long time ago.* He could certainly now understand what his mother had meant by this, but the falls were awe-inspiring nonetheless. The otherworldly guardians of nature were much harder for Kyle to spot in the physical realm. Yet, when he concentrated hard enough, focusing on his third-eye area, the entities could be vaguely made out as a shadow on a branch, a movement of a rock, a dance of light on the water, or the soaring force behind a sudden burst of wind.

'Do you think Tim meant we were to follow him in?' Matt queried, filming the spot where Tim had submerged.

'God, I hope not.' Kyle sat himself down on a warm rock.

'He's certainly taking his time.' Zoe was starting to worry. 'Do you think there're crocs in there?' She took a step back from the edge.

Matt lowered his camera, starting to entertain the idea that he might have to dive in after Tim. 'He couldn't possibly have held his breath for this long.'

Kyle stood up. Surely creation was not so cruel as to take his father from him now. Were a few hours all they would have together?

'Bubbles.' Zoe pointed to the still water beyond the falls, where Tim finally surfaced and everyone breathed a sigh of relief.

'That must be some sort of record,' Matt shouted out as Tim swam closer, clutching something in his fist.

'Are there crocs in there?' Zoe wanted to know.

'Nope.' Tim replied.

'It's freshwater. Are you sure?'

'Very sure.'

'How could you be sure?'

'I'm not dead, am I?' Tim climbed out of the water and planted a large rock in her hand.

It was pretty clear what the rock was composed of. 'This is a solid gold nugget,' Zoe decided as she tried to break off bits with her fingers, but the rock proved too tough.

'This is literally a mountain of gold,' Tim informed her. 'The locals have always known this and your uncle strongly suspects that he's on to a gold mine here.'

'That would seem to explain the big fence to keep the locals out,' Kyle supposed, 'but I don't understand why Nivok didn't mine it sooner.'

'Well, he couldn't,' Tim said. 'When Zoe's parents died they left all their worldly possessions to Zoe, along with this piece of land. The courts decreed that although James

Nivok was Zoe's trustee, he could not mine the land on her behalf — even though the government of Queensland had granted him a mineral development licence in the hope that a full scale mining lease would follow, along with much revenue. The judge decided that your uncle had the option to keep renewing his licence until such time as Zoe came into her inheritance and sold him the land, or gave him permission to proceed with his investigation.'

'Permission which he requested a few days ago,' Zoe summed up. 'Did my parents know about this? I mean, how did my uncle manage to get a mineral development licence on a piece of land my parents inherited?'

'From what I understand, after Halifax died and left that piece of land to your father, James tricked his brother into getting an exploration permit. When his plan was discovered, James lied to your father, saying he planned to surprise him if they had had any positive results from the survey. Your father did not take legal action against his brother, but he probably should have. I was the geologist who worked on that exploration survey and when I reported my findings, James and your father,

David, had a distinct disagreement about what should happen next.' Tim wrung out his trousers, as best he could with them still on his body. 'You see, once your father learnt James was carrying out a mineral survey, your father hired a botanist to do an environmental impact study at the same time. She had actually been applying for permission to do an environmental report on the area for years, and David figured it was an apt time to give her the go-ahead.'

'Wasn't she the woman you eventually married?' Matt asked Tim, having read something about that in Tim's file.

Tim nodded. 'The same month I met her.' He forced a smile but said no more.

'Do you mind me asking what her interest in this land was?' Zoe requested cautiously.

'Her interest was ancestral,' Tim replied. 'For her grandmother's people, this mountain, and the waterhole, were sacred male ground and all the descendants of her family group are bound to protect and honour it.'

'There's no native title claim against this land, is there?' Zoe wondered if this was something else her uncle had failed to tell her.

Tim shook his head. 'Those rights were destroyed over a century ago, when this land was sold by the government to the Nivoks as a freehold estate. However, no mortal law can release the Indigenous people of this land from their obligation to the spirits of the Dreamtime, who created this earth for them.'

'Oh.' Zoe drew back, concerned, and folded her arms, thinking female rights were being threatened. 'And why, may I ask, is it considered sacred *male* ground?'

Tim smiled, knowing the reason would seem incredible to western ears. 'Because this waterhole hosts a bunyip who likes to eat women and children.'

Zoe fixed him with a look of scepticism. 'You don't believe that, do you?'

'That's why I can trust that there are no crocs in here,' Tim replied. 'Bunyips don't tolerate other predators in their waterholes.'

'*Cool.*' Kyle confirmed his belief in Tim's story, as the man moved past him to fetch dry clothes. 'Have you seen it?'

'Seen it?' Tim echoed. 'It guides my destiny.'

Kyle's smile broadened. He thought of telling Tim about his yowie, which led him to wonder how Tim knew the bunyip was his guardian … Kyle decided it was not the time to pursue this line of inquiry.

'I was under the impression that bunyips were mythological creatures.' Zoe risked voicing her limited understanding.

'Such a creature has an ability to shift dimensions,' Tim explained. 'It's an understandable misconception.'

'So you can see otherworldly creatures, Tim?' Zoe ventured to say on Kyle's behalf, knowing he would be excited to learn of someone else with his talent.

'I don't want to strike you as a loon or anything,' Tim observed, 'but yes, I have been known to see them.'

Zoe looked at Kyle, thrilled for him, and was surprised when Kyle changed the subject.

'Well, how about we break out some of the groceries we have in the car and make ourselves something to eat?' he suggested.

Everyone seemed very keen on the idea.

By the time their hunger had been appeased, the afternoon shadows grew long across the landscape.

Matt had wandered back over to the waterhole. He had it in his head to experiment with the night vision function on his camera, in the hope of capturing a bunyip on film.

'Can I help?' Kyle offered as he joined Matt by the water.

Matt was peering through the camera, which he'd mounted on a tripod, and was adjusting the focus. 'Um ... I suppose.' He considered the offer with an air of distant ill will.

Matt had been suppressing his feelings ever since they'd met up again, and they hadn't had the chance to speak alone until now. Zoe had gone to lie down in the back of the car, and Tim was relaxing by the fire. Kyle wanted to talk to Tim, but clearing the air with his best friend was a more pressing concern.

'You can stand on that rock by the water there.' Matt directed Kyle to his point of focus and as Kyle made a move to comply, Matt added. 'And try to be taken by a mythological beast while you're at it.'

Kyle looked back to Matt, feeling he was not joking about his desire. Matt wore his jester's grin, but it was not as sincere as normal. 'I know I've really stretched the friendship lately.'

Matt looked away, wanting to avoid the subject.

Kyle had never thought to see Matt so hurt, or that he would be the cause. 'It seems you were right about me pissing people off so they won't get too close. I knew you liked Zoe, and yet I pursued her anyway.'

'What did you do?' Matt looked back to Kyle. 'I mean, one minute she hates you and the next...'

'I don't know what happened,' Kyle defended, and when Matt appeared disappointed by the response, Kyle endeavoured to explain. 'Zoe and I connect on another level.' Kyle fumbled for the words that would save his friendship, but Matt was clearly not impressed.

'Which is supposed to mean, what?' Matt raised both brows, eager to learn.

In his frustration Kyle suddenly realised the confession he was avoiding. 'There's something about me that I've never told you Matt —'

'Spare me.' Matt held up a hand, feeling that Kyle had confessed all his horrors in one drunken stupor or another.

'I see things,' Kyle blurted out and began to tremble at the thought of confessing that which had always caused him grief. 'Creatures, visions, prophetic dreams ... Zoe tells me it's clairvoyance.'

Matt was stunned a second, bombarded by suspicion, doubt, then anger. 'Bullshit!' Matt left the camera to charge at Kyle.

'It's true, that's how I knew you'd be in Nivok's office that night,' Kyle blurted out and winced as Matt grabbed hold of his shirt, of a mind to punch his lights out. Kyle was fearful for his injury and had no desire to make it worse, what's more he was already freezing and feared ending up in the drink. Matt, hesitating to digest the information, gave Kyle the chance to add, 'In the vision Nivok shot you.'

Matt backed down. 'So it was my life you saved that night.' With the revelation, Matt let Kyle go.

Kyle shrugged off his heroic gesture, as he didn't feel it justified betraying his best friend. 'So, I saved your life ... what was stealing your girlfriend? Payment?'

Matt figured Kyle was being a little hard on himself and he hesitated, reluctant to admit: 'Zoe was never my girlfriend. She's a good friend though,' he granted, cracking a smile.

'As she is such a dear friend, you had better start treating her better than you have in the past.' Matt threatened to belt Kyle over the skull, but avoided contact and released his frustration with a growl. 'Now get over there and stand on that bloody rock!' Matt shoved Kyle along, the ill will dispersed, and their friendship resumed its merry course.

'Thanks for getting me to a doctor and finding Tim.' Kyle started remembering all the instances he'd yet to thank his friend for.

Matt waved off the sentiment as he returned to his tripod. 'You saved my life, let's call it even.' Matt resumed his focusing. 'Still, I don't understand why you are thanking me for hunting down Tim Burke.'

Kyle took a deep breath; he wasn't prepared to admit what he so strongly suspected, until he'd had it from the horse's mouth. 'I'll get back to you on that.' He left his mark to go resolve the issue.

'I'm not finished with you yet,' Matt protested.

'Sorry,' Kyle appealed. 'There's something else I really need to do. But, I'll be back.'

* * *

252

Tim had thrown down his jacket and was lying not far from the fire with his head resting on a log. His eyes were closed, but Kyle knew he wasn't asleep.

Kyle took a seat by the fire and stared into the flames to psych himself into asking Tim something that had been playing on his mind for hours. 'How do you know the bunyip is your guardian, Tim?'

Tim decided to humour Kyle, although he suspected the kid was taking the piss out of him. 'I read it in a book long ago.' Tim thought his answer was rather clever.

'The *Book of Dreams*.' Kyle was astounded by the revelation. He knew he'd guessed correctly from the astonished look on Tim's face.

'I've never mentioned that to anyone,' Tim uttered, as he sat up. 'How could you know?'

Kyle was distracted by his own deductions, however. 'I assumed I inherited this sight from my mother's side of the family, but it was yours ... you have it.' Kyle abruptly ceased his verbal theorising when he realised he'd let the cat out of the bag.

'You know who I am, Kyle?' Tim seemed mildly relieved by the possibility.

Kyle nodded.

'How?' Tim was amazed, and a little perplexed. How should he handle this development?

'I read it in a book recently.' His smug confession triggered so many emotions in Kyle that he found himself struggling to hold back tears. The relief of finally finding and confronting his father conflicted with the sorrow he felt at misplacing Book before he'd finished his own story.

Tim was intrigued and inspired by Kyle's admission. 'My time under Book's tutelage was so long ago that it was starting to seem nothing more than a dream.' Tim crawled over to take a seat nearer Kyle, but not too close; he didn't want to make this situation any more awkward than it already was. 'But everything I foresaw at that time is now coming to pass. And there can be no doubt that you are my son,' he concluded in earnest.

'Were you in doubt?'

'Well,' Tim shrugged, 'they moved you around a lot as a child. It became harder and harder to keep track of you. The last time I saw you, you were about nine years old.' Although

Kyle was silent, he seemed open to hearing more, so Tim continued. 'You were riding a skateboard on one of those park ramps and you took a bad fall. I ventured over to see if you were okay and —' He shrugged, trying not to laugh at the memory. 'You told me to piss off or you'd shove your skateboard up my arse.'

The story made Kyle laugh. 'I don't remember, but that sounds like me at nine.'

'I'm hoping you've changed a bit since then,' Tim commented, leaning away from Kyle. 'I understand that your life has been anything but a bed of roses and that you might not be very well disposed towards me. In fact, I'm surprised you're even talking to me.'

Kyle shook his head and offered Tim his hand to shake; he wasn't ready for the fatherly hug yet. It was still a bit strange having family. 'If there's one thing Book has taught me, it's that I choose my own path and I alone am responsible for walking it.'

Tim took Kyle's hand and clenched it in both of his own. His son's offer of friendship after all these years of worry, guilt and remorse was a true gift from the gods.

Tim's parental guilt was still evident in his face; Kyle's forgiveness was a comfort to him, but he obviously thought that it did not absolve him for the neglect.

'I know why you never came for me and although it has taken me a while to get over it, I want you to know that I really respect what you did and what you are still trying to do.'

'I never should have left Alex that night,' Tim muttered under his breath. This piece of knowledge had plagued him for twenty years.

'I know you had no choice and that the choice you made was under extreme duress,' Kyle said, and for the first time he accepted that this was the simple truth of the matter. 'Whoever killed Zoe's parents is to blame for our past sorrows. What happens between us from here on in, that's our own responsibility.'

'True. And James Nivok was the catalyst of whom you speak,' Tim informed him plainly. 'He had my best friend, your mother's youngest brother, killed the same way only yesterday.'

'That was the other little accident that Nivok wanted arranged the night he shot me,' Kyle realised. 'You were the target but Nivok's hired killer missed.'

'And my parents were the previous little accident that my uncle referred to that day.' Zoe stood alongside the car, the malice she felt visible on her face as she now approached the men. 'He killed my parents so that he could brainwash me into selling him this land as soon as I was old enough.'

Kyle didn't have a whole lot of energy left, but what he had he used to get to Zoe and give her a hug.

'Son-of-a-bitch must pay,' she sobbed into Kyle's shoulder. Her resolution firm, she eased away from Kyle to look at Tim. 'Can we do it? Can we bring him to justice?'

'I have dreamed of little else for twenty years. I want my life back,' Tim answered, 'but before today I seriously doubted my chances. United, we stand a better chance of exposing Nivok. Still, even if we can prove our case against him, preventing this land from being mined is a completely different kettle of fish.'

'Well, it's my land and there's no way I'm going to sell it now,' Zoe reassured him, 'so you need hold no fear of that ever happening.'

'Your uncle is in very tight with the Queensland government and they can still enforce their mining rights if the right company has enough money to pour into the area,' Tim said.

'But that's highway robbery!' Now Zoe was fuming, her determination dented.

'That's the law,' Tim concluded flatly, not liking it any more than she did.

'I do believe that saving Turrammelin mountain is my quest,' Kyle announced, and then, noting how he shivered, he added, 'or at least it was.'

'Did Book tell you that?' Tim asked.

'Who *is* Book?' Zoe wondered, as they bandied the word around like a nickname.

Kyle shook his head and smiled. He knew Tim would be interested in hearing what he had to say: 'My mother told me.'

Both Zoe and Tim were shocked by this news. Tim broke the silence. 'You've spoken to Alex?' He was overcome by joy at the prospect.

Kyle nodded, looking around the moonlit clearing. 'She still inhabits this place and will do so for as long as her soul-land remains under threat.'

Zoe was staring at Kyle, enchanted, and then her eyes drifted to Tim. 'I take it that etheric

258

sight runs in the family.' She'd overheard part of their earlier conversation.

'Book gave me the sight,' Tim confirmed. 'I did not bear the burden of having it my whole life.' He looked at Kyle with sympathetic eyes.

'Who *is* Book?' Zoe appealed to them once more, and Kyle and Tim both cracked a smile, aware now that they were teasing her by avoiding the topic.

'Hey, guys.' Matt tried to yell in a whisper as he ran. 'There's something weird going on down at the pool … you should really come take a look at this!'

'Define weird,' Kyle requested, as they moved to meet Matt halfway.

'Um …' He was reluctant to spit it out, as it seemed so fantastic. 'Well … a ball of fiery light rose out of the water and then split into many smaller balls, which are darting all over the place. I've got it all on film,' he was quick to add, and was surprised when no one expressed disbelief.

'Min min lights,' Tim supposed, though when they reached the pool of water there was no sign of the mysterious phenomena.

'I swear they were here,' Matt said defensively, rewinding the cartridge in his camera to view the footage he'd captured.

'We believe you, Matt,' Zoe assured him, having glanced back to see numerous yellow-orange lights dancing around their campfire.

'Shit!' Matt fast-forwarded his tape again, not wanting to tape over the extraordinary footage he already had.

'They look like fairies,' Zoe observed with delight.

'What are they?' Kyle asked Tim, as he seemed to know more than anybody else did.

'They are fairies of sorts ... salamanders in western thought,' Tim replied.

'Aren't salamanders some sort of lizard?' Matt raised his camera to shoot.

'No,' Kyle quietly corrected him. 'They're fire spirits and they're looking for me.' Kyle looked back at Tim to explain. 'I never finished with Book. I got interrupted — twice!'

'So you've not discovered Book's identity?'

'No.' Kyle frowned. 'I never reached that chapter.'

Tim said nothing more about it, although the

smile on his face was suggestive. 'We'll wait here,' he decided. 'You should go have your audience with Burn-a-debt.'

Tim's naming of the entity confirmed for Kyle his father's claim to have read the book. 'Hopefully she wants to give me my body heat back. That would be nice.' Arms crossed tight around his chest, Kyle wandered forth to the fateful meeting.

'Have I missed something?' Matt didn't want to stay put. He sensed something was going on between Kyle and Tim, as their private banter was very perplexing.

'So that is why he's been so cold since his Near Death Experience,' Zoe reasoned to herself, completely forgetting his father stood beside her.

'Kyle nearly died?' Tim was rocked to the core by the information.

'But did not.' Zoe, although slightly confused by all that was transpiring around Kyle, was thrilled for him to have finally found a loved one; more and more the coming together of this small band of people seemed fated. 'Your son is the most extraordinary person I've ever known.' Zoe and Tim looked at Kyle as he approached the mysterious anomaly that hovered around their campfire.

'I had nothing to do with that, unfortunately,' Tim replied.

'And yet he is so much like you.' Zoe expressed her opinion, wanting to help Tim and Kyle through their awkward adjustment. 'You gave him your genes and that was obviously enough.'

'He's even more like his mother,' said Tim, fondly, mildly comforted by Zoe's perspective.

'Oh,' uttered Matt, now enlightened on the vital development that he'd missed. However, afraid of putting his foot in his mouth regarding the sensitive issue, he made no further comment and crept closer to the min min lights with his camera.

The lights, each about the size of a pingpong ball, ceased their whirling movements and became stationary as Kyle got within metres of them.

'Bernadette?' Kyle queried, halting as the lights ceased their movement; he counted eight of them.

All the lights rushed towards Kyle at once,

darting about his body to tease him with their warmth. *Burn-a-debt, no regret, a challenge met, a death forfeit.*

The chant of eight or so young female voices built up in Kyle's mind, and once their riddle had been repeated several times over he begged them to stop. 'I think I get the deal ... what's the challenge?'

The eight balls of light merged into four; each doubled in size but the choir of voices was reduced to a quartet. *Gift to fire, stop desire, to inspire, what's admired.* The four lights moved to circle above Kyle's sports bag and as they ascended higher into the air the boomerang rose from its hiding place.

'Ah, I don't think I'm qualified to use that thing.' Kyle hesitated to take it as the fire spirits brought the item to him. 'When you said I had to *stop desire*, I thought you were speaking metaphorically.'

Warrior energy, comes with me, flows through thee, with courage, valour and loyalty.

'All right, if you say so ... but this was your idea.' Kyle took the weapon in hand. 'So where is this rogue emotion I have to bring to an end?'

The four lights merged into two, now the size of basketballs, and then sped off towards the damaged fence.

'Oh, great, a trek. Just what the doctor ordered.' Kyle meandered along behind them, and they circled back to encourage him.

Make haste, pick up pace, must win this race, to have a case.

'All right, I'm moving.' Kyle wasn't much of a runner, especially with his current injury, but he did work out and so was fit enough to make a show of enthusiasm.

'Where are they taking him?' Zoe protested. 'He can't run far in his condition.'

'Best find out.' Tim gave chase, with Zoe and Matt in hot pursuit.

On the flat land between the road and Mount Turrammelin, a car was parked. Both the interior and exterior lights were ablaze, and loud drunken laughter emanated from the area.

Kyle took advantage of a small cluster of bushes not too far from the ruckus, where he crouched to assess the situation. The two balls of light had raced ahead to whirl around his target: three drunken youths who seemed oblivious to the anomaly that had taken an interest in their activities. *I don't get what it is I'm supposed to do here?* It was no crime of passion to get drunk. Higher and higher into the sky the earthlights rose.

'Okay, let's do it,' decreed the loudest of the three, as he placed a hood over his head and pulled a gun. His two mates also put on hoods, before they all moved around to open the boot of the car.

They pulled two people from the boot, their arms bound behind their backs, their mouths gagged. As the two young hostages were Indigenous Australians and the three hooded youths — in their late teens or early twenties — were not, Kyle had a pretty good idea of what was going down.

'Tie him up over there.' The youth in charge pointed to a large log lying on its side. 'He can watch.' The lad struggled to free himself as he was dragged towards the stump by two of his abductors. 'I wouldn't if I were you.' The ringleader held a gun to the temple of his female captive.

Kyle looked at the boomerang in his hand. *This is going to be useless ... give me a gun, and maybe*. He feared he would fail Burn-a-debt's test. He recalled the vision he'd had upon seeing the boomerang for the first time after its storage, and this seemed to suggest he'd once trained in the art of throwing the weapon. Would his subconscious remember what he did not?

Once the male captive was secured, the ringleader tossed his gun to one of his mates, and cast his female captive face down on to the bonnet of the car. 'We can't have a half-caste like you breeding with a blackfella. That would just make for more blacks,' he told her, holding her down with one hand as he fumbled with the belt on his trousers, his friends cheering him on.

Kyle stood to take aim with the boomerang. He was surprised to feel very certain of how to hold the weapon; it felt comfortable in his grasp. He took aim at the fellow with the gun and was yanked to the ground by Tim.

'Your aim is all wrong for this weapon,' his father explained. 'This is a returning boomerang, not a hunting weapon.'

'I beg to differ,' Kyle whispered back, 'but this is the only boomerang I've ever thrown, and it flew straight the last time I hunted with it.'

Tim realised it didn't matter whether Kyle was right or not, as the distraction would give them time to charge. 'Have a go by all means,' Tim granted. 'The three of us will charge as you let fly.'

'Four,' Zoe protested, and Tim shook his head.

'You stay put.'

Matt handed Zoe his camera, and although she was exasperated by the ruling she did not argue — there was no time.

Kyle stood and looked to the heavens, where the celestial lights could barely be seen. *Guide my aim, burn my debt.* His focus shifted to the gunman as he let the weapon fly. The boomerang sped straight into its target's forehead and knocked him out cold.

Kyle and Matt charged the remaining observer, whilst Tim ripped the ringleader from his yet to be mounted victim. Tim slapped the lad around the head a few times and then dragged him to where they'd tied the male captive. As Matt and Kyle had wrestled their drunken target to the ground and Matt now held him in an armlock, Kyle moved to untie the captive male from the log so that they could make use of his rope and gag. Zoe headed to the girl's aid, untying her hands. She was surprised that the girl wasn't distraught; she was furious and pushed Zoe out of the way.

'You fucking arseholes!' She raced to retrieve the gun from the ground close by and aimed at the now unhooded, bound and gagged youths, one of whom was still unconscious. 'You're going to die!'

Kyle stood in front of their captives to prevent this girl making a grave error. 'I didn't prevent a rape to aid a murder. I'm sure you have a life that does not need to be ruined because of this mindless incident.'

'Of course you'd defend them. You're one of them!' she protested, glancing around at his all-white company, when her gaze came to rest on Kyle's father. 'Tim?' She peered through the darkness to be sure it was him.

'Hello, Kimba.' Tim approached the irate girl cautiously. 'I'd like you to meet my son, Kyle, your cousin.' When he motioned to the man she had her gun aimed at, Kimba was so shocked she handed Tim the weapon.

'This is the lost one?' She smiled now, approaching Kyle, and hugging him. 'Welcome home. Thanks for coming to our rescue.' Kimba retreated to hug her boyfriend in the wake of their ordeal. 'This is Felix.' She introduced him to everyone.

'How did you do that?' Felix asked Kyle and then laughed, amused. 'Only a whitefella could throw a *bubbera* boomerang as straight as a *maki*.'

With the mention of his weapon Kyle moved to retrieve it. 'I know I'm no expert, but I think you all have your facts screwed up.' Boomerang in hand, Kyle returned to Kimba and Felix. 'It flies straight,' he insisted, taking aim at one of the ringleader's legs. 'Observe.' He cast the weapon, which induced a muffled wail from the gagged target upon impact.

'So it does.' Felix smiled broadly at Kyle's game. 'Might I try?'

'By all means.' Kyle retrieved the weapon and handed it to Felix.

Kimba clapped her hands in delight, seemingly satisfied to settle for this less troublesome form of revenge. 'Aim for his balls,' she said, suggesting her preferred target, whereupon their conscious targets both rolled on their sides to take it in the hip.

Felix's aim was a little high, however, and the boomerang cracked a rib of the ringleader.

'Aw.' Felix made it sound like a shame that he'd missed his actual target, as Kyle retrieved the boomerang once more.

'Nice form though,' Kyle said, as the target groaned. 'I think you've winded him.'

'Top points,' Matt decreed as he applauded. 'Legendary effort.'

'Okay, enough.' Tim hated to be the grown-up; personally he would have liked to string the three offenders from the nearest tree.

'Can't I just try a hooked shot?' Kyle appealed playfully, teasing their captives, who were now pleading for mercy through their gags.

'What are we going to do with them?' Tim said reasonably, feeling Kyle's request didn't warrant a response.

'What I'd really like to do is strip them naked and leave them here to rot, but ...' Zoe screwed up her nose, 'the stench would be awful and they might never be found by anyone who gives a shit. And besides, we don't want such trash on this property.'

'We could just strip them naked and send them packing,' Kimba compromised and Zoe nodded in agreement. 'The car belongs to Felix, so I'm afraid they'll have to walk ... and carry their mate.'

'Excellent,' Kyle rubbed his hands together, 'more target practice.'

'Uncle Tim ...' Kimba looked about the huge clearing. 'Where's Dad? He went to fetch you from prison. Didn't you meet up?' The look on everybody's face set Kimba's mental alarm bells ringing.

'You haven't heard the news?' Tim knew his in-laws didn't watch a lot of TV, and they wouldn't have expected any incidents to occur on his release from prison.

Kimba shook her head. 'What's happened?' She left Felix to pursue her uncle. Tim tossed Kyle the gun and led Kimba away to break the sad news in private.

Kyle got Matt to untie their captives whilst he covered them with the gun.

'No way I'm taking my clothes off,' the ringleader announced, once he'd removed his gag. 'You can shoot me first, nigger lover!'

Kyle's impulse was to pull the trigger. Thankfully, he thought better of it. He knew if he went to the trouble of humiliating these idiots, they'd cause him further grief and he didn't need the attention. 'Just bugger off,' Kyle instructed, wanting them out of his sight. They made him sick. 'And take your mate with you.'

They grabbed their unconscious friend and dragged him away as fast as they were able.

'This is dangerous territory,' Felix yelled after them. 'In the wilds you would do well to remember that there's a black man in every shadow.'

Kyle fired a couple of shots after them to speed their departure and then passed the gun to Matt. 'Add this to our collection.' Having fired the gun, Kyle decided he much preferred the feel, and skill, of wielding the boomerang; its silence was another advantage. He'd completely forgotten about Burn-a-debt until the two balls of light suddenly swooped to earth, startling Matt, Zoe and Felix most of all. The three backed up to distance themselves from the fiery balls of light.

'*Mooroop burra*,' Felix muttered aghast, as Kyle just stood there allowing the two free-floating anomalies to circle him.

'Pardon?' Matt queried the meaning of his words.

'Spirit lights,' Felix explained in a whisper. 'I've never heard of them getting this close to anyone before. Or rather, I've never heard of anyone allowing them to get this close ... many believe they are evil.'

'They led us to your rescue.' Zoe surprised Felix with the news. 'So it would seem that the opposite is true in this case.'

Tim and Kimba had been drawn back into their midst at the sight of the min min, and the dance of light that was taking place around Kyle brought a smile of wonder to Kimba's tear-stained face. 'He is the one the Matong Bargi Arika has been waiting for,' she whispered under her breath.

Tim caught the comment, however, and suppressed a smile of pride — he suspected Kimba was right.

The two balls of light ended their frenzied dance when they collided with one another right in front of Kyle to become one large ball of light.

Most wise, your compromise, in my eyes, your debt dies. The fiery ball spoke in one young female voice and Kyle was the only one who perceived her dialogue.

'Your blessing will be most welcome.' Kyle could feel the cold again now that he was standing still. The warmth the entity was giving out was very welcoming; Kyle wanted to move into the light and immerse himself in it. And so he did — much to the dismay of most of those present.

'No.' Tim warned the others to stay back. 'He'll be fine … I've done this myself,' he stated, to assure those who doubted his word. 'It is a blessing. No harm will come of it, only good.'

Zoe stared at Kyle, unable to stop fretting at seeing a large fiery mass consume her boyfriend's head.

Kyle was unaware of the outside world; his entire focus was centred around the warmth returning to his body — a sensation that was much like sinking into a hot bath at the end of a frosty winter.

Inner eyes, open wide, rise inside … this one survives, Burn-a-debt decreed.

In that instant his body began to vibrate and it felt as if all the molecules in his body were being sucked clean of wear and tear, and then pumped full of warm, refreshing vital energy. He had lost all physical sight as soon as he'd made contact with the fiery elemental, but his inner eye was perceiving a vision of a very old Indigenous woman seated at the base of an even older, gnarled tree.

I can arrange the audience you seek, Matong Bakkare. A voice emanated from the woman, but she did not move her mouth, open her eyes, or make any movement whatsoever; to all appearances she could have been dead. *I am the origin of the story.*

This vision faded to another of a cave, where gold lined the walls and half the floor appeared liquid. Kyle sat before a fire, his eyes seeming lost in it, his mind whirling from the sound of clapping sticks keeping time with a didgeridoo. *Heed the Bullroarer, the voice of Baiame!* a male voice demanded, before the vision abruptly withdrew and Kyle found himself wavering in his stance, back on the dark land, staring at Turrammelin mountain in the distance crowned by a waxing moon.

'Who is Baiame?' he mumbled deliriously. His knees gave up the struggle and his weary form collapsed unconscious.

'I thought you said it wouldn't harm him?' Zoe directed an angry rebuke at Tim as they rushed to Kyle's side; she was relieved to find Kyle still breathing.

'It didn't hurt him.' Tim whipped open Kyle's shirt, and removed the bloody bandage from his side. 'It healed him,' he announced. Kyle's wound had completely vanished.

'Oh my ...' gasped Zoe, having seen the terrible state of the wound only hours ago. 'That's miraculous.'

Tim eased the boomerang from Kyle's grip to inspect it — Kimba took an interest in it too. 'I recognise this workmanship,' he commented, somewhat awed by the realisation.

'That's one of Uncle Rex's,' Kimba noted curiously.

'It is and all,' Tim agreed. 'And if I recall correctly, this boomerang was fashioned as an offering for a very important ritual held here over twenty years ago ... the night Kyle was born.'

'So how did Kyle end up with it when he has been lost all these years?' Kimba wondered.

'A very good question,' Tim replied. 'I saw this weapon fed to the flame that night.' He gazed around at those present, so that they might see how serious he was. 'It was reduced to ash.'

CHAPTER
NINE

MATONG BARGI AND
THE TURRAMULLI

When Kyle awoke he was staring at a ceiling, which was rather unexpected, and he sat upright to look around. He didn't recognise the small bedroom, and what was more puzzling was that he felt no pain or cold. In fact, he was rather on the warm side.

'I must have burned my debt.' It was the only thing that could explain his fast recovery, and upon checking his side Kyle was gobsmacked to discover his wound had vanished altogether.

I can arrange the audience you seek, Matong Bakkare. I am the origin of the story.

'The old woman.' When Kyle thought back over his encounter with the earthlights, she was the first thing he remembered. *Who is she? And, more importantly, where is she?*

She'll send for you.

He turned around to find Kyron sitting in the corner. 'Kyron!' Kyle suppressed his shock to a whisper. 'I can see you, buddy.' He rushed to wrestle with the creature, but it was transparent and Kyle's hands passed right through his guardian.

I know you can, Kyron stated proudly. *You're really connected now, just like you used to be when you were little.*

Kyle noted that he only heard Kyron's voice in his mind. 'Connected?'

Uh-huh. Burn-a-debt's blessing extended the rainbow serpent in you fully ... your line of communication with the Great One is open once more. Now all you need to do is persuade the men of the local clan to help you place a call to Baiame.

'I need to have a ritual?' Kyle felt very disillusioned by the task of convincing the local Indigenous men that this white boy deserved their help to get an audience with God. But then again, the second vision from his earthlight encounter had indicated this. Kyle looked back at Kyron, noticing that he did not appear stressed to be frequenting the physical world. 'Doesn't being here with me make you feel uncomfortable?'

'Well, I'm not all here.' Kyron referred to his transparent form. 'I've always been with you in this capacity, but you haven't been able to perceive me in a long time.' But Kyron's tone did not infer that Kyle was to blame for this. 'And your courage of late gives me courage. I feel more comfortable about being here, especially now that we're almost home.'

'Almost home? Are you referring to Turrammelin mountain?' Kyle was unsure. 'We've already been there — yesterday.'

'Only the exterior,' he said sadly.

Kyle opened his mouth to question this further, when Matt's voice diverted his attention to the next room.

'He's not himself at all,' Matt was saying.

'He's got very wise all of a sudden and he hasn't asked for a drink or a *smoke* since his near death thingy and that is totally out of character for Kyle, believe me.'

'So you think this Great Spirit might have possessed Kyle, Tim?' Zoe queried and Kyle crept closer to make sure he overheard the response.

'It's just a possibility. I know that one does not just pick up a boomerang and wield it so precisely.' Tim knew this from personal experience. 'This particular boomerang was a gift to the Great Spirit, Baiame, and as Felix pointed out yesterday it is a *bubbera* returning boomerang not a *maki* hunting weapon; it shouldn't fly straight, and yet it does. It was hoped that the offering would placate Baiame, so that he would allow the guardian of Turrammelin mountain to return to protect the sacred site.'

'The bunyip?' Zoe asked.

'No.' Tim corrected her misconception. 'The bunyip is the guardian of the pool ... the outer defence as it were. However, it does not possess the same glamorous powers as the true guardian spirit of the mountain, who was exiled during the bloodletting of Bargi Arika's time.'

'The bloodletting?' Zoe questioned warily.

'That is not for me to speak —' Tim began to advise.

'The guardian of the mountain was a yowie.' Kyle stepped out from hiding to interrupt Tim's explanation.

Tim nodded to confirm Kyle's words, only half surprised that Kyle knew about the legend. 'In these parts it was known as the Turramulli.'

'Turrammelin means "makes big noise". It was named after the creature's howl,' Kyle added for everyone's information.

'How do you know so much about the guardian when you've never even been here before, and know next to nothing about our cultural heritage and history?' Kimba had to know; her curiosity was driving her nuts.

'The creature's name is Kyron, or Ron for short,' Kyle responded lightheartedly. 'He's the one who gave me the boomerang.' He motioned to the item in Tim's hand, and when everyone looked at him thunderstruck and disbelieving, Kyle added, 'Ron's the one who taught me how to use it too.'

'Bullshit.' Kimba coughed, she clearly didn't believe him.

She was a tough little nut this one, friendly but proud and self-righteous. Her dark hair was cut very short but it had already begun to direct itself into small ringlets. Her attire was all denim and black, which suited her rebellious nature and made her look similar to Kyle.

Kyle shrugged off her scepticism. 'You're right ... in reality, I just pulled the flaming boomerang from the ceremonial fire and fully restored it, all with nothing but the bare hands of my pre-natal form.' He held his arms up to flex his muscles, as if proclaiming himself as some sort of super-being.

Kimba shook her head, unfazed by his mockery. 'I'll figure out how you got it, don't you worry.'

'Good-oh,' Kyle encouraged her. 'And while you're at it, you could explain where my wounds have gone and why fire spirits did a dance on my head last night.' He realised he'd got a bit carried away with his teasing, because everyone was staring at him as if he had two heads.

'What *is* going on with you?' Matt ventured, sounding a little concerned for his friend. 'Are you possessed?'

'I'm not possessed,' Kyle objected, with a laugh. 'And I haven't gone nuts either!' Kyle glanced back as Kyron came to stand behind him in the doorway. 'Ron's right here.' He motioned to his ghostly guardian, expecting everyone before him to suddenly cower in fear.

Only you can see or hear me, Kyron advised him, a little late to save Kyle the embarrassment.

'But ... only I can see him,' Kyle added, wincing, as he knew what kind of a response he'd fetch.

'Bullshit,' Kimba and Felix said in accord and even Matt was smiling in disbelief.

'I don't know about that,' Zoe defended. 'Kyle has told me about his yowie before.' She looked at Tim. 'You have the sight. Can you see it?'

'I cannot.' Tim shrugged at Kyle in apology, as everyone else felt vindicated by his words. 'But that doesn't mean it isn't there. The creature may choose not to present itself to me.'

'Yeah, sure, whatever.' Kimba waved off the possibility, having a chuckle with Matt and Felix.

'Why speculate either way?' Tim pointed

out. 'Bargi Arika will see the truth, sure enough, and no one will doubt her word.'

'Who?' Kyle queried.

She is the old woman you seek, advised Kyron.

'Oh, her.' Kyle waved off an answer before anyone could give one. 'Kyron said she was going to send for me.'

Kimba folded her arms. 'This could really get annoying. How long do you plan to keep up this charade?'

'What charade?' Kyle grinned broadly.

'There's nothing here,' Kimba insisted, walking past Kyle and then backwards and forwards through Kyron, who began to laugh hysterically.

Make her stop, it tickles!

Kyle grabbed Kimba's arm to prevent her passing through the creature again. 'Ron wants you to stop it because moving through his space like that tickles him.'

Was Kyle a brilliant actor, or did he really believe what he was telling her? 'I think those earthlights blew a fuse in your brain.' She took her arm back. 'Matong Bargi will see through you to the truth.'

'I sincerely hope so.' Kyle smiled, infuriating his cousin all the more.

Kimba would have pursued the argument but there was a knock at her front door. She moved to the window to peer through the blinds and see who the caller was. 'It's cool. It's Uncle Rex,' she announced, so that everyone could relax.

'Bargi Arika said that Tim was here.' Rex stepped inside as Kimba nodded, but before proceeding into the lounge he hugged Kimba.

'You know about Dad then?' She assumed as much by his comforting gesture.

'Yes. I'm sorry.' Rex hugged her close and then headed off to find Tim.

The two men embraced each other and spoke quietly of Harry's demise, before Tim handed Rex the boomerang. 'But here's the good news.'

As Rex looked the weapon over his jaw nearly hit the floor. 'This proves the claim. The lost one *has* returned.'

Tim pointed to Kyle.

'Bargi Arika has asked to see you,' Rex informed the newcomer, who, despite his olive skin, was nearly as white-skinned as his father.

Yet his mother's ancestry was reflected in his dark eyes and his nearly black straight hair. 'Bargi said you were expecting her summons.'

'That I am,' Kyle concurred, looking at Kimba who was obviously both flabbergasted and annoyed to be proven wrong. 'But who is the Bargi Arika?'

'That's Matong Bargi Arika to you,' Tim explained. 'It means great-grandmother, the small blue water lily, and thus white people have always called Arika, Lily.'

'She's my great-grandmother!' Kyle had always thought about his parents; he'd never got as far as thinking about aunts, uncles, cousins, grandparents, or great-grandparents.

Tim smiled, delighted by Kyle's reaction. 'She's ninety-seven years old and knows the history of Mount Turrammelin like the back of her hand.'

'Then I would like to speak with her too,' Zoe requested.

'You must be the wife of Bargi's Matong Bakkare.' Rex clicked his fingers as he recalled: 'Arika said you must come also.'

Zoe was shocked and strangely delighted. 'I'm not Kyle's wife,' although she did not say this with any dismay.

'Oh, really.' Rex chuckled, looking from Zoe to Kyle, but he made no further comment on the subject. 'I'm to take you both to her resting place.'

Kyle looked at Matt, who'd not been included in the summons.

'He has other plans.' Rex explained why he hadn't extended the invitation to Matthew. 'Arika said that she did not want to keep the film maker from his purpose.'

'Matt?' Kyle prompted a response from him, as Matthew looked at Rex, stunned by his knowledge.

'Well, yeah … I do.' Matt waved a finger in Felix's direction. 'Felix dabbles in amateur film making. He's got a video editing suite set up on his computer at home, so I was going to head over there and check out what I shot last night … and the Nivok tapes.'

'I can do audio too, so I might be able to enhance the sound quality a bit,' Felix added. 'Well, I guess this means we've got a date then.'

Matt appeared to be happy about that. He was only just starting to investigate spiritual matters and, quite frankly, the phenomena that were manifesting around Kyle lately defied his sense of adventure. Kyle had Zoe and Tim to support him through whatever it was he was going through. Matt was happy to stick to chasing facts, evidence and avenues of inquiry that they might pursue to keep Nivok's bulldozers away from Turrammelin mountain.

Kyle and Zoe followed Rex's car in their four-wheel drive. Tim and Kimba were in Rex's car so that they could discuss a burial ceremony for Harry with him.

'So how does it feel to have a wife?' Zoe found the notion amusing and she wanted to test the shallow waters of their relationship.

'Bloody marvellous!' Kyle stated emphatically, which thrilled Zoe. 'For me, that is.' Kyle became more serious. 'For her, I fear it sucks.'

'You're not so bad,' said Zoe, affectionately. 'I can think of worse people to be stuck with for life.'

'But how could you know that I wasn't just after your money?' Kyle reasoned.

Zoe laughed away his fears. 'Well, you know, Kyle, you haven't exactly been trying to romance my money out from underneath me, now have you?'

Kyle cracked a smile; he was a bit slack in the romance department.

'You took a bullet on my behalf, which I very much doubt you would have done if you were only in it for the money,' Zoe continued, hoping to entice him into expressing his feelings. 'And, if otherworldly creatures think you're worth befriending ... you can't have a better recommendation than that in my book.'

'Well,' Kyle smiled, 'that's a relief.' He knew she wanted him to say more, but he wasn't too sure how to say it. 'Kyron really likes you too,' he thought to add, pointing to the back seat.

'Does he now?' Zoe was mildly surprised by this news. 'Then why won't he let me see him?'

Kyle turned in his seat to appeal to his guide. 'Please, buddy, you trust Zoe, I know you do. Just let her see you so she knows I'm not a complete psycho. Please.'

The yowie thought hard on this and then nodded.

'He's says okay. You can see him,' Kyle advised her.

'Oh yeah.' Zoe glanced in her rear-vision mirror to find it filled with the face of a huge, horned, fanged gorilla. The car started swerving all over the place. 'Oh my God!' She brought the four-wheel drive to a screaming halt on the side of the road and hit Kyle a few times. 'Did you have to do that while I was driving?' She jumped out of the car before turning to view the creature in her back seat. 'There's the ghost of a yeti in my car,' she said, bewildered and excited. 'And I can see it! He's just like I imagined!'

Kyle and Kyron just looked at each other in a blasé fashion, as Zoe screamed into her cupped hands to calm herself down.

'Okay, I'm calm.' She looked at the placid monster. 'Hello, Kyron. I'm very pleased to meet you.'

Always a pleasure, Kyron replied.

'And he's telepathic!' She hugged both hands to her heart, delighted. 'This is so great,' Zoe exclaimed, her whole body shaking with excitement.

'Perhaps I should drive,' Kyle climbed into the driver's seat, 'before we lose our guide.' He motioned to the car disappearing down the long stretch of road.

'Oh.' Zoe ran around to the passenger door, climbed in and closed the door. 'Thanks so much, guys.' She looked from Kyron to Kyle.

'This is the best gift I've ever been given.' Zoe hugged Kyle and kissed his cheek. 'I knew you weren't lying.'

'Who'd want to seem this weird on purpose?' Kyle got the car moving.

'I love it that you're weird.' Zoe rested her head on his shoulder, taking advantage of this short time alone — well, sort of alone.

'That's what I love most about you too,' Kyle managed to say without his voice wavering under the stress; speaking of love was still shaky ground for him.

Still, it was enough to make Zoe feel wonderfully secure about where she stood with Kyle. The misconception of the Matong Bargi — that Zoe was Kyle's wife — was playing on her mind. This mysterious woman seemed to know so much, so was this more like a prophecy? Zoe was dying to know.

They brought the cars to a stop at a thick patch of forest, not far from Turrammelin mountain. This forest did not appear to be a natural formation, because concentric rings of different trees had been planted in such a fashion as to make the interior impenetrable.

'This is Matong Bargi's place?' Zoe walked around the perimeter with Kyle.

'She grew every tree herself,' Tim told them, rather proud of the old woman's achievement.

'And this is not Nivok land?' Zoe noticed how close they were to the mountain.

'It will be once Bargi passes on,' Tim corrected her, a little mournfully. 'This place was granted to Arika by the Nivoks for as long as she lives, then the land reverts to the original owner ... well, you now,' Tim realised.

Zoe then noticed a small stream trickling through a gully that extended from the mountain. 'The front door?' she guessed.

'The only door,' Tim confirmed as he, Rex and Kimba moved ahead. 'Wait here, we'll announce you.'

'So kind,' replied Zoe regally.

Kyle was happy enough to wait around. He'd brought his boomerang along and the flat land only thinly dotted by trees between here and the thicker forests on the mountain proved the perfect place to have a play.

The first thing he wanted to try was to make the boomerang return to him. 'I have a theory about this boomerang, Ron,' Kyle said in an aside to his guardian when the yowie sat in the shade of the trees to watch and see what Kyle had remembered.

Really?

'Yep. I believe that it has otherworldly properties and is enchanted to respond directly to the will of the wielder.' Kyle had walked out onto the plain a little way and he looked back to see what his guardian had to say about it.

Well, that's a good theory, Kyron replied, as if none the wiser.

'Twelve metres diameter, return,' said Kyle, flinging the weapon off in such a way as to encourage its spinning. It completed a perfect circle and returned to Kyle's grasp.

'Yeah!' Zoe applauded, taking a seat beside Kyron.

'I knew it!' Kyle was disappointed. 'It's not that I'm so talented … I have a weapon that can't miss.'

'But you cast the boomerang differently that time from how you cast it last night,' Zoe pointed out. 'Surely that denotes a certain amount of expertise.'

'I taught him that,' Kyron boasted proudly. 'He was quite the prodigy too. He nearly wiped out the entire feral cat population around his orphanage. That is, until his carers deemed Kyle's obsession with killing wild cats to be unnatural. They threatened to take the boomerang away and that's when Kyle locked it up and threw away the key.'

Kyle was entranced by the recollection that had been locked away with the weapon; he knew Kyron spoke the truth. 'I was a lovely child.' He grinned at Zoe and let the horrible memory go, for he could finally admit that he might have been a bit of a worry as a youngster. 'But I have control now,' he stated. As Kyron and Zoe both nodded to agree with him, Kyle spied Rex and Kimba returning. Kimba was looking at him very differently now, as if she was in silent awe of him.

'Bargi will see you now. Just follow the stream to its end,' Rex directed, forcing a smile of reassurance.

Rex, too, seemed to treat him with a certain respect, which Kyle had not been expecting, and it made him wonder what his great-grandmother was telling everyone about him. Kyle was used to being a closet psychic cum psycho, not a Messiah.

Zoe caught the change in mood also. As they walked into the forest, branches and foliage arching over the stream, it felt as if they were entering another world, somewhere she'd visited in fairytales, or in a dream.

'It doesn't seem quite real, does it?' Kyle caught a glimpse of the wee bear-like beast that had once played guardian to the *Book of Dreams*. Then Kyle was seeing the creatures from his past everywhere, whipping in and out of the undergrowth that had almost overgrown the tiny stream. 'Book?' Kyle recognised the ambience of the place, and picked up his pace, eager to discover if his hunch was right.

'Who *is* Book?' Zoe begged to know.

'I think we're just about to find out.'

The tunnel of trees ended in a large clearing filled with native flowers and obviously it provided a home for the local fauna. By the pool at the end of the stream stood a very large spindly gum tree and seated inside the hollow at the tree's base was an old, withered woman. A gap in the canopy allowed soft, filtered sunlight to penetrate and dance upon the ground where the aging woman resided. Her skin was as wrinkled as the tree bark, her hair grey and wiry. Her eyes were closed and she made no movement; Kyle feared he'd come too late.

Welcome, Matong Bakkare. You have been a long time in coming.

Zoe and Kyle both stopped in their tracks when they heard the female voice in their minds. The old woman had not moved her mouth — she still had the appearance of a wax cast. They looked at Tim, seated near her, for an explanation.

My physical senses left me years ago ... I have remained of this world only to attend to the business of this meeting.

'How have you remained here?' Kyle voiced his curiosity as he took hold of Zoe's hand and led her to a seat before his great-grandmother.

By the grace of the Great Spirit I have been sustained in order that I could convey my story to you.

Kyle was still frowning. 'You can't just live on air, though?'

Can I not? She sounded surprised that he would think so. *During your experience of detachment from the physical realm, did you hunger or thirst or feel any physical discomfort?*

Zoe looked at Kyle, confused by the question. Did Matong Bargi refer to his Near Death Experience? Kyle was grinning broadly.

'You are Book,' he concluded surely.

'What?' Zoe muttered under her breath, completely perplexed.

I am the Book of Dreams, Arika granted, *the story of dreams lost and dreams found.* The telepathic voice of the old woman changed into that of the distinguished male voice that Kyle had come to associate with the book. *Your next questions will be, why a book; why disguise my true heritage, sex and colour behind the guise of a white man?*

This is exactly what was running through Kyle's mind. 'Well, why?'

Would you have listened to the tuition of an old coloured woman? No, I think not. I think the mentality bred into you would have made you argue every step of the way and we never would have made it past the foreword.

Kyle was a little ashamed to concede this was quite true.

If I had come to you in the form of a

bullroarer you wouldn't have known what to do with me. You probably would have mistaken me for a piece of jewellery and hung me around your neck!

'Ah ... what's a bullroarer?' Kyle knew he was just proving the old woman's point, and Tim had a quiet chuckle.

'It's a divining tool,' Tim advised his boy.

'Oh.' Kyle had figured it was something like that. 'You understand the ways of the world very well, Matong Bargi.'

'Bargi understands the ways of many worlds,' said Tim, rising to take his leave.

'Aren't you staying for the story?' Kyle asked, surprised.

'You forget ... I was made privy to the book's secrets long ago.' Tim smiled and looking at Arika, he clasped both hands to his stomach. '*An ungune*,' he said to her, throwing his arms wide, then resuming his retreat.

'Should I go?' Zoe wondered if she was intruding.

Please stay. What I have to say involves you too. Although I should warn you that my tale is sad and terrible, so if you feel compelled to depart at any time, please feel free.

'I'm sorry, Matong Bargi. I know you are anxious to tell your tale,' Kyle worried that his childish curiosity was delaying her, 'but, I still don't understand how —'

How I could take the form of a book to convey my knowledge and guidance to you?

'If you're implying what I think you're implying,' Zoe attempted to help out, 'that's shape-shifting coupled with bilocation — which is a highly skilled psychic practice, but not entirely unheard of.' She had read of spiritual masters and psychics who had been accredited with such gifts, but Zoe had never met anyone so adept herself.

'It's unheard of by me.' Kyle admitted to being none the wiser.

It's just creation ... it happens every day. The old woman employed her aged female voice for thought projection once more and her tone was one of amusement. *Focused will creates the forms of this world and the reality we experience in it, with a lot of help from our elemental friends, of course!*

The creatures from the book's cover emerged from tree and shrub, puddle and stone, to gather around Arika, but the creatures of the otherworld were very respectful of the old woman's person.

Zoe's gasp drew Kyle's attention her way. 'You see them?' he asked hopefully.

Zoe nodded, her eyes fixed on the source of her wonder. 'And Arika is —' Zoe lost her voice in amazement.

Kyle looked back to his great-grandmother, who was growing younger by the second. When she had regressed in years to her prime, her eyelids parted and she looked at Kyle.

'We are all just thought forms pulling matter unto ourselves to form a body to inhabit,' she said, 'and if you understand this, metamorphosis is possible.'

The young woman focused on a patch of ground in front of her and chanted.

'Warrawee, bimble thambaroo,'
Come here, earth spirits,
'yappulum nganauwe peggeralin,'
enter my dreaming,
'warrina yetni tumpinyeri.'
give it life.

The *Book of Dreams* began to materialise as the forest's otherworldly inhabitants, quite literally, threw themselves into the Matong Bargi's creation. When the book contained numerous entities and was completely solid of substance, Arika clasped both hands to her stomach and said:

'*An ungune.*'

Thank you.

She threw her hands away from her stomach before lifting the book. 'I appear youthful to you now because that is what I will you to perceive. My physical body has not changed, only your perception of the illusion of form that I am presenting.' She handed the book to Kyle.

'It seems I still have much to learn.' Kyle conceded as he took possession of the familiar item. The book was solid and just as he remembered it.

'You never had a problem, Kyle.' Arika smiled, 'You have been given a gift and should learn to use it.'

'Why me?' Kyle asked the question that had plagued him most of his life.

'Because the night your weapon,' Arika pointed to the boomerang Kyle had laid down on the ground beside him, 'was fed to the flame in offering, you were the one amidst those gathered who the Great Spirit chose to bless with the gift that might save the land which once belonged to our people. I know this, because Baiame assigned the banished guardian of the mountain the task of guiding his chosen warrior towards this destiny. Turramulli found himself hindered by your despair, and as I had a vested interest in your development I agreed to aid the creature that had been the beginning of my woes. By so doing, I began to heal the wound that this land and I have shared for over half a century. I brought forth my *Book of Dreams*, devised decades before to open the eyes of a non-believer —'

'Tim,' Kyle granted.

'And a most worthy recipient of sacred knowledge he has proven to be,' she assured Kyle. 'He never stopped agonising over your separation and it was only when I assured him you would return to the mountain of your own accord that Tim refrained from retrieving you too soon.'

Kyle felt the old resentments rising in him, but rather than fly into a fit of rage to protest at how hard done by he had been, Kyle allowed his tears to flow. 'It was tough, Bargi,' he told her, although he was sure she knew all that he'd endured.

'Now you are tough,' she stated proudly, 'and you have as much of my wisdom as your psyche can stand. You are healthy, strong, extremely psychic and *in love*.' She motioned to Zoe, who had placed an arm around Kyle as soon as his tears had started to flow.

'I don't feel very tough.' He brushed away the tears, but Arika reached out and stayed his hand.

'It is tough to release the past and forgive, for then you have no one to blame for your failures.' Arika's glance touched briefly on Kyron, for the creature appeared to be experiencing the emotional turmoil of his charge. 'By taking responsibility for our own actions, thoughts and aspirations, we find the courage to believe in our own ability to create a better life, for ourself and for others.'

'I have much to be thankful for,' Kyle realised. He was not compelled to deny how he felt about the woman at his side; quite the contrary.

'If Tim had changed the course of your life, Kyle, you and Zoe would not have met under such favourable circumstances,' Arika pointed out and Kyle was rocked to discover that there was a silver lining to his life's story.

'You'd be on opposite sides of the fence doing battle over this mountain, most likely,' Arika continued.

Kyle turned and looked into Zoe's eyes and found she was also rather teary. 'Then my youth alone was a small price to pay,' he told her and was pleasantly surprised when Zoe collapsed in a flood of sentimental tears and kissed him.

'Well, that's the great-great-grandchildren taken care of,' Arika jested, which got the couple's attention very quickly. 'Just kidding ... Maybe?' she teased, cocking an eye questioningly. 'Is your curiosity now satisfied?'

'How rude of us,' Zoe said, as her question regarding 'being seen as Kyle's wife' seemed to have answered itself. It was lovely to think that they were destined to be together. 'Here we come all this way to hear your story and we've asked about everything but!'

'Please forgive all our questions, Matong Bargi Arika.' Kyle handed the book back to its author, whereupon the otherworldly creatures dispersed from the cover and the book dematerialised. 'I for one am *dying* to hear the history of Turrammelin mountain.' He made himself comfortable next to Zoe to hear the tale.

Arika smiled to make it clear she was not offended. 'Then I shall tell my story one last time.'

In 1905 Arika was born into a land that was only sparsely populated by those white people who owned or had been granted large portions of land to develop for farming. Her tribe had lost ownership of the mountain many years before her birth, but her people had been allowed to live around their sacred land in return for the work they did on the sugar cane farm which had spread out around the mountain since their dispossession.

Zoe's great-great-grandfather, Barnett Nivok, had owned and run the property at the time. Both the Europeans and the Aboriginal locals saw him as a fair, hardworking man. Some of the other landowners had considered Barnett too fair in allowing blacks to live on his land. They warned that he should drive them off or remove them to reserves, because they were not fit to work and live alongside decent white folk. Barnett laughed off their racist ideas, saying, 'But then I'd have to find extra farmhands, and feed them, and house them … it works better for everyone this way.'

Barnett had two sons: Parker, who was ten years old, and Lance, who was born earlier in the year that Arika was born. Through living in such a remote location, those at the Nivok homestead rarely had visitors, or themselves went visiting, and thus the children of the Turrammelin tribe had grown up with the Nivok children. Lance and Arika were virtually inseparable before the age of ten, after which time both Arika's parents and the Nivoks made a concerted effort to keep them apart. All the adults saw it coming and although Barnett was considerate of the local people in his employ, he would not tolerate his son fraternising with a black girl lest the worst happened.

Just before Arika's sixteenth birthday, the worst did happen. Arika fell pregnant and Lance told both their parents that he wanted to marry her. His proposal was rejected by all, and the young lovers were dragged their separate ways home.

Having predicted this reaction, Lance and Arika had arranged to meet at the sacred pool at the base of the mountain two days hence. They planned to run away together; Lance had been wielding an axe since the age of five and held no fear of not being able to carve a home out of the wilderness for Arika and himself. Arika had all the knowledge of the land passed on from her people, so they would not starve to death, or want for medicines.

They had picked this spot to meet because they thought it would be the last place anyone would expect to find them. All through their childhood Arika's parents had told them scary tales of the creatures who frequented the waterhole and ate little children. As teenagers, they felt that the purpose of these tales was to prevent children going near the deep waterhole and possibly drowning. The site was considered a sacred male place, so none of the locals ever swam there or used it as a water source — there were other little streams and pools that ran off the mountain which were preferred.

Unbeknownst to Lance, he and his family had angered the guardian of the mountain by their slaughter of the trees in its territory. When the lad was the first to arrive that evening, it was right on Turramulli's hunting time.

Arika arrived to find her lover in pieces. The beast that had murdered him was holding up the head of its victim in triumph.

Her scream was heard for miles and brought all and sundry running to the scene. The beast vanished into thin air, leaving the hysterical Arika to explain. The teenage girl cited the Turramulli as the murderer of her lover, and yet, in her heart, she felt some of the blame for Lance's death must fall on her shoulders — she should never have challenged the taboos of her people. Arika had chosen this as their meeting place, for, in accordance with sacred belief, only the mountain that stood behind the waterhole and fed it and the waterhole itself were sacred ground. She had assumed they would be safe as long as they met around the environs of the site. This assumption proved fatal and ultimately Arika had to concede that she might have been a catalyst for all the suffering that followed.

As Lance was the golden boy of his family, the one everyone favoured, his death hit his family hard — very hard. Barnett rejected Arika's monster story as a feeble attempt to cover for a member of her clan who must have taken revenge on Lance for impregnating one of their women. Barnett gave his workers two days to produce the murderer, and when no one came forward he handed the matter over to the local law enforcement, who had their own way of dealing with the blacks.

'I'll kill every one of those murdering blacks if I have to, to find who killed your son.' And the law officer proved true to his word.

Barnett demanded that Arika be spared and taken to the local Reserve so that when her bastard child was born it would be taken away from her and she, too, would feel what it was like to lose a child.

'My great-great-grandfather allowed your whole clan to be slaughtered?' Zoe cried, shocked and sickened.

Arika nodded, empathetic to Zoe's difficulty in understanding the rude truth about her ancestors. 'They didn't bother burying the bodies, however. They just weighted them all with stones and threw them in our sacred billabong.'

'They're in the pool?' That was it; Zoe was running for a place where she could throw up in private.

'Zoe?' Kyle stood to go after her.

'Stay away,' she ordered. 'I'll be back in a —'

Kyle took the hint and sat back down. 'But if Barnett was so pissed at you … pardon the language.' Kyle had never before bothered reining in his swearing.

'I've heard far worse,' she assured him with a smile. 'Why did Nivok grant me this land?' She pre-empted his question, pleased that he was so interested. She held up a finger to indicate that she was just coming to that. 'Obviously the bloodshed cursed the billabong. The guardian of the mountain was also cursed, for he had indirectly caused the massacre of the people who protected and tended to his mountain's needs. Turramulli had never killed for any reason other than food, and in Baiame's eyes killing to revenge the trees was killing for one's own gratification, so the creature's otherworldly powers were removed.

Its immortality, ability to shape-shift, its glamour, super-strength and ability to move freely between dimensions all ceased to be, and Turramulli was rendered mortal, condemned to live in the material world.'

I was very angry and frustrated. Kyron joined the conversation. *I needed someone to blame for my undoing.*

'Barnett,' Kyle guessed and he didn't need confirmation. The mournful look on Kyron's face said it all. 'You killed him, too?'

It wasn't until several years after I'd killed his son, that I had the opportunity to unleash my frustration on Barnett. He was out walking the property alone when I attacked. The old man managed to aim and fire at me during the clash and the sound of the shot brought people to the old man's rescue. I was forced to flee but I left a trail of blood that was easy to track, even for a white man. Barnett's son, Parker, hunted me down, captured me and after much torture, he had me drawn and quartered.

'Hence your fear of human beings and their realm,' Kyle figured.

Upon my mortal death, the Great One took pity on me and returned my powers — except for my courage and strength — and confined me to his ethereal realms. To the victim in this affair, Arika, he granted otherworldly skills. We were promised that there would come a day when I would be given the chance to appease the Great Spirits, and Arika, to regain the guardianship of my beloved mountain. That opportunity came the night you were born.

Kyron was by now looking and sounding rather distressed, so Arika took over the telling of the tale. 'Barnett and everyone now knew that I'd been telling the truth all along, and that my entire family had been slaughtered unjustly. Barnett only lived for little more than a day after the attack, but that was long enough to change his final will and testament. To me he left this piece of land for the duration of my days and let me know where to find the child I'd lost. For, as mad as Barnett had been about my association with his son, he still hadn't been able to bring himself to lose track of his first granddaughter, and in his will he made provision for her. Barnett left everything else to his son, Parker. However, in a separate document Barnett decreed that Turrammelin mountain was never to be disturbed by any descendant of his family, lest they be cursed.'

'What!' Zoe came rushing back to the gathering. 'That's why my father was reluctant to allow my uncle to develop this land. He must have known about their great-grandfather's dying wish.'

'And do you know what else?' Kyle posed to Zoe. 'We're distantly related.'

'That's right,' Arika smiled. 'Kyle is from Lance's line and you, Zoe, are from Parker's side of the family.'

'So you're like my second cousin, twice removed, or something?' Kyle was ecstatic; he was suddenly related to everyone — even James Nivok!

Zoe's smile had broadened too, having always been a little short on relatives herself. 'And you, Arika, must be like my great-great-aunt!' They all had a bit of a chuckle at this. 'So even I am related to the Turrammelin clan by marriage.'

'My people have a saying.' Arika took hold of Zoe's hand, as the girl sat down beside Kyle once more. 'We are all black, we are all white. If you're white now, you were black in your last life, or will be in your next. In the beginning and the end we are all one and we are all the creation of the Great Spirits of the Dreamtime, who await our return to their midst.'

They were all teary now, Zoe most of all. 'I have always believed that,' she told Arika in all sincerity, 'and whatever I must do to save this mountain, you may rest assured that I shall see it done.'

'I know.' Arika stroked Zoe's face and then gave her a hug. 'I don't doubt your ability to take on your uncle and win. You have a far stronger will than he will ever have in this life.'

Arika smelt like the Australian bush at Christmas time and this scent immediately calmed Zoe's erratic emotions and filled her with childlike happiness. One of Arika's little creatures, a half-marsupial, half-gnome that walked erect, approached Zoe and offered her a drink of water in a wooden handbowl and she accepted it gratefully. Knowing something of the lower orders of the otherworld's nature kingdom, when she had drunk her fill and felt much improved, she removed one of her bracelets and gave it to the elemental, who was most delighted by the gift. He held up a finger to

Zoe as if to say, 'You shall be rewarded for this delight,' which, from an earth elemental, would usually mean financial reward of some kind.

'The first thing we must do is to get the guardian of the mountain reinstated.' Arika looked at Kyle. 'You have passed my initiation; therefore, the males of your clan will agree to a corroboree to witness Baiame's judgement of you and your guardian. May he be pleased by your efforts and extend his otherworldly protection to the resting place of all our families.'

As Kyron stood up, Kyle assumed it was time to go. 'Do you have any advice for when I face Baiame?' he thought to ask before rising.

Arika smiled and shook her head. 'You have accomplished much as a spiritual warrior of late. Your soul is very beautiful and that will speak for itself.' She urged Kyle hither with her hands and then hugged him close with her free arm, the other being wrapped around Zoe. 'Your ancestors are very proud of all you have endured for their cause during your short life. Know that you have their support, and the gratitude and admiration of the *Book of Dreams* and its minions.'

The wee beasts mobbed the three seated humans like a pack of domestic animals seeking their owner's affection, and the moment was a perfect joy.

Kyle's emotions were all over the place when he staggered along with Zoe towards the tunnel that led back to the real world. Zoe, too, was an emotional wreck. He could literally feel the tremors of awareness rushing through her petite body in intermittent trembling. At the exit, Kyle looked back once to see that age had again beset his great-grandmother's form, which had returned to its serene, still pose. *Don't go dying on me yet, Matong Bargi.*

I am the least of your worries, her age-old voice replied in his mind. *This book needs a conclusion and I'm not going anywhere until I get it.*

CHAPTER
TEN

THE LAW OF THE LAND

The world beyond the sacred grove seemed a harsh place in comparison, and Kyle felt strangely drained and stimulated by all the information that he was processing.

'That was the most abstruse, intense experience of my entire life!' Zoe had the half-horrified, half-delighted smile of someone who had just disembarked from a roller coaster.

Kyle swung Zoe around and into his arms. 'Marry me?' Zoe's eyes boggled. The question was too much to handle at a moment's notice. Kyle knew it would be, but it made his next suggestion seem mild by comparison. 'Or at least have sex with me at your earliest possible convenience?'

Zoe burst out laughing. 'You read my mind.' She hugged his muscle-bound body close and kissed him.

Something changed in that moment; their relationship sank to a deeper level and they both realised it was love.

'I *will* marry you.' She let him know she intended to take him up on the proposal. She knew he was what she wanted; how could any other man compete after today?

It was not Kyle's idea of a serious marriage proposal, but it was good to learn that she was all for it. 'No rush,' he teased. 'So long as we both understand where this is headed.' He tried to sound possessive.

Zoe was growing rather fond of his games. 'I'll get you to the altar sooner or later, Kyle Burke, don't you worry.' The name just slipped out. 'I mean ... well, what is my second name to be?'

Kyle had a think about this. 'Well, I'm a Burke

now.' He liked it better than Norton, which he'd inherited from a brief adoption period.

Zoe approved of his decision. Tim was approaching them and she saw by his smile that he'd heard the comment too.

'Kyle.' Tim called ahead for his attention. 'You have to come with us now.' Tim referred to Rex and himself. 'If Zoe could give Kimba a lift back to town, that would be great.'

Zoe knew they were off to do secret men's business and she knew they wouldn't let her come along. 'You be careful now, you hear.'

'I've been through worse, believe me.' Kyle backed away, reluctantly letting her hands go as he followed Tim back to the car.

Kyron waved to her as he pursued his charge. *Don't be sad ... if we're successful tonight, I'll give you special permission to enter into Turrammelin's sacred place, and I'll assure you safe passage.*

Kyle could see that the promise satisfied Zoe by the broad smile on her face. 'Could I interest you in a date tomorrow?' he asked.

Zoe laughed out loud. Here they were, talking about marriage, and they hadn't even dated. 'Sure. If you're up for it?'

Kyle looked at Tim for his professional opinion.

Tim looked at Rex and they both appeared to be amused by the question. 'He'll be good to go by the afternoon,' he declared, and climbed into the car.

'It's a date then,' Zoe confirmed. 'I'll see you *after*.'

'A reward at the end of my quest ... I'll look forward to it.' Kyle waved and joined his father and Rex in the car.

Kimba wandered over to where Zoe stood watching the vehicle depart; she was eager to know Zoe's mind on her visit with Arika. 'You've got more insight and balls than I first gave you credit for. I thought Arika's tale would send you packing for sure, but it is clear it has got you thinking.'

'Yes, indeed,' Zoe replied, pleased to have proven herself to her new kinswoman. 'And I'm thinking I need a good solicitor.'

'For marital advice?' Kimba jested.

'Heavens, no.' Zoe was amused but kind of delighted by the question. 'I need to know more about land law.'

Kimba smiled broadly and fished in her

pocket. 'How fortunate that that's what I have a degree in.' She handed Zoe her card and after reading Kimba's qualifications, Zoe laughed at the synchronicity.

'You're hired.' She slapped a hand down on the older girl's shoulder. 'And while they're off with the boy's club, let's see if we *girls* can figure out a way to save this place.'

Kimba liked Zoe's attitude, ignorant though it was. 'What the men are doing will prove every bit as beneficial to our cause as anything we might come up with. Higher forces decide the outcome of everything in this world. Without the support of the Great Spirits our efforts will come to naught.'

'God, I believe that!' Zoe wanted to kick herself. 'I'm so sorry, I —'

Kimba laughed. 'I know you do. Matong Bargi told me all about you … and my lost cousin,' she teased with a grin, heading back to the car.

'What did she say?' Zoe could hardly contain her excitement, as she galloped after Kimba.

'What do you want to know?' Kimba asked, as if she couldn't guess.

'Well, you know ...' Zoe shrugged coyly. 'Will Kyle and I end up together?'

Kimba laughed, as the girl had proven predictable. 'I think you already know the answer to that.'

Zoe's smile was making her face ache. 'But did Arika predict whether it would be a lasting relationship?' She wanted Kimba to be more specific.

'You're not ready to know the answer to that question,' Kimba said, strolling around the car to the passenger door and hopping in. 'The truth is too deep for a relationship so new.'

Now Zoe was doubly interested. 'Look, I know I haven't known Kyle long.' She quickly climbed into the driver's seat to appeal to Kimba to spill the beans. 'Ours has been a short intense friendship and yet it is the most meaningful relationship of my life! Nothing you could tell me is going to scare me away from your cousin.'

Kimba still wasn't entirely convinced.

'I've been shot at, chased by police, confronted by a yowie, and introduced to an oracle, who informs me that my ancestors murdered her entire clan. If I was going to abandon you all, I think I would have done it already.'

'You can see the yowie now?' Kimba queried, as this was not the case in the morning.

'Kyron granted me leave to see him on the way down here, just so that I'd know Kyle wasn't conning me,' Zoe explained. 'Not that I ever thought he was.' She gazed fondly into space, recalling all the otherworldly incidents that had inspired their romance. 'I'd never met anyone as psychically gifted as Kyle, until today, when I met his great-grandmother.' She started up the car.

'I guess I've been a little hard on him,' Kimba admitted. 'I just hadn't expected the lost one, the saviour of our ancestral lands, to be so *white*. Racist, I know, but there you have it.' Kimba realised an apology was in order.

'I wouldn't worry. Kyle does have a tendency to rub people the wrong way upon first impression ... me included,' Zoe admitted, wanting to get back to their original subject. 'Now, are you going to tell me what Arika said about my future with Kyle or not?'

Kimba shook her head. 'Just know that it's all good and as it should be.'

* * *

As the Aboriginal population in this, as in every area of Australia, had dwindled, the members of different neighbouring clans had been ordered, persuaded and bullied into a few small settlements in each district.

So it was that Kyle found himself at an Aboriginal community to meet the male elders of the local clan. This was the same settlement that Arika had been taken to to see out her pregnancy. All the members of this community had been done out of their ancestral lands long ago — Mount Turrammelin had been one of the last bastions where they had been allowed access to a sacred site. Since the systematic slaughter of the Turrammelin clan in the 1920s, the locals visited their sites to perform rites at great risk of arrest, a beating, or worse.

Kyle met many relatives this afternoon: uncles and aunts, cousins, nieces, nephews and in-laws. He bore the brunt of many jokes, half of which he didn't understand as he didn't speak the language. He was very pleased to have his father there to speak for him, though, because Tim brought an end to their mockery and disbelief quite a few times with a few well-chosen words; everyone would just suddenly stop laughing and look Kyle's way, wearing the same awed stare Rex and Kimba had worn after speaking with Arika about him.

'We cannot delay,' Tim concluded in English for his son's benefit. 'We must make this happen tonight.'

'Aw.' The younger males threw down or placed aside their beers and bottles of drink. 'There goes Saturday night,' whined one.

Although a drink and a smoke had been offered to Kyle, he'd declined. He felt on a high and he knew his old vices would drag him back down if he went anywhere near them. As far as his old demons knew, Kyle was dead and he had no desire to attract them into his life again.

Still, most of the men here gathered seemed well disposed towards the idea of an impromptu sacred rite. The elders had much preparation and planning to do beforehand, so Tim offered to brief Kyle about the forthcoming event and invited him to take a walk.

'I suppose Arika has already prepared you for tonight,' Tim asked, unsure of how in-depth this discourse had to be.

'Book did, yeah,' Kyle confirmed with a casual shrug and a nod, not really too worried about it.

Tim found Kyle's easygoing attitude amusing. 'I was far more nervous than you are about my audience with Baiame,' he admitted. 'You're about to meet a mighty architect of the universe. Don't you find that daunting?'

Kyle stopped, disconcerted. 'Well, I didn't until you put it that way.'

Tim laughed out loud. 'It will not be at all as you expect, and you shall remember only that which the Great Spirit deems essential to your quest.'

'Are we going to Mount Turrammelin to perform the rite?'

'We are going into the mountain,' Tim replied.

Goody, goody, goody, goody, goody, goody, goody!

Kyle looked behind him to see Kyron doing a happy dance. 'Ron seems very keen on that idea.'

'The secret cave was once his home and Turramulli has been banished from there a long time. I'm sure tonight has seemed an eternity in coming for your guide.' Tim let Kyle know that he believed in the yowie, just as Kyle believed in the bunyip.

'So what did Baiame tell you?' Kyle probed, hoping to learn a little more about the great entity he was to meet.

Tim's smile was a little strained as he thought long and hard on the question. 'I was told about you.'

'What about me?' Kyle pursued the topic, although Tim clearly didn't want to.

'Many, many good things,' Tim assured him, before his mood darkened a little. 'Your mother's death was never mentioned, however. I thought I was to have something to do with your development, but ...' He took a deep breath and decided not to go there. 'I was warned that you'd be fiercely independent. I just didn't realise *how* independent.'

'Forget the past, Dad.' The word just slipped out of Kyle's mouth and surprisingly it didn't feel awkward to say it. 'I'm over it. It's repressing and it will cause dis-ease in you if you hang onto it for too long. So, do us both a favour and give it up. I bear you no malice, or my mother either.' Emotional tears were welling: Kyle felt like his being had been plugged into an energy grid ever since his encounter with Burn-a-debt. Pivotal revelations seemed to trigger a surge of emotion, which manifested in his physical form as a rise in temperature accompanied by a flood of tears. 'I'm really happy to finally know who I am.'

Tim couldn't keep his distance any more. He'd wanted to hug his boy for some twenty years and the moment finally felt right.

'I don't know why I'm crying,' Kyle mumbled. 'I'm happy, really.' He pulled away from the long silent embrace first, to find Tim teary eyed as well.

'Happiness is catchy,' Tim explained. 'I never thought I'd ever have your friendship.'

'Well, you do.' Kyle slapped his father's shoulder. 'No need to doubt that, *ever*.'

Their stroll led to a group of tall gums, which provided some nice shade from the afternoon sun.

'So do I have to do anything special to prepare for tonight?' Kyle sat himself down at the base of one of the trees.

'When I take you back to the gathering, all your male kin will come together.' Tim sat at the base of a tree close by. 'Just be respectful and you'll fare well … in fact, your success has already been foreseen.'

'By Matong Bargi?' Kyle asked.

Tim shook his head. 'By me, during the same rite you are about to take.'

'Did you partake in this rite in order to marry my mother?' Kyle wondered what Tim's motivation had been. 'Or was it Book's encouragement that led you to participate?'

'Book had a lot to do with it,' Tim granted. 'Although I didn't undertake the rite in order to marry her, I undertook it in order to understand Alex's way of life, and I learnt so much more than I ever imagined I would. A brush with the divine can't help but change a man.'

'Are you talking about Baiame, or my mother?' Kyle suspected the latter by the vague smile on Tim's face.

'I knew her for less than a year of my forty-five years on this earth and I had seen nothing as divine in this world until you showed up. I have never quite forgiven Baiame for not warning me of her death.'

'She is very beautiful,' Kyle conceded, his gaze lost in space as he summoned her image to mind. He emerged from his reminiscing to find Tim staring at him very strangely.

'You spoke with her, you said?'

'She told me you'd met at Turrammelin, been married there and that I had been conceived there.' Kyle conveyed what he remembered of their conversation.

Tim chuckled. 'Not necessarily in that order. I found out about you the night we were wed.'

'Some wedding present!' Kyle hammed it up.

'It was the best wedding present I could have asked for,' Tim assured him, leaning his back against the tree to stare at the clear blue sky. 'Those were good times.'

'So what happened?' Kyle fished for the part of the saga that had only been touched upon thus far.

'James Nivok.' Tim looked at Kyle. 'I would never have imagined that one man could do me so much damage, especially someone I originally got along with so well. I suppose I did turn on James unexpectedly, but had he not lied to his brother, David, then I would not have had to go behind his back.'

'Please, Dad,' Kyle appealed with a confused frown, 'could you just start at the beginning?'

'Fair enough.' Tim realised he wasn't being very clear, but he hated going back to the time of his undoing. He remembered the period just prior to that time as the best days of his life. 'I suppose it really all started the day I found the nugget, which was also the same day I met your mother.' The memory brought the warmth back into Tim's face.

On the day in question Tim had been out at the mountain, doing the initial surveying before they brought the big equipment in. The sun was a real scorcher by midday and the pool beneath the waterfall was just too inviting to ignore.

Diving deep into the cool water, Tim spied a rock glittering on a rocky outcrop at the edge of the deep pool. He surfaced to find he'd discovered gold without so much as lifting a shovel. And that seemed especially good, considering this was his first major job since earning his degree.

'The bunyip who frequents that pool is not going to like you invading its space.'

Tim looked up to see a goddess standing over him. She was dressed in trekking gear, her long dark hair flying in the warm breeze.

'Men are not really to the creature's taste,' she told him, 'but then I doubt it has ever seen a white man before. It might fancy you as a bit of a delicacy.'

'You're joking.' Tim honestly thought so, until he heard something large surface in the pool not too far behind him.

He didn't look back. He took the woman's helping hand out of the pool and was quite a few metres from the water before he turned to see a large trunk-like neck, with a dog-cum-seal-like head on the end, as it sank back into the watery depths of the pool. 'What the hell was that?'

The beautiful fair-skinned, dark-eyed beauty was not at all disturbed by his alarm; she was more interested in the gold nugget he was holding. 'I think the more important question is, who are you, and what do you plan to do with that?'

When Alex discovered that Tim was working for James, who was executing a mineral surveying licence, she tried to warn Tim that something fishy was going on. Alex was working for David Nivok, who had conservation plans for the site. But Tim wasn't about to forgo the glory of his first major discovery and it was his job to hand over the nugget to Nivok — which he did the very next day.

'Idiot!' Kyle exclaimed, getting caught up in the story and forgetting it was Tim they were talking about. 'Sorry ... then what happened?'

Tim, however, was nodding in agreement with Kyle's first assessment. 'Book happened,' he explained simply. 'Mine was a different story to yours, but the journey was still very much the same, I'm sure. Arika made me realise what a self-absorbed prat I was and how blind I was to the great love that had crossed my path.'

'Sounds pretty familiar,' Kyle joked. 'And you finished Book's tale?'

'Yes, I did,' Tim concurred. 'And you know, the funniest thing was that I returned to the exact same moment in time as when I'd taken up the book to read. I didn't lose a second, but I gained a world of knowledge and a whole new perspective on the situation I was now in.'

'Hold on a second,' Kyle objected. 'Book never mentioned the time anomaly. That means I didn't have to return to save Matt. I would have been given the opportunity anyway. Shit!'

Kyle calmed down and looked at Tim, who had both eyebrows raised in a questioning manner. 'Sorry, do go on.'

'The first person I sought out was Alex, to confirm if what I'd learnt about Turrammelin mountain from Book was true. Over a week we spent time together and talked and fell in love in the process. Alex had told David Nivok about our run-in and he was in the process of trying to uncover the story of the mineral mining lease affair. I divulged all I knew, to aid David in his private investigation into his brother's dealings. Meanwhile, I continued to work for James, prolonging the initial surveying as long as I could. I married your mother during this time and had no reason to suspect that my wonderful life was about to be taken away. David Nivok fully intended to take his brother on in the courts, and if he had, our lives would have been very different. James had tricked David into signing an application form for a mining survey on the land. By the time Alex and I flew down to Sydney to talk about our testimonies in legal proceedings, David had cooled. James had sworn that the survey was to be a gift to

David, to let David know what the land was truly worth, and as getting a licence for mining surveys and the rest was a costly process, David's suspicions abated. He forgave his brother and did not press charges or go on record about the dishonest dealings at all.'

'Big mistake,' Kyle emphasised.

'Yet David was still suspicious enough to completely rewrite his will the very same evening that he let James off the hook. A month later David and his wife were dead, and I was on the run.'

'But how on earth did Nivok frame you for their murder?'

'James' story was that David was all for the mining of Turrammelin mountain and that I had joined the extremists in the area who wanted to save the mountain.'

'Say no more.' Kyle waved it off, as the topic seemed to cause Tim some distress.

'Of course, they never found any evidence connecting me to the car bomb, but it did distract everyone from the possibility of James' involvement in his brother's death. Everything was left to Zoe, so there was no motive to point the police in James' direction either.'

'Thus the death of Zoe's parents remains an unsolved mystery,' Kyle concluded.

'Only for some.'

Zoe and Kimba arrived back at Kimba's house to find Matt sitting on the doorstep. He explained that when Felix had heard on the grapevine about the ritual being held for Kyle this evening, he'd dropped Matt off and headed out to join the ceremony.

'And you're not interested in joining the rest of the men?' Zoe nearly said 'boys' club' but didn't, knowing Kimba would take offence.

'Spiritual matters go way over my head,' Matt admitted, 'and Kyle tells a good yarn, which I'll look forward to hearing. I actually thought it more important that I speak with you.'

'What have you come up with?' Zoe noted Matt was wearing a confident air that hinted he was on top of the situation.

'Any chance of a cuppa?' Matt grinned, cheekily delaying his response to Zoe's question as he looked at Kimba.

'If you've found something to assist our cause, I'll give you anything you like.' There was a touch of flirtation in her tone as she unlocked the door and invited everyone inside.

Zoe pretended not to notice and she wondered if Matt had. 'So what have you found?' Zoe started grilling him as soon as they were seated at the kitchen table.

Matt pulled a slim file and a thick file from his bag. 'Well, it seems to me that our biggest problem with saving the mountain is debunking James Nivok. We need to link what I have him saying on tape to hard evidence that he was responsible for the murder of your parents and Kimba's father.'

'Tim hasn't been able to do that in twenty years of trying,' Kimba commented, having been over this a million times already.

'But he didn't have these.' Matt placed his hands on the files. 'Tim hasn't been successful because he's been chasing the wrong man.'

'What?' Zoe opened the slim file on top to find a picture of her uncle's hired thug. 'Ivan Zevron ... my uncle's bodyguard?'

Matt nodded. 'To prove your uncle was responsible, we need this man's confession.'

'You think Ivan killed my parents on my uncle's say-so, Matt?' Zoe quizzed. 'Because of what they said to each other in my uncle's office the night before Kimba's father was killed?'

'Because of what Nivok said on my recording, and because I was there when Harry picked up Tim. I saw a man slide out from underneath Harry's car. I thought it was some guy having car trouble, until I saw Harry get into the same car. I tried to warn him once the penny dropped.' Matt looked at Kimba to assure her he had tried, albeit too late.

She had a single tear trickling down her cheek, which she promptly wiped away. 'And this was the man you saw climbing out from under my father's car?' Kimba pointed to the photo in the open file, a contemptuous look on her face.

'I was eighty percent sure, then I started looking through these old company wage statements — obviously from before the days of computer programs — now I'm ninety-nine percent sure.' Matt opened up the file to where he'd circled payments to Ivan Zevron, who had earned a steady wage each week from Nivok Industries for his services as James Nivok's bodyguard. 'Here, he received a large bonus.' Matt pointed out the irregularity.

'So,' Zoe shrugged. 'My uncle gives bonuses to all his high-performance employees.'

'Look at the date.' Matt pointed it out.

It took a moment to click before Zoe gasped in shock. 'That was the same month my parents were killed.'

'Exactly,' Matt confirmed. 'And I'm betting that if we could check this week's wage report, we'd find Mr Zevron was getting another big bonus.'

'I know all the entry codes to the computer systems at Nivok Industries. All I need is a mobile phone and a computer and I can confirm that guess ... I'll go shopping.' Zoe sat back in her chair, sickened by the whole affair.

'I'm sorry, Zoe.' Matt reached out and took one of her hands. 'This must be hard for you.'

Zoe shook her head, on the verge of tears. 'I just want to set things right.' Her tears overwhelmed her, as did the prospect of the challenge she was facing. 'There's so much history that's created this godawful mess. Sorry ...' She pulled herself together and took a deep breath.

'We're here to help,' Matt assured her, and

Kimba's timing with the cups of tea proved perfect.

'You tell me what you want to happen,' Kimba took a seat facing Zoe, 'and I'll make it happen.'

'I want my uncle convicted.' Zoe voiced her first wish.

'Granted,' Matt said. 'We're well on our way to doing that.'

'I want to give Mount Turrammelin back to its people.' Zoe was reduced to tears again. 'Arika's natural memorial will stand for all time and the resting place of her people shall never be disturbed.'

Tears were now streaming down Kimba's face, as she thought Zoe's sentiment was beautiful and selfless. 'If only you could do that.' Kimba held a hand to the sobbing woman's cheek. 'Once extinguished, Native Title cannot be revived. The freehold estate must return to Crown ownership if not inherited or sold by the owner.'

'What!' Zoe stood, enraged. 'I can't even *give* it back if I want to. Who the hell makes these laws anyway?'

'However,' Kimba clicked her fingers, 'you could sell it back to us.'

'No, I don't want your money,' Zoe objected strongly, 'I have excess already.'

Kimba smiled, thinking Zoe was too sweet for her own good. 'If this is truly what you want to do — and I believe it is unprecedented in Australia for any freehold landowner to want to give back Native Title —' Kimba sniffled back her tears of pride and excitement, 'there is an Indigenous Land Fund which can purchase land on behalf of our people, for those who have some connection with a piece of land but cannot make a Native Title claim to it.'

'Yes!' Zoe jumped at the idea. 'Perfect. Why not channel public money into something worthwhile for a change?'

'It won't be nearly as much as your uncle would have given you for it, I'm afraid.' Kimba winced at the understatement.

'I don't want anything for it,' Zoe emphasised. 'Any money I make in the process is blood money and I shall wash my hands clean of it in the hope that the curse my family created will be lifted. I could use the money to employ the local clan to create a memorial to the Turrammelin people who died there.' She felt incredibly good about her resolution. 'I don't want anyone to forget Arika's story.'

'In that case,' Kimba nodded, 'there is also a department of the National Trust for cultural heritage projects which we could approach. You might be able to ensure the land is as protected from mining as it possibly can be. There are no absolutes as far as mining is concerned. The best we can hope for is to keep the mountain's treasure a secret, as my ancestors have managed to do for the last two hundred years,' she concluded on a confident note.

The mention of a story had set Matt's mind ticking. 'We could make a documentary … the dark history of Mount Turrammelin.'

Kimba looked intrigued by the idea. 'It could serve our cause to lay down the entire history on film. I could present it to the boards as part of our proposal.'

'And it would give us something to send to the press and stir up public support.' Zoe liked the idea of having that kind of insurance policy.

'I haven't called the TV station to see if I still have a job, now that I'm a kidnapper.' Matt rolled his eyes. 'Still, I'm pretty sure I could get a tape to the right people in the newsroom.

Hell, I met most of them a few days ago. I've got business cards coming out my ears!' He tried not to sound discouraged at the possibility that his media career was ended before it had even started, but a documentary would be a foot in the door to film making, which also had appeal.

'It's all good.' Zoe smiled, relieved to have the skeleton of a plan. 'Thanks guys, I feel better.'

'Now the only question is,' Matt posited, 'that after we save the land and convict your uncle, what are you going to do with Nivok Industries?'

Zoe's eyes parted wide. She hadn't thought about that eventuality yet. 'That's a very good question.' Her horrified expression turned to a smile as she mulled over the alternatives.

'When is your birthday?' Kimba wondered how much time they had to gather a case before Zoe had to present herself at the solicitors to claim her inheritance.

'Two days from now.' Zoe wasn't looking forward to her big day of independence as much as she had been: instead of flying off to see the world she'd be entering the world of big business. *I don't doubt your ability to take on your uncle and win.* Arika's words gave her strength and determination. 'Let's write a script, Matt. And Kimba —'

'I'm on it,' Kimba stood up to leave for her home office. 'I'll make some preliminary investigations and see who I can get on board. If I can arrange meetings ...?'

'I'm good tomorrow morning and the next day,' Zoe advised.

'Ah yes, the big date.' Kimba remembered that Kyle had booked Zoe for tomorrow afternoon.

'Try and get round it.' Zoe realised that the land issue was more important. 'But if you can't ...' She shrugged.

'I shall move mountains,' Kimba vowed, as she left them to their scriptwriting.

'So things are working out well with you and Kyle then?' Matt assumed.

Zoe nodded, her smile returning. 'I think I shall marry him,' she casually announced.

Matt wasn't really hurt by the announcement. He was warmed by it actually. 'Then the mountain will end up being returned to the Turrammelin clan via your kids anyway.'

Zoe found his reasoning invigorating. 'Now, if we can just keep the gold a secret, we'll be laughing no matter what happens.' She'd never had any close friends that she could really trust, confide in and rely upon, but now she was surrounded by them. It seemed the Great Spirit had sent aid, just when she needed it most.

When Kyle awoke on a small bed on the floor of a small room, he didn't know where he was and the previous night was a complete blur. He felt groggy — as if he'd had too much to drink. He sat up, scratching his head as he observed two other beds in the room, which appeared to have been slept in but were now empty. There was a long mirror on the wall, which Kyle crawled towards to inspect himself.

'Bad hair day.' He ran his fingers through the knotted mess to find all sorts of grit, but his skin was clean of all the ceremonial paint that his relatives had covered him in for the ceremony. 'Well, I'm glad they didn't leave me painted up for the ride home.' On the other hand Kyle was sort of disappointed. He already had a couple of tattoos and had rather liked the mask and body paint. All he wore at present was his jeans, as he'd been stripped to the waist before being prepared for the ceremony. His jeans felt damp and Kyle's feet and hands were filthy — even by his standards. 'What the hell did I do last night?'

Panic began to set in when Kyle tried to remember that night and realised that he could recall absolutely nothing.

'Kyron?' He couldn't see his guide anywhere either. 'Where are you, buddy? Ron?' The yowie did not respond.

Kyle bolted out of the room and discovered he was at Kimba's place and had been recovering in her spare room. 'Tim!' Kyle bowled into the lounge room to find Matt shooting footage of Tim, whilst Kimba and Zoe looked on.

'Shhh!' the two girls urged quietly and looked back at Tim, who was talking about his early days with Nivok Industries.

'But I can't remember anything about last night!' Kyle appealed. 'And Kyron is missing!'

'Cut,' Kimba decreed, as Kyle was clearly not going to co-operate. 'We're a little pressed for time here, cuz.'

'I told you that you wouldn't remember much,' Tim rose from the lounge and approached Kyle, 'but fragments will come to you as required.'

'But Kyron?'

'Well, everything went swimmingly and the Turramulli was reinstated as the guardian of the mountain. So I imagine he's still in his cave, revelling in his homecoming.'

'And what if I need him?' Kyle crossed his arms, a little saddened by the fact that Ron clearly wasn't bound to traipse around after him any more.

'His commitment to you is complete and you shall be assigned a new guardian if one is needed, or compelled to assist you in some way,' Tim explained. 'You've reached the stage, in the eyes of the Great Spirit, where you can handle the situation on your own. Do you think my bunyip follows me around night and day? No. Why? Because he has his own responsibilities to see to; his own existence to experience.'

'Oh. Well, at least I still have my boomerang.' Kyle began to look around for it and when Tim started shaking his head, all of Kyle's senses were hit by a vision.

Kyle was holding out his treasure in offering

to a bright presence, and yet at the same time Kyle saw himself standing before a fire offering the boomerang to the flame. *'Then I return this to its rightful owner with much gratitude, as all weapons are now redundant to me.'* Kyle's own words rang in his ears.

'Now you're remembering,' Tim assumed from the way Kyle had suddenly spaced out.

'Kyle, are you okay?' Zoe asked, concerned. Her boyfriend hadn't even acknowledged her presence.

'Um … no,' he decided, giving Zoe a kiss on the forehead without breaking from his thought. 'There's something really important that I was supposed to remember.'

'How do you know if you can't remember it?' Kimba added sarcastically. Not that Kyle noticed.

Don't forget to bring Zoe to the pool tomorrow, Kyle recalled Kyron saying. 'No, that's not it. There was something else.'

'Sweetheart.' Zoe took hold of Kyle's chin and directed his eyes her way. 'You're talking to yourself. Perhaps a shower will refresh your memory … and the rest of you.' Zoe noticed how dirty he was and took a step away since she was wearing white. 'You haven't forgotten about our date, have you?'

'Our date,' Kyle suddenly woke up. 'No, of course I haven't. What time is it?'

'Around noon,' she advised amiably.

'I'll be right back,' he assured. 'Kimba. Can I —'

'Yeah, sure.' She pointed him in the direction of the bathroom. 'Towels are in there. And keep it down, will you. No singing in the shower, we're filming.'

Kyle gave Kimba the thumbs up. 'No probs, cuz. I wouldn't want anyone to hear my singing voice anyway.'

The hot water pelting down upon his head was most welcome.

Kimba mentioning singing had prompted Kyle to remember one of the chants they'd sung the night before, which he began humming to himself.

As Kyle hummed, his mind wandered back to the ceremonial fire, from inside of which came a blinding light filled with golden sparkles. He was drawn into the light, and on the other side Kyle was propelled upon a technicolour journey into the vast wilderness of times long past.

Boundless forests filled with masses of exotic creatures and plants, rolling rivers fed the great oceans and long sandy beaches stretched for miles along the coastline. Glittering aqua waters rushed the white sandy shores and the only high-rise to be seen were the eroding cliffs that bordered the shoreline. The sea abounded with life, and it was hard to conceive that such vast populations of sea life could dwindle as much as they had. In this world, mankind didn't really figure at all and it was extremely beautiful. Sadly, it bore little resemblance to the Earth Kyle knew. Yet the wilderness he viewed was distinctly Australian and the large percentage of Caucasian blood coursing through his veins made Kyle feel deep remorse for the damage; when his vision turned ugly he felt it even more deeply.

People, animals and sea life slaughtered; forests torn down; rivers dammed; mountains mined; the sea pumped full of sewage and toxic waste products; the ocean bed drilled for oil and littered with wrecks of old ships, cars and barrels of obnoxious chemicals. The world was turning into one giant graveyard, he feared.

Out in the lounge room, Tim had been distracted in his discourse by Kyle's chant as it gained in volume, much to his cousin's, and everyone's, amused annoyance. Tim suspected Kyle had discovered that the chant aided recall of events from the night before.

'He's just unbelievable.' Kimba chuckled, and then paused to assess his talent. 'He actually sounds more like a relative of mine than he looks.' She turned on her heel to go shut him up. 'Do you think you can raise your voice a bit, the people in America can't hear you!' Kimba thumped on the door, whereby Kyle's chanting ceased.

Matt was on the way to get himself a drink, when he spied a police car pulling up out front. 'Company. Police!' He made a beeline for the bedroom, grabbing Zoe on his way through and Tim cottoned on quick-smart.

'Do you think they traced us here?' Matt queried once they were huddled in the spare room with Zoe and Tim.

'Not likely,' was Tim's opinion.

Kimba knocked on the bathroom door. 'Stay put. Okay?'

'I got it,' Kyle mumbled, switching off the shower.

Kimba was most relieved when she discovered that the police were here to question her about her father's death, and not about harbouring kidnappers and trespassers. They did ask after Tim's whereabouts though, because her father had been picking Tim up when he was killed. She answered their questions obligingly, keeping them at the door, eager to be rid of them. She said she hadn't had much contact with her father and that his movements and other associates had been largely unknown to her.

'That's all then,' the policeman doing the talking advised her, putting his notebook away. 'Would you mind if I borrowed your bathroom? It's a fair drive back to town.'

Kimba didn't want to refuse and raise suspicion. Hopefully, when the officer ran into Kyle he wouldn't recognise him. 'Sure you can use my bathroom,' she said rather more loudly than she normally would have, hoping Kyle would attempt to hide.

The officer entered the bathroom and Kimba held her breath. The door closed. She waited for the alarm to be raised. The toilet flushed, the tap was turned on and off and the officer exited. 'Thanks.' He put on his hat on his way out the door. 'My condolences for your loss.'

Kimba forced a smile and seeing the officers on their way, she rushed back to the bathroom to see what Kyle had done with himself. She was amazed to find the bathroom empty. 'Well, I'll be.' she marvelled, feeling movement behind her. Kimba turned to see Kyle wander out of her bedroom with her hairbrush in his hand.

'I hope you don't mind, I couldn't find one in the bathroom,' he explained.

'But I told you to stay put.' Kimba placed hands on hips, frustrated, wondering why she'd been disobeyed.

'I thought you told me to shut up.' Kyle justified, seeing that Kimba was plainly annoyed with him. 'Geez, could you be more specific with your abuse in future.' He returned to the bathroom and closed the door, completely oblivious to his close brush with the law.

'Completely infuriating,' she muttered. She really couldn't justify being mad at Kyle, even though he could have easily walked straight into a disaster. 'No wonder he needs divine guidance.'

CHAPTER
ELEVEN

THE GOLDEN CAVE

As Matt had shot Zoe's interviews and speech for the documentary the night before, the heiress was dismissed for the afternoon so that she and Kyle could go on their long overdue date. Zoe had already decided to take the indirect route out to the mountain via town, enabling her to purchase the makings of a picnic lunch, a portable computer and a new mobile phone using her fake ID. If they detected her digging around in the computer system at Nivok, they'd trace Lisa — her alias — to a false address. And if, by some miracle, someone linked Lisa to the plane hire a few days ago, by the time they came to Queensland looking for her, Zoe would be back in Sydney.

It was a lovely day out at the mountain. The atmosphere of the place had changed entirely since Zoe's last visit: instead of feeling ominous it now felt tranquil and homely.

They found a nice, shady spot not too close to the pool to lay out their blanket and picnic, and Zoe managed to pinpoint a spot with good reception for the phone.

'So, what's with the hardware?' Kyle licked his fingers after devouring a fresh jam donut. 'Wasn't this supposed to be a date? You know, one of those rare opportunities when we get to shower affection upon each other.'

'I'm just chasing up something for Matt. It won't take a second now that I'm in.' Zoe reached over and brushed his cheek affectionately, then went straight back to her new toy.

'That's putting another man before me.' Kyle faked a perturbed tone. 'I don't think I find that acceptable.' He crawled towards her, a large grin on his face.

'Just one second,' she giggled as he attempted to bowl her over with a hug to the waist. 'I'm almost there.'

'So am I.' Kyle kissed her neck a few times, then as much of her bare back as the halter top she was wearing allowed.

'Oh my ...' Zoe was finding it hard to concentrate and she was just about to give up on the task, when she found what she was looking for. 'Matt was right!'

'I'm so pleased.' Kyle looked at the spreadsheet, which was incredibly uninteresting; more intriguing to him was the knot for Zoe's top that he spotted underneath her hair.

Zoe copied the file and got offline quickly, racing against Kyle's slow tug on the end of the bow at her neck. She was excited and saddened by her discovery, but she wasn't going to allow it to spoil this afternoon. 'All done.' She switched off and pushed everything aside.

'Me too.' He slipped a finger beneath the loose knot remaining.

Zoe returned his beaming grin as she whipped her top off altogether and lay beside

Kyle, her arms raised high above her head in abandon. 'I'm all yours.'

'Making me the luckiest man on the planet.' Kyle moved closer to bestow one of those consciousness-altering kisses on her, and the act drew his attention completely to her. Her scent, touch, taste, and the feel of her breast in his hand, was like a divine spell come to steal him away from all worldly strife. When their attire allowed them to get no closer, there was a mild frenzy to discard the few clothes that stood between them and their first sensual experience of each other.

Matt had yet to film any footage of Matong Bargi Arika's natural environment, so Kimba offered to drive him out there before they went to Felix's to start editing the documentary.

Matt was most impressed by the subject matter and the view of Turrammelin mountain that this place gave him. For two reasons he did not ask to go through the tunnel to film whatever was at the end of it: firstly, because it was probably considered sacred ground and secondly, because he was a little apprehensive about meeting the old oracle herself. Instead,

Matt ran around shooting the exterior from all angles. Satisfied with his coverage he turned the camera on Kimba.

She was staring at the mountain and hadn't noticed that she was being filmed.

Unlike most of the girls Matt had known, Kimba stood tall and proud and she had the kind of fearlessness about her that Matt had come to associate with Kyle. She also had that same dark, intriguing air and he was disturbed to feel suddenly attracted to her. Was he just drawn to her because she reminded him of Kyle? *No way*, decided Matt. Or was it that Kimba's aura was so akin to Kyle's that Matt felt like he'd known her for years and so felt comfortable around her. Kimba turned and caught his intense focus upon her, which startled him.

'Why are you shooting me?' She placed both hands on her hips, but picking up on Matt's apparent discomposure, she smiled.

'I was just thinking that this is a terrific backdrop for you to relate your great-grandmother's story,' Matt covered himself.

'Well, I can do it in voice-over at Felix's.' She recalled their existing plan.

'But it might be better if you presented it,' Matt explained. 'You look great on camera,' he blurted out, thinking that was more information than he'd intended to offer.

Kimba was on to him now. 'Are you flirting with me, Matthew Ryan?' She grinned and cocked an eye in question.

'No, no,' he assured her, suppressing a guilty smile. 'I wouldn't dream of it.'

Kimba was immediately insulted. 'Because I'm black!'

Matt was horrified by her rash assumption. 'No, no. Because you're with Felix.'

'Oh.' Kimba was embarrassed by her error.

'Geez.' Matt shook off the unexpected change in mood. 'You and Kyle could be twins sometimes, I swear.' Matt returned to shooting the scenery.

'Now you're really trying to insult me,' Kimba replied in a huff.

'Ah, no,' Matt corrected. 'That would be a compliment. Kyle is one of the bravest, truest people I know.'

'You obviously don't get out much.'

'God,' Matt cried out frustrated. 'You two are so much alike it's scary!' If Kimba had been trying to piss him off, she'd succeeded. 'What is your problem with him anyway?'

'I don't have a problem with him,' Kimba yelled back, denying Matt's claims.

'Bullshit, you don't!' Matt slipped the camera beneath his arm, so he could deal with Kimba directly. She was a little taken aback, as he was usually so good natured. 'Is it because he is *white*?'

'No!' Kimba was defensive, knowing Matt was inquiring after her prejudices. 'That's not it at all.' She only realised the truth of the matter in that same instant.

'Then why antagonise him?' Matt softened his tone.

Kimba exhaled heavely; it was hard to admit the truth. 'I'm just jealous,' she began reluctantly. 'I've been here since birth, true to my culture, my people and to the cause of saving this land ... I've devoted my life to little else. So why is it that *he* gets our ancient guardian and divine abilities? Why did the Great Spirit choose *him*? Because he was born a *man*!'

No. I am proof that the Great Spirit shows no bias in that regard.

Matt and Kimba looked to find a young woman standing nearby. Unlike Kimba, she was a full-blood Aboriginal.

'Matong Bargi,' Kimba gasped under her breath. Her great-grandmother had not been seen beyond her inner sanctum in over twenty years.

'What?' Matt didn't understand at all, surely this young woman could not be Kimba's great-grandmother; Tim had said she was ninety-seven years old. Then Matt noticed the woman was not entirely solid in form — he could see the landscape through her. His fear of the unknown was outweighed by his desire for good pictures and Matt discreetly hit the 'record' button on the camera under his arm.

Kyle was chosen because the Great Spirit owed him the opportunity to reclaim his identity, Arika explained to assuage her great-granddaughter's anger.

Although Matt saw her speak, her words seemed to bypass his ears to register inside his mind.

You've always had family support in your endeavours, Kimba, and your life has always been within your control ... the same cannot be said of your cousin. And if you think you have suffered for your cause, know that Kyle has suffered infinitely more, because of his unusual talents.

'Now I understand why all Kyle's foster parents thought he was mentally unstable,' Matt gasped as he realised the truth about Kyle's past. 'It wasn't just his temper that he was being medicated and locked up for.'

'He was committed?' Kimba nearly choked on the information.

'Several times,' Matt told her, sadly. 'But Kyle would not appreciate you knowing it, or about the many times he copped a beating for rebelling against his circumstances.'

The truth hurt, for underneath her jealousy Kimba was becoming fond of Kyle.

You all have a special role to play in the preservation of this place ... and you must support each other if we are to stand any chance of succeeding.

Kimba nodded in understanding, too ashamed of herself to speak, but she also knew that her great-grandmother did not need an explanation, for she always knew one's mind and heart.

The ghostly woman broke into her native language to speak with her great-granddaughter and whatever she said caused the very sombre Kimba to giggle.

I predict great things for you film maker ... although at present I fear you are just ruining your film stock, Arika informed Matthew, who with an embarrassed smile, switched off his camera. *Your service to my people has been at great personal expense and this has not gone unnoticed ... the Great Spirit is keeping track of all.*

Arika's smile filled Matt with wonder. It finally dawned on him that he was speaking with some kind of supernatural being, and she had predicted great things for him! When Arika disappeared into the wall of trees, Matt's theory was looking even stronger. 'What just happened?' He wanted to get Kimba's slant on things.

'I got a well-deserved kick up the arse.' Kimba gave a happy sigh, as she felt lightened of a great load.

'What are family for?' Matt commented. 'So, what did Arika say just now to make you laugh?'

Kimba grinned. 'She said that ... you *were* flirting with me.'

Matt was amused and speechless a second. 'Well, I guess I can't deny it then.' He smiled at Kimba and she smiled back. 'Although it would probably be much simpler if I did deny it.'

'Probably,' Kimba agreed, some of the joy slipping from her expression. 'Well,' she ended the closeness of the moment with a clap of her hands, 'I guess we're all done here.' She turned and headed for the car.

'Looks that way.' Matt followed, sensing that he'd somehow blown the moment — but maybe that wasn't such a bad thing? After all, he really liked Kimba and Felix, and he didn't want to create any bad karma between them. 'Do you think the Great Spirit could send me a girlfriend who is not attached to one of my best friends?' he mumbled as he traipsed after Kimba.

Late afternoon came upon the couple far too quickly.

'I suppose we should think about getting dressed and heading back,' Zoe mumbled from her position curled up alongside Kyle. She was half wrapped in the picnic blanket they were lying on, whereas Kyle was perfectly happy to be butt-naked in the afternoon sun. Unlike most men, Kyle looked better naked than he did dressed — in Zoe's opinion. She would have been quite happy to remain, running her fingers over the washboard muscles on his stomach, for some time yet. 'Oh,' she complained when Kyle rose and pulled his jeans on.

'We can't go yet,' Kyle informed her with a cheeky grin. 'I have a birthday surprise for you.'

Zoe was immediately delighted. 'But it's not my birthday yet.'

'I thought I'd get in early, before the shit hits the fan.' He winked. 'Get dressed. We're going swimming.'

'Why get dressed to go swimming?' Zoe wondered.

'Well, we need Kyron's assistance,' Kyle advised, 'but if you feel comfortable —'

'Right you are.' Zoe complied in haste. 'Is it safe to go swimming with the bunyip and all?' She felt silly asking the question as she had not seen the creature; yet, if a yowie could exist, why not a bunyip?'

'A bunyip fears nothing, except a yowie.' Kyle smiled as Kyron manifested beside him, in full physical form.

'Oh, my God!' Zoe pulled her shorts on to complete her outfit, and congratulated the beast. 'You got your powers back! That's wonderful!'

Kyron nodded, pleased with himself. 'Yes, the Great One was most impressed with my work.' He looked at Kyle.

The creature's smile was rather odd; it looked more like a sneer because it exposed his large teeth.

'And through me, Kyle may draw upon my talents too,' he added, excited about telling them.

'What!' Kyle and Zoe exclaimed at once.

All weapons are now redundant to me. 'That's why I gave the boomerang back.' Kyle found he already knew Kyron wasn't kidding.

'And that is why I wanted you both to come here today,' he explained, 'so I could instruct Kyle on his new capabilities. And as chance would have it, the perfect opportunity to test your new skills shall be supplied before sundown.'

'Really?' Kyle looked about him.

'Don't you remember?' Kyron prompted.

'Yes ... well, no.' Kyle was perplexed by the question. 'I know there was something important, but ...'

Eyes wide open, Kyle found himself staring into the sacred fire from the night before and then, whoosh, he was back at the picnic site. It was later in the day. A car drove up beside Zoe's and out climbed —

'Nivok's bodyguard is on his way here now.' Kyle's attention came rushing back to the present. 'He's going to find our stuff,' he panicked. 'We should pack up and get out of here.' Kyle's first concern was for Zoe.

'Leave it. Believe me,' the yowie sounded very relaxed and placed a hand on Kyle's shoulder, 'it doesn't matter what your enemy finds.'

'Are we still going swimming?' Zoe wondered.

'Well, technically Kyle doesn't have to go swimming. If he wills it I can extend him my skill to pass through matter.'

'Whoa. Really?' Kyle walked up to a big tree and slowly extended his hands towards the thick wooden base. They passed through it, as if Kyle was back in the subtle realms of existence. When his arms penetrated easily, he stepped right through the solid tree base at will, and as with the walls of Adreana's fortress, he was momentarily blinded by the colour and texture of the substance through which he moved. When he tried to pass back again, however, Kyle rebounded from the forehead.

'Just kidding,' laughed Kyron, motioning for Kyle to move through the tree again — Kyle chose to walk around however. 'He's got no sense of humour,' Kyron commented to Zoe, who was so gobsmacked that she didn't know what to say. 'The Great Spirit gave me the choice of supporting Kyle's will or not supporting it, in case the human was tempted to abuse my attributes. But I'm afraid the Great Spirit will only allow me to extend my expertise to Kyle. *You* we shall have to take swimming,' the beast concluded.

'What else can Kyle do?' Zoe finally found her voice.

'Can I fly, like superman?' Kyle tried a lift-off that failed dismally, much to Zoe and Kyron's amusement.

'All right. So I'm not Superman.'

'Bah, Superman was a klutz compared to a rainbow warrior,' Kyron scoffed.

'You've watched Superman, Kyron?' Zoe was surprised.

'Kyle used to watch it all the time … and Spiderman and Mighty Mouse. You name the superhero and we've watched it.' This last comment almost sounded like a complaint. 'You don't need to fly when you can will yourself from place to place.' The creature raised its arms and shot upwards, where it grabbed a large branch and swung up to perch on it. Kyron waved, before vanishing and then yelling to them from the opposite side of the pool. He then disappeared and reappeared in their midst.

Kyle was smiling very broadly and his heart was pounding ten to the dozen. He felt a foreign power surging through his being, a fearlessness that came from knowing he was connected to all things that were more powerful and knowledgeable than himself. He was not alone and never had been. How could he be alone when he was not a single entity, but one tiny fragment of an awesome intelligence that carefully orchestrated outcomes and new challenges based on the choices and actions of its smaller parts?

'Well, come on then,' Zoe prompted. 'Let's see it.' She could see Kyle was dying to give it a whirl.

There was no doubt or hesitation on Kyle's part; he followed his guide's actions, willing each step in turn. He looked up at the branch overhead and imagined himself rising swiftly to brace it; he perceived the arms of his astral body extend forth to grip the tree trunk and the next thing Kyle knew he had hold of the branch. He had done some gym work, so swinging up to perch upon the branch was not a problem. He looked to the opposite side of the pool and imagined himself standing there looking over at Zoe and Kyron. No sooner did Kyle espy his astral body standing on the far side of the pool, than his perception altered and he found himself standing in his desired destination. 'Yahoo! I have *always* wanted to do that.' Kyle envisioned himself back where he started, and there he was, as if he'd never left. 'This is *mad*!'

'You can also will things to you,' Kyron added, to Kyle's further elation.

Kyle immediately turned and focused on the car keys lying on the ground, whereupon his auric arm extended and brought the keys into his possession. 'Excellent!' But then he had to wonder. 'Why have I been extended this gift?'

'So that you can protect the new custodian of this land,' the creature replied.

'But you already have these powers,' Kyle reasoned.

'Not *me*.' Kyron bonked Kyle on the head. '*Zoe* ... and her offspring.'

'Ooooh!' Kyle was enlightened and understood.

Offspring! Zoe was a little alarmed by that suggestion, having just had unprotected sex, but she chose to ignore the implication. 'But I intend to sell this land back to the people it was stolen from,' Zoe pointed out.

Kyron shrugged. 'I'm just the messenger of the Great Spirit. I don't pretend to know the divine agenda.' The yowie looked at Kyle. 'And there's more for you to learn yet, like how to wield *the glamour*.' Kyron made it sound a treat and both Kyle and Zoe took the bait.

'The glamour?' they echoed in unison.

'Is that like spell casting?' Zoe wondered.

'Pretty much,' Kyron said casually.

'As in, like, a wizard!' Kyle really took to the idea.

'So that's what happened this afternoon,' Zoe teased Kyle, wrapping her arms about her new lover. 'You enchanted me with your glamour.'

'I didn't, did I?' Kyle was concerned about the possibility and looked to Kyron for an answer. The beast was shaking his head as if Kyle should know better, but Zoe placed a finger on Kyle's chin and attracted his attention back her way.

'I've been falling in love with you since you read me like a book in my uncle's office that first day,' she confessed. 'Otherworldly glamour had nothing to do with it.'

Kyron stood, tapping his foot, while the couple reassured one another with a kiss, and then another, and then another, and then Kyron cleared his throat very loudly. 'Zoe's birthday present!' he prompted, and they both looked his way.

'Oh, yes.' Kyle got with the program.

'So my present is underwater?' Zoe asked.

'Come on, I'll show you,' Kyle led her by the hand towards the waterfall. 'Kyron will take care of the bunyip.'

Zoe was pleased to turn and find Kyron following closely behind them.

They stopped on the bank at a point that was close to the waterfall, but out of reach of the spray and turbulence. 'Here is good.' Kyle imagined that this was where his mother had fished his father from the water on the first day they'd met.

Zoe noted bubbles rising in a section of the pool and gasped when the large, dark dog-like head rose out of the water. The head was supported on a long neck attached to a body that was about the size of a horse. The creature was staring straight at Zoe and licking its lips. 'Kyle?'

'It's all right,' Kyron advised, looking to the offending presence. '*Thrunkkun! Iterra!*'

With a snarl the beast faded from the physical world.

'I gave him the day off,' Kyron explained. 'Feel free to proceed. You are completely safe now.'

'Excellent, I'm roasting.' Kyle dived right in, taking Zoe with him.

Kyle encouraged Zoe to follow him to the outer perimeter of the waterfall. 'Actually, there's something else I should do while we're here. Won't be a second.'

Zoe grabbed Kyle to prevent him diving. 'What are you doing?'

Kyle fixed her with an odd look. 'Checking Arika's story.'

'You're going to look for bodies?' Zoe was suddenly a little freaked by her predicament.

'There's probably nothing left after all this time, but there's no harm in checking.' Kyle dived before she could query his motives further.

A short time later, Kyle surfaced with a few splinters of bone in his hand. 'I dug these out of the mud at the bottom of the pool.'

'Are they human?' Zoe asked.

Kyle nodded. 'Pretty sure,' he advised her, letting the splinters return to the bottom of the pool. 'I found part of a skull, too, but I thought I'd spare you the gruesome details on your birthday. I have a far better gift. Take a deep breath and follow me.'

Zoe nodded, game for the challenge, and took a lungful of air before going under to follow Kyle down below the fall of the water. There was an underground tunnel in the mountain that quickly led into another pool, where they surfaced into a naturally formed palace of gold.

A rocky opening high on the cavern wall allowed some exterior light to penetrate. A fire burned on the cavern floor and supplied the bulk of the lighting; the smoke rose to escape out through the opening in the wall. Huge veins of gold ran through the cavern and great chunks of it lay on the floor, having fallen from the walls.

'The tribal elders wanted you to see this place, so you would know that it remains untouched,' Kyle explained as he climbed out of the water.

'God, my uncle would have a fit if he even suspected that there was *this* much gold here.' Zoe pulled herself up beside Kyle. 'It's so beautiful,' she said quietly. 'It's almost a pity that no one else will ever get to see it.' She reassured him that the wealth of the mountain made no difference to her decision to sell the land.

'Aren't you afraid the locals might be conning you?' Kyle played the devil's advocate. 'Buy the land cheap and then sell out to mining companies anyway?'

Zoe shrugged. 'I'd like to think not, but even if they did, that won't be my bad karma, it will be theirs, and they'll have the *Book of Dreams* to deal with.' She laughed. 'And Kyron.'

'Wow! I misjudged you so badly,' he admitted. 'I can't believe you'd give away millions, just like that.'

'Well, you're giving it away too, you know.' Zoe hugged him. 'You're going to marry me, don't forget, so what's mine is yours.'

'In that case, we have more than enough. What's five million!'

'We've got company.' Kyron entered through the wall of the cavern to alert them.

'Ivan,' Zoe guessed. 'Is he alone?'

'No,' Kyle told her as his vision of the event returned and he saw three other men climb out of the car with him. 'There are four of them, and they're all armed.'

'See,' Kyron smiled, reassuringly. 'A nice little challenge for you.'

Kyle was smiling, but Zoe was not. 'You can't take on four armed men by yourself, even with the powers you have. You're not experienced enough.'

'Well, thanks for the vote of confidence,' Kyle teased, and almost succeeded in making her feel bad.

'I love you, and I don't want —'

'No need to stress.' Kyle looked at his guardian. 'But I do believe Kyron means to give me a crash course in glamour.'

The yowie began to chuckle as it nodded its head to confirm Kyle's statement.

When Kyle materialised on the bonnet of the intruder's car, not one of them noticed. Ivan Zevron was inspecting Zoe's new computer, while the other three men had spread out to look for the missing picnickers in the little light that remained of the day.

'Are you guys looking for me?' Kyle bounced on the bonnet a few times.

The four men came to form a half circle opposing him, their weapons drawn and fixed upon his person.

'Yes, we are.' Ivan grinned, considering the lad's appearance was a rather stupid move.

All weapons to me, Kyle decided. Every weapon his enemies possessed flew towards Kyle and stuck to his body as if he was one large magnet.

'What the ...?' Ivan grabbed for his departing weaponry to no avail.

Kyle chuckled at their perplexed expressions and at the extraordinary amount of hardware they carried. He counted about nine guns, plus ammunition, a few blades, and some sort of electric prodder. 'Well, you guys have quite an armoury here. These will go very nicely with the rest of my collection.' Kyle selected the most powerful looking gun, Ivan's of course, to hold his attackers at bay with. 'I've been waiting for you, Ivan.' Kyle waved his hand in the direction of the three other men and they froze, entranced.

Ivan's hardened visage was beginning to crack. 'What are you?'

'No, Ivan, the question is *who* am I?' Kyle tossed the weapon in the air and it never came down. 'I am the son of the man that James Nivok tried to frame for the murder of David Nivok. You do remember that little incident, don't you, Ivan?'

'What have you done to them?' Ivan tried to divert the subject.

'You ought to be worrying about what I intend to do with you,' Kyle said, and when Kyle pointed his finger towards a rock, Ivan found himself seated there, unable to move.

'What *are* you going to do?' Ivan struggled to keep his cool, but his fear of the unknown was making him angry.

'First, let's deal with your friends.' Kyle looked at Ivan's three accomplices, who seemed like ex-military types. He clicked his fingers to wake them up. 'What are you guys? Ex-commandos?'

'Yeah,' they all replied.

'Well, I've got a new mission for you.' Kyle pondered what it should be. 'You're on a quest to find ...' He raised a finger when he thought of something remote, yet beneficial. '... the last Tasmanian Tiger.'

'Yes,' the men agreed.

'And as the only thing you'll ever be shooting with again is a camera, you'd better gear up on your way south,' Kyle advised.

'South?' queried one of the men.

'Well, you're not going to find a Tasmanian Tiger in Queensland, are you? So take the car, Ivan won't be needing it, and get on the case immediately.' When the three men promptly complied with his orders, Kyle shrugged. 'Hell, you guys need to chill out a bit. Why don't you do a spot of fishing while you're there?'

The last of the men gave Kyle a thumbs-up as he climbed into the car with his buddies, who were very enthusiastic about their new orders.

'Is it hypnosis?' Ivan tried to fathom what was taking place. He breathed deeply and couldn't smell any gas, so he didn't suspect he'd been drugged.

'You're not drugged,' Kyle guessed what he was thinking, 'but it is hypnotic suggestion of sorts. It's just a trait I picked up from my mother's side of the family.'

'The old, black witch,' Ivan gasped, and he cast his mind back twenty years.

James Nivok had been of the mind to evict her from the land, but after one meeting with the witch, James had abandoned the idea and settled for putting fences around the waterhole.

'So you've met my great-grandmother.' Kyle nodded, figuring James had tried to bully her from her home at some stage. 'She gave you a good *spook*ing, did she?' Kyle was delighted to make Ivan jump; Arika must have really freaked him out.

'What do you want, Burke?' Ivan hardened his voice.

'I wish,' Kyle paused for emphasis and continued in a taunting fashion, 'that by your heart you will die, if you should ever tell a … fib.' He smiled warmly.

'So?' Ivan scoffed.

'So …' Kyle turned on his heel to pace as he questioned the witness. 'Did, or did you not, plant the bomb in David Nivok's car that resulted in the death of both David and his wife?'

Ivan said nothing.

Answer the question. Kyle silently urged the subject to conform to his will.

'No,' Ivan spat out when compelled, then began to feel a pain in his chest.

'You're hoping to die, Ivan.' Kyle winced at his wrong choice. 'Just tell the truth and all will be well for you.'

Ivan's face had gone bright red. 'Yes,' he squeezed out. The relief was instant and he began to breathe normally. 'You son of a bitch,' he snarled, 'take this curse off of me.'

'And it was James Nivok who hired you to plant the bomb in his brother's car, wasn't it?'

Ivan started going red again.

* * *

Kimba always woke early. It was a habit she'd formed when studying for her degree which she'd never managed to shake. Not that it bothered her greatly. She loved to take in the sunrise. It was the most comfortable part of the day, temperature-wise.

Opening the back door to let in the warm rays of the morning sun, she was greeted by the magpie's song, which dominated the sounds of all the other creatures in the vicinity. Sighting Kyle seated in the middle of a dirt patch in the unfenced wasteland that was her backyard, Kimba refrained from closing the back door, unsure if she wanted to be in or out.

She had been avoiding spending time alone with her cousin. She still had issues with him that she hadn't wanted to confront. But now did seem the perfect opportunity to prove to herself and her ancestors that Kyle had her full support.

She walked down the back stairs and across the yard to take a seat alongside Kyle. 'Our hero,' she announced, in praise of his capture of Nivok's thug the day before. 'Tim told us the news last night when we got back from Felix's place. How did you do it?'

'I used Kyron's glamour.' Kyle's eyes remained fixed on the horizon. The landscape was barren except for a few old gums scattered here and there. 'I know you don't believe that I see —'

'Yes, I do,' Kimba cut in and Kyle turned to look at her, surprised. 'Look, this is hard for me, as I'm a bit of a hard-nosed bitch, as you know —'

'Nah,' Kyle jeered. 'I hadn't noticed.'

'But,' she spoke over him, determined to get this apology over with. 'The truth is, I was —'

'Jealous and resentful,' Kyle finished for her.

Her insult melted quickly into shame. 'That obvious, huh?'

'I'd be sore as hell if I were in your shoes,' Kyle proffered in support.

'You would?' Kimba frowned. She hadn't expected this response.

'Yes.' Kyle stood up, energised by the topic. 'And don't think I haven't wondered why you weren't chosen instead of me. Our whole plan was your invention ... I've done nothing to deserve divine favour.'

'Whoa.' Kimba rose to stand beside him, scarcely believing her ears. 'Don't tell me wonder boy is doubting himself?' Kyle was always so cocky and confident, it scared Kimba to see him in this light.

'That's just an act,' Kyle appealed. 'You don't know what it's like in here.' He pointed to his own body.

That's when Kimba noticed: 'Kyle, you're shaking.'

'No shit.' His voice was now trembling in time with his body. 'I feel like I've been plugged into some giant cosmic energy grid. I was doing okay until after my run-in with Ivan last night. Since then I've felt like I'm on overload.'

'You probably are on a kind of spiritual overload.' Kimba took hold of his shoulders, but Kyle couldn't calm down.

'I used to only see otherworldly creatures, but now I'm having visions, *world visions*, and most of them aren't very pretty. I don't know what the hell I'm supposed to do with all this information, Kimba ... I thought I could cope with this superhero business, but I'm beginning to think not.'

Kimba realised her folly; psychic talent had its downside too. She was now secretly relieved that she was not standing in Kyle's shoes. 'You think I could have coped with such circumstances better?' She shook her head in the negative. 'I was an idiot to undermine your confidence, when you're our ace in the hole. Believe me, everyone who has undergone a rite such as you did can expect to experience large shifts in their energy field and moments of revelation. But it will pass.'

Kyle calmed a little, wanting to believe her.

'You *have* been plugged into a giant energy grid, and downloaded a whole heap of information that you're still struggling to process. You probably didn't have the chance to really absorb the information until last night ... did you sleep at all?'

Kyle shook his head.

'When is the last time you ate?'

'Lunchtime yesterday,' Kyle answered.

'Well, no wonder you're feeling weak.' She put emphasis on this as being a major cause of his self-doubt, although she could not imagine the inner shake-up he was experiencing. 'I'm betting bacon and eggs will have you feeling your old cocky self in no time.'

'Perhaps you're right.' Kyle sounded hopeful, willing to give her the benefit of the doubt as he accompanied her towards the house.

'I know I'm right,' Kimba assured him. 'If the Great Spirit, Matong Bargi and all the males of our people say you're up to the task, then it's the gospel truth that you are.'

'Do you really believe that?' Kyle didn't know any of them as well as Kimba did.

'I'll stake my ancestral lands on it.' This was, in reality, exactly what she was doing.

Kyle didn't know if that made him feel better or worse. 'Then I'd best get my shit together, huh?'

Kimba smiled and gave a confirming nod. 'I'll cook and you can tell me more about Kyron's glamour,' Kimba offered. 'That sounds like a talent we might be able to put to good use.'

Kyle liked her reasoning. 'And have already.'

In the office of Hackerman & Partners, the law firm for all Nivok's private and business affairs, James Nivok was discussing what would happen in the event of his niece never being found when his niece walked through the door, accompanied by a young, smartly dressed Aboriginal woman. This was most unexpected and most inconvenient for James.

'Zoe, sweetheart. Where have you been?' He approached to embrace her, but his niece sidestepped him. 'I've got half the country out looking for you. We thought you'd been kidnapped.'

'Don't be ridiculous, uncle,' she scoffed. 'I told you I was going up north to view the land you wish to purchase. So you'd best have one of your henchmen call the police and explain the misunderstanding.'

James was not happy, but he glanced aside to his private secretary and gave the nod. 'You haven't seen Ivan in the course of your travels?'

'Why would I have seen him? He's your bodyguard.'

'Because, as with most of the police department, I sent him looking for you,' James informed her, most put out.

Sent him to kill me, you mean. Zoe presumed Ivan was meant to ensure that she never showed to collect her inheritance, and then her murder could have been blamed on Kyle and Matt. It was very hard not to become irate and start yelling accusations, but today was not the day of reckoning, just the prelude. 'I understand a few of Ivan's friends are on holiday in Tassie at present ... perhaps he went with them?' She smiled smugly, pleased to put her uncle off balance. He obviously didn't know what to make of her banter. 'This is Kimba Nura-Jirrand. She'll be representing my legal interests from now on.'

'That's a huge responsibility to hand over to someone with so few years experience,' protested the leader of the four solicitors in attendance, attempting to make his objection sound like concern for Zoe.

'I know perfectly well what I'm doing,' Zoe advised all those seated across the conference table from her, but when Zoe saw her uncle's condescending grin, it made her angry. 'Is something funny, Uncle James?'

'No, no ... the name just sparked a memory of that cartoon you used to watch, you know ... Kimba, the *white* lion.'

Kimba took a deep breath, having copped this joke all her life. 'In the language of my people Kimba means *bushfire*,' she stated in a cool, ominous fashion. 'Nura-Jirrand means *you fear*.'

'I was never much inclined towards the great outdoors myself,' commented James snidely, confident that Zoe would still be selling her stock and assets and had only brought in this legal adviser in the hope of sweetening the deal.

'Can we please get on with this?' Zoe requested. 'I have other meetings to attend today.' She could almost hear the word *meetings* ringing in her uncle's brain as one of the team of solicitors pulled out a mound of paperwork.

When all the documents relating to her inheritance had been signed and taken care of, the solicitor moved on to a new pile of papers. 'These are the documents pertaining to the purchase of your company stock and the piece of land in northern Queensland.'

'I'll take the offer on the land deal to look over.' Kimba slid it into her briefcase.

'I was under the impression we were going to settle all this today.' James was a little put out by the proposed delay.

'I will not be selling my controlling interest in Nivok Industries at this stage,' Zoe advised him calmly, much to his team's shock and horror. 'I will have my lawyer look over your offer for the land in Queensland, but I tell you now that I am considering other offers.'

'Other offers!' James stood up, enraged. 'You can't consider other offers, darling heart, because the courts gave me first option on buying that land twenty years ago.'

Zoe just looked at him blankly and rose, not prepared to argue the issue. 'If you have a problem with my decision you'll have to discuss it with my lawyer.'

Kimba placed her business card on the table and stood to accompany her client out of the room.

'We'll see what the courts have to say about your decision.' James had friends in high places in the legal system and he figured he would have that piece of land one way or another.

'If you feel the need to take me to court,' Zoe tried to sound as if the threat was neither here nor there to her, 'then so be it.' As she approached the conference room door, it swung open and in walked Ivan. A momentary look of shock crossed his face as he confronted Zoe. 'There you are, Ivan,' she commented on her way past him. 'I do believe my uncle is looking for you.'

'And I've been looking for you,' Ivan replied, astonished.

'Mission successful then,' she concluded. 'Bye.' Zoe waved.

Kimba paused at the doorway and put down her briefcase to clasp both hands to her stomach. '*An ungune*,' she said to all present, throwing her arms wide. Retrieving her bag she followed her client from the room.

Shortly after Zoe received her summons to court, she released a press statement that was similar to the script of their documentary.

She outlined the ancient history of the land dispute and her reasons for wanting to sell the land back to the Turrammelin people: that the mountain remain as a monument to those who had died there. She advised that the Indigenous Land Fund was currently reviewing the case and were hoping to make an offer on the land within days. The Cultural Heritage Projects Department of the National Trust had also expressed interest in the initial proposal to have Turrammelin mountain, and the forest home of the Matong Bargi Arika, declared as significant sites. Whatever profit was made on the sale of the mountain, Zoe announced, would go into the Mount Turrammelin Trust for its preservation.

Zoe also mentioned that she aspired to steer Nivok Industries into a cleaner, safer tomorrow by focusing the company's portfolio on renewable resources and conservation. She suggested that anyone interested in seeing this major corporation move in an environmentally-conscious direction should ring Nivok Industries and voice their support for doing something positive for the nation's natural heritage.

The press statement concluded with the information that the documentary 'The Dark History of Mount Turrammelin' would screen on national television the following evening. Having been cleared of kidnapping charges, Matt and his story had been embraced by his new employers.

The documentary did not contain any references to the death of David Nivok, nor any references to James or Nivok Industries, only telling the story of the Matong Bargi and Zoe's grandfather's dying wish. It also showed the footage of the earthlights that Matt had taken at the mountain, and suggested this kind of phenomenon might have been the reason why the people of Turrammelin mountain considered the place sacred. They decided it was best not to mention the yowie, outside of the creature's direct involvement in Arika's story, or the bunyip, as they didn't wish to attract hunters to the area or create a tourist destination. All they needed was to stir up a bit of media interest and public support as they knew that was what governing bodies responded to best.

CHAPTER
TWELVE

HUNTERS

'Where the hell did she dig up all this ancient history?' James Nivok sat before his wall of TV screens, watching the plea for public sympathy unfold; his niece had truly astounded him with her tactics.

Ivan shrugged and took a guess. 'The old black witch?'

Nivok's stare quickly diverted to his bodyguard. 'Surely she's dead by now ... didn't you check?'

'I'm not going back there,' Ivan retorted. James was surely joking? 'Have you forgotten what happened last time? You need a priest, not a hitman, for that little chore.'

Obviously James did remember, because he shuddered and looked back at his screens.

There was a knock at the door and Nivok's head of staff entered. 'Mr Nivok, incoming calls are blocking the phone lines. I'm going to have to bring in more staff.'

James was furious. 'Take the phones off the hook, and send your people home!' The woman quickly departed to comply with his wish.

'You know that's just going to give the impression that the public outcry was such as to jam the phone lines all night,' Ivan pointed out. 'The press will have a field day.'

'Not if you'd done your bloody job,' James roared as he rose from his chair to get a drink. 'This is a fucking nightmare!' He stormed to the bar, and having his back to his bodyguard he failed to see the smug grin that had formed on Ivan's lips.

* * *

Zoe's apartment was a hive of activity, this being where the members of the Mount Turrammelin Project were basing themselves during their short stint in Sydney.

Matt had just arrived with the take-away food he'd picked up on his way back from work. 'They're not sending me to cover the court case, of course,' he announced, trying not to sound disappointed. 'They have to send a more experienced cameraman to cover such a big story.'

'Do they?' Zoe scoffed. 'Well, I won't give an interview unless you are accompanying me,' she announced to brighten his mood. 'And, for you, it'll be an exclusive.'

'That would be *sweet*,' Matt smiled.

'My pleasure.' Zoe handed him a beer from her fridge. 'Felix called today to say that "The Dark History, Part 2" is coming along well, and should be completed by the time we go to court.'

'To the whole truth and nothing but.' Matt clinked his can against Zoe's wine glass.

'Surprise, surprise!' Kimba ripped a fax from the machine in the sunroom, now converted into a temporary office. This room was an extension of Zoe's lounge room, which Kimba entered waving her fax about. 'Nivok has made an even bigger offer. Boy, is he desperate to settle this dispute out of court. And Hackerman & Partners have finally found the personal note written by Barnett Nivok that was attached to your grandfather's will and are sending us a copy. Although the document is not legally binding, we can present it as a cause of dispute between your uncle and your parents.'

'Excellent.' Zoe was pleased about that. 'I wonder if my uncle's desperation stems from noting Ivan Zevron's name on our witness list?' The heiress glanced over all the zeros attached to the numbers on the offer document, then screwed up the fax and tossed it in the bin. 'No way is he escaping now.'

'I wonder how Ivan is enjoying his stay at the Aboriginal settlement?' Matt pondered the scenario with a smile.

'I'm more worried about how Kyle is doing trying to keep up Ivan's identity.' Zoe had been worried sick since she'd passed him on her way out of the solicitors' office.

'Yeah, what if Kyle sneezes and looses his disguise unexpectedly?' Matt pondered, knowing nothing of occult matters.

'Kyle's just the puppet,' Kimba reminded them both. 'It is his guardian who is the master shaman and the one pulling the strings. Turramulli has a lot to prove after his long time in exile, and he won't leave his charge exposed. Besides, we have other things to worry about.' Kimba handed over the letter and tried not to wince. 'We finally have an initial offer from the Land Fund.'

'One point five million.' Zoe was disappointed. 'That's not going to maintain the area for very long. The Land Fund gets forty-five million every year, and this money is all funds they won't have to pay out in future. This is a win-win situation for all of us and as this is all just figures on paper, let's make it look competitive ... I want to see three million at least.'

Kimba couldn't repress her glee. 'I'll see what I can do.'

'Hey, baby, I'm home.' Kyle breezed in through the door, still in the guise of Ivan. 'How about a kiss.' He chased Zoe into the kitchen.

'Aw, Kyle, please.' She held him off, thinking this was the stuff nightmares were made of.

'I promise I'll turn into a handsome prince,' he suggested playfully.

'Oh ... all right.' Zoe closed her eyes and gave him a very tightlipped kiss.

'Tada!' Kyle was in his own body as they parted.

'Disappointing!' Kimba, who witnessed the transformation with total awe, disparaged Kyle's talent. 'I'd be asking for a refund if I were you, Zoe.'

'Don't listen, honey.' Zoe blocked Kyle's ears. 'You're a prince in my eyes.' She gave him a more welcoming kiss.

'I'll say he's anything he wants if he learnt something useful today.' Kimba folded her arms and waited.

Kyle looked at Matt, who was leaning in the kitchen doorway, looking astonished and holding a beer. 'It's okay, Matt. I'm still me.'

'Yep,' Matt agreed, 'and you get scarier every day.'

'He's still an amateur compared to Matong Bargi.' Kimba continued to downplay Kyle's skill.

'But I'm learning.' Kyle appeared in Kimba's face suddenly, startling her. She finally gave him an amused smile. 'Do you want to hear about my day?'

'Yes, I do.' She grinned at him defiantly, deliberately not stepping back to get Kyle out of her personal space. 'I hope you weren't slacking off.'

'Slacking off!' Kyle said with such animation that Kimba began to chuckle. 'I'll have you know I've thwarted a corrupt attempt to derail our Land Fund deal today, and apart from that I've endeavoured to get up Nivok's nose as often as possible.'

Matt and Zoe applauded, but Kimba was curious. 'What sort of a corrupt attempt?'

'Nivok planned to pull in a few favours from a friend of his in federal parliament who could affect the flow of funds to our bidders.'

'And what did you do?' Kimba persisted with the inquisition.

'I willed that the person to whom James was speaking was deeply moved by our cause and paranoid about the public support we had already gained.' Kyle smiled as if expecting praise.

'But maybe the parliamentarian in question really was touched by our cause and was aware of the extent of interest we've stirred up already?' Kimba posed.

'Either way, we thwarted the threat.' Kyle gave her a chummy hug.

'What's this *we* shit, white man?' Kimba teased. 'It looks like *our* campaign is working.' She referred her congratulations to Zoe and Matt.

Zoe knew Kimba was just teasing, as Kimba had already confessed her faith in the spiritual side of their campaign led by Kyle and his guardian — the girl was just jostling for her super-cousin's attention and so Zoe said nothing.

'You'd be right about that,' Kyle agreed, jumping onto the lounge, his feet hitting the coffee table at the same time his bum hit the seat. 'The phone lines at Nivok got so crammed that they had to shut them down. The staff couldn't cope.' Kyle was pleased to finally get his audience a bit excited.

'I knew it.' Kimba hugged Zoe and they bounced around in a circle together. 'The time is right,' she concluded as they came to a standstill.

'Is my uncle *really* furious?' Zoe asked.

'*Absolutely* spewing.' Kyle picked up that day's paper to read about their venture. 'And if you ask me, he's shit scared.'

'So he should be,' Matt averred, with a firm nod.

'I don't think his motivation is money either. He wants power,' Kyle disclosed.

'Judging from some of the figures he's been throwing at us today,' Kimba observed, 'I'd say money isn't an issue with him.'

'And if he craves power so badly,' Kyle debated, 'that leads me to understand that Nivok has at some time felt vulnerable and powerless ... he must have, if he could need power more than the love of his own family.' This was something Kyle found hard to fathom, having always craved a family.

'I don't think James and my grandfather, Halifax, got along very well.' Zoe offered up the little she knew, as her grandfather had died before she was born. 'After all, Halifax did leave Turrammelin to his younger son, David, and two-thirds of his company in my parent's hands too, which leads me to believe that my father was the favoured son.'

'Aw, boo-hoo, poor billionaire, playboy,

jetsetting arsehole!' Kimba wandered back to her office, having more important things to think about.

Kyle had to admit that not too long ago he would have thought the same thing. But something inside him wanted a good outcome for everyone, including the emotion-starved, self-obsessed man he'd spent most of the day with. Kyle knew what it was to fear. On this level he could empathise with Nivok; they were not so different. But Kyle had never taken a life and James Nivok had to atone for all the lives his selfish actions had destroyed.

Kyle followed Nivok around for the next few days and even scored a free flight to Queensland for the court hearing. He knew James was nervous about Ivan being put on the stand, but Kyle was sure he'd managed to lull the tycoon into a false sense of security by assuring James that he would lie to save them both from being thrown in prison.

James, however, was not quite as gullible or had such a closed mind as everyone had assumed. Kyle didn't know James well enough to know when he was acting oddly — in this case overindulging his friendship with his bodyguard to ensure Ivan kept close, where James could keep an eye on him.

For James had bought the apartment for Zoe, his name was on the lease and he had spare keys. It was no problem whatsoever to have the place wired while Zoe was out of the city. James had had surveillance people record every conversation since Zoe had made her play at the solicitors' office. And, as hard as it was to believe, James had come to realise that supernatural forces were working against him — right alongside him in fact. From what he'd learnt listening into the conversations in his niece's apartment, and from her wonderful documentary, the lad wearing his bodyguard's image was, incredibly, drawing his power from a yowie, known to the local people as the Turramulli. The documentary reported that the creature had been drawn and quartered by James' grandfather, Parker, but obviously this was not the entire truth.

Ivan wasn't the only gun for hire James was acquainted with and he'd sent a crack team of hunters to deal with the monster before the trial. Zoe's documentary had even enlightened him as to the best means to get to the monster — through its beloved trees.

On the night before the hearing, Kyle managed to slip away from the tycoon. The real Ivan Zevron would assume his rightful place alongside Nivok for the court case the next day. Ivan would have all memory of where he'd been excised from his mind, and the only thing he would realise was that he was required to join his employer in court that morning. When asked to take the stand, Ivan would be compelled to tell the truth.

Rex and Tim were flying down to the city from Mount Turrammelin with Ivan on a small jet that Zoe had hired. They were to arrive first thing in the morning, so that the real Ivan Zevron and Nivok didn't have too much time to chat before the hearing. Kyle planned to meet his father at the airport to ensure Ivan was well under his control before they packed him off in a cab to the courthouse.

Tim and Rex took the road past Turrammelin mountain on their way to the airport.

Ivan's hands were tied behind his back, and he sat quietly in the back of the car. The bonds were just a precaution since the thug had been as sweet as a kitten from the time Kyle had left him in their charge.

The sun was just rising in the distance and a warm, reverent calm blanketed the land. Tim loved the sunrise here and cherished the precious few he'd watched with Alex; he was missing his wife more than usual today.

It seemed like Rex had read Tim's mind, because he pulled in at the Mount Turrammelin lookout.

'A short smoke break won't hurt,' Rex insisted.

'Short,' Tim emphasised, knowing his Indigenous family normally had little regard for time schedules.

'We're heaps early.' Rex waved off Tim's concern and climbed out of the car.

'Stay put,' Tim instructed Ivan, who simply nodded to confirm that he understood.

The men sat down on a log and Rex lit up a smoke while Tim took in the view and the happy memories. *Not long now, my love.* 'The nightmare just might end today.' Tim could hardly believe the hour of reckoning was finally upon them.

'What do you mean, might?' Rex slapped his friend's shoulder. 'We finally have the Great Spirit on side. What could possibly go wrong?'

A loud grinding noise was heard in the distance, spurring Tim and Rex into leaping up — the sound emanated from the mountain's direction.

'That sounds like a chainsaw.' Tim voiced his observation warily. Suddenly, on the distant mountain, he saw a large tree topple to the ground. 'No! That's what started this whole mess.' Tim began to run towards the mountain, when a blood-curdling howl was heard and he paused to hear it echo across the land. A whistle from Rex urged Tim to turn back and witness Ivan stagger from the car.

'Where the fuck am I?' the hitman snarled, and tried to pry his hands out of their binding. 'This is kidnapping!' he yelled at Rex and Tim, and then attempted to do a runner down the road.

'Oh, no,' Tim muttered, his fear building. If Ivan had regained his sensibilities, then something had happened to either Kyle or

Kyle's guardian. 'Catch him and get him to court.' Although it was obvious that it would do them little good to get Ivan on the stand if they couldn't still compel him to tell the truth. 'Nivok, you insidious bastard.' Tim resumed his sprint for the mountain.

'Watch your back.' Rex raced after Ivan and caught him with ease. 'I'll take care of our friend here.' He headed Ivan back to the car and pushed him into the boot.

Tim kept low as he ran across the dry, grassy flat land, heading towards the mountain forest as far away from the fallen tree as possible. He did this to avoid being seen by the trespasser — or trespassers. He didn't seriously think the yowie was in trouble; it was far more likely to be Kyle and the yowie's howl was a protest against this tree-felling incident. However, if the yowie again killed to protect the trees, the Great Spirit would definitely revoke his powers. Was that what had happened?

When Tim reached the cover of the trees, he grabbed his mobile phone from his back pocket and, locating a signal, phoned Zoe's mobile number, as she would have reached her accommodation in Brisbane by now.

'Hello?' Zoe sounded sleepy.

'Zoe? Is Kyle there?' Tim whispered.

'Well, yes, but he's dead to the world right now. Do you want me to wake him?' She was obviously surprised to be hearing from Tim at 6.30 a.m.

'No. If you're sure he's okay?' This seemed to indicate that the yowie had either killed or been killed, but Tim didn't want to panic everyone until he was certain as to what had happened. 'How was Kyle before he went to sleep?'

'Um … energetic. Cocky, amorous —'

'Sounds pretty normal,' Tim warranted.

'Are you on the plane already?' Zoe yawned the last part of the sentence.

'No, I had a change of plans. Rex is bringing Ivan down. I'll explain later —'

'Why are you whispering? Are you okay?'

'At present.' Tim felt that that might not be the case for very long. 'Talk soon.' He hung up and moved to rise when several darts skimmed past him to lodge in a tree in a lovely straight line. They looked like tranquiliser darts as they were filled with liquid — they could also have contained poison. 'Hunters.' Tim grabbed the darts as he made quickly for thicker cover — their liquid had been wasted upon contact with the tree, but the tips looked like they were made for elephant hide and would serve him as a weapon.

Tim moved with great pace and near silence further into the forest before he scaled a tree near the pool to await his pursuer. It wasn't long before the hunter crept past Tim's perch, and he was easily overcome by an attack from above. Unfortunately, the intruder managed to shout for help before Tim knocked him unconscious with a head butt, which indicated that the hunter had friends in the vicinity. Tim was about to disappear back up the tree when two more men with similar weapons came charging down the forest path that led to the far side of the pool — the track had been seldom used as an approach to the water. Tim snatched up two of the darts from his belt, one in each hand, and threw them into the legs of the man who led the charge. The wounded man hit the ground, losing his weapon in the fall. Spotting the gun of the unconscious man,

Tim grabbed it up and took aim, only to find that, in the excitement of the chase, his pursuer had forgotten to reload the weapon.

The remaining hunter laughed as he realised Tim's predicament. 'All out of luck, hey?'

As the gunman took aim at Tim, the sound of bubbling water became audible. The hunter suddenly took more interest in a target that lay beyond Tim, and Tim figured the cavalry had just arrived.

'Not quite,' Tim replied.

The familiar disgruntled snarl of the bunyip strengthened Tim's faith in cosmic justice.

The ringing phone was sweet relief to Zoe's ears. She'd been so worried since Tim called, but hadn't wanted to call him in case the sound of his phone exposed Tim to danger. 'Thank God it's you. Something has happened to Kyle. I can't seem to get him to wake. He's all groggy.'

'That could be because his guardian has been pumped with enough sedative to kill an elephant!' Tim explained angrily, but then calmed down enough to deliver the bad news. 'He's going to be out of action for at least twelve hours.'

Zoe gasped; the realisation that her uncle had outsmarted her yet again nearly stopped her heart. 'No, no, no, he can't win. How could he have known?' In the documentary, they had made it clear that the yowie was deceased. 'That bastard has got my apartment wired!' She knew in her heart that it was entirely possible and easy to do, and therefore probable — what better way to keep tabs on her loyalty? 'I'm so *stupid*. I should have rented an office in Sydney. Shit!'

'It'll be okay.' Tim lied through his teeth to ease her fears. 'As soon as I get your uncle's thugs tied up and out of harm's way, I'll head across country to see Bargi and explain what's happened. She'll know what to do.'

'I'll get Matt to meet Rex at the airport, and we'll await your word. If necessary, I'll see if Kimba can get the trial postponed, or we'll stall, or … something.' Zoe forced a smile, knowing faith in divine order was all she had left.

'Chin up,' Tim advised gently and with more optimism. 'Even if the very worst should happen today, we both know that karma will have her way in the end, should we live to see it or no.'

'Thanks, Tim, for everything. I won't forget what you've suffered for my family.'

'Our people became one when Arika gave birth.' Tim indicated that there was no need to thank him. 'Our pain and dreams are entwined, and our hopes for tomorrow depend very much on each other.'

'They certainly do,' Zoe granted, stroking Kyle's hair, 'but I'm really glad you're on my side, all the same.'

'Ditto,' said Tim. 'Keep the faith. Speak soon.' He hung up.

Zoe placed the phone on the side table and looked at Tim's son, still unconscious on the bed beside her. 'I fear karmic justice has taken the day off.'

'No . . .' Kyle almost stirred.

'No what, baby?' She slid down closer to him.

'F—' He stirred again, and his eyelids raised for a fraction of a second to reveal his dark, blurry eyes. 'Fe—' was all he said before sinking into a deep slumber once more.

'No fear?' Zoe took a guess as to what Kyle was trying to convey. Even in this state he could manage to be supportive and Zoe really appreciated his effort. 'I promise.' She kissed him, in the hope that like Sleeping Beauty he might be stirred by the kiss of true love — but no such luck.

Although Matt was disappointed at not being able to sit in on the court case, he was still going to get his exclusive afterwards, provided there was a trial at all today. He was a bit worried at first that the TV station, who had given him time off to fly to Queensland and attend the case, would feel ripped off if they discovered that he'd missed most of the hearing. However, Zoe had vowed to fill him in on *everything*.

Matt was on his way from the hotel to meet Rex at Brisbane airport and help keep Ivan under control, in case by some miracle they could still use him as a witness. Matt took his mostly unconscious mate with him to the airport.

In the hope that Kyle might come around, Matt tried to encourage conversation when his mate started to babble.

'T— two.'

'Nah, it's only about nine-thirty,' Matt replied.

'Teams ...' Kyle's head rolled to rest on his other shoulder.

Matt wasn't too sure what to make of that. 'Are you talking cricket? Football? I'm not too sure what's on today. Hey, hold on, you hate sport!'

'No!' Kyle shouted loudly, his eyes opening wide for a second as his body stiffened. 'Felix!' His eyes closed and his head dropped as he continued to mumble. 'Stop ... Matt's ...'

'We're nowhere near Felix.' Matt looked around at the highway they were following to the airport. 'He's back up north, editing,' he explained, realising that his friend was now snoring again.

The girls spoke briefly to the press on their way up the courthouse stairs and then escaped the commotion when security cleared their way to the foyer.

'I do love the way the press refer to me as Ms Nura-Jirrand,' Kimba commented to Zoe, having handled the media masterfully.

Kimba was quite the rebel in her private life, but as a professional she saw being able to dress up and play power games as all part and parcel of beating the enemy at their own game.

'I'm —' Kimba's phone rang and they stopped their journey up the interior stairs to take the call. 'One second . . . hello?'

Despite the holes Nivok had shot in their beautiful plan, Kimba was still confident that they'd somehow win out. She'd waited forever for *this* day in court and nothing, but *nothing*, was going to destroy her belief that it was the will of the Great Spirit that they be victorious.

Zoe stood back to give Kimba some privacy to speak, and noting the commotion on the stairs outside the glass entrance doors she guessed that her uncle had arrived. He spoke to the press briefly to say he was confident that justice would be done today. When Zoe looked back at Kimba, the expression on the face of her defence counsel had been transformed from determined to devastated.

Kimba closed her mobile and shoved it in her pocket. Reaching into another pocket she retrieved a tissue to stem her sudden flow of tears.

'What has happened?' Zoe asked gently. Aware that Kimba was very good at suppressing her emotions, she knew the news must be dreadful to have upset her to this extent.

'Felix's studio went up in flames last night,' Kimba said, still in shock. 'Destroyed, along with everything in it.'

'How is Felix?' Zoe ventured to ask, as Kimba had vagued out.

'He died on the way to hospital.' Kimba stated this rather more serenely than expected, as she had spotted Nivok's party entering through the courthouse doors.

If looks could kill, James Nivok would have been dead on arrival at court. Both women, still in shock, glared at him as he passed, eyes like daggers and revolt in their hearts and minds.

James blew Zoe a kiss and waved to her before he moved on up the stairs to the courtroom, with all his cronies and advisers in tow.

'By sundown, that smug grin of his will be redundant,' Kimba vowed. 'The slaughter stops *today*.'

When Matt got Zoe's call, they were just piling Zevron into the back seat of the car. Rex got in to sit beside their captive, leaving Kyle in the front passenger seat.

'What's up?' Matt asked after updating Zoe on their progress.

The news of Felix's death sent shock waves through Matt's body. He may not have known Felix long, but he'd planned to get to know him a whole lot better. He was a good man and shaping up to be a good friend. 'How is Kimba?'

'She's a rock,' Zoe replied, 'as always.'

'Fuck!' Matt exclaimed, as the revelation hit him. 'That's what Kyle was mumbling about before. Two teams! He must have meant your uncle had sent two teams north, one to deal with the Turramulli and the other to take care of my footage.'

'Oh, my God!' Zoe had her own revelation. 'Kyle tried to tell me too. He wasn't saying 'no fear'. He was trying to tell me that Felix was in trouble.'

'Well, Felix isn't the only one Kyle has expressed fear for during this delirium of his.' Matt walked further away from the car, so that Ivan wouldn't overhear him. 'I thought Kyle was just having a few nightmares about people he knows, because he's also been calling out to Tim and Bargi. If there are two teams of hitmen up north and Tim's only taken care of one —'

Zoe gasped. 'Tim and Arika could still be in danger. I'll call Tim right now.'

'I'll worry about Tim. You get your arse into court,' Matt demanded, albeit in a friendly fashion. 'And don't worry about Tim and Bargi. They're more capable of dealing with danger than the rest of us put together.'

'We could really use Kyle though.' Zoe's concern and longing were apparent in her tone, although she tried to downplay it. 'How's my lad doing?'

'Well, even unconscious, you've got to figure that Kyle isn't lying idle.' Matt wanted to say something encouraging. 'We both know he has contacts beyond this world, and I feel he's up to something in that head of his.'

'Magic happens ... right?' Zoe picked up on where Matt was coming from.

'Especially where Kyle's concerned,' Matt agreed.

'Our luck can turn just like that!'

Matt heard the click from Zoe's fingers. 'Done,' he granted, feeling that their situation couldn't really get much worse.

He was pleased that Zoe seemed to be in better spirits when he said goodbye. Matt dialled Tim's number straight after he'd hung up from Zoe. The recorded message informed him that Tim's phone was unattended or out of radio range. 'Damn it!' He climbed back into the car.

'What's wrong with Mr Wizard?' Ivan referred to Kyle, as having lost the glamour of ignorance Kyle had cast, Ivan now remembered everything Kyle had put him through. 'Not even the supernatural will stop my boss.' He chuckled with delight.

'Gag him, will you?' Matt beseeched Rex and handed him some gaffer tape that was in Matt's all-purpose car repair kit.

'Won't that look mighty funny, him sitting there gagged?' Rex pointed out.

'Shove him in the boot then,' Matt suggested. 'Half the seat folds down, so you won't attract any attention.'

The tape was across Ivan's mouth before he could protest.

Rex was well bearded and Ivan, usually clean-shaven, had whiskers from his stay with the local clan, which the industrial strength tape would rip out by the roots upon removal. 'Look on the bright side,' Rex teased. 'When this comes off you won't need to shave for a week. Better than wax.'

Matt tried again to raise Tim by phone, while Rex shoved Ivan headfirst into the boot and closed the seat behind him. 'I sure hope Tim's battery ain't dead.' Matt figured Tim had made a few long-distance calls that morning.

'There's a black spot in the shadow of the mountain, so if Tim's there he won't have reception,' Rex explained.

'Great!' Matt tossed Rex the phone. 'Keep trying anyway.' He turned to Kyle, being held upright in his seat by the belt. 'I have to tell you, Kyle, the situation is *not* looking good. I can't warn Tim; his phone is dead. I don't want to guilt you out or anything, but we could really use your help right now.'

CHAPTER
THIRTEEN

NATURAL SELECTION

This was so damn frustrating! He didn't seem to be able to get anyone to hear him.

Since the hunters downed his guide, Kyle had been using the crystal ball Crystaleyes had given him to zip around with Kyron in the causal world, and warn those close to him against the tragedies unfolding in the north. Kyle had talked to Zoe in her sleep, but she'd forgotten everything when she woke up. Unfortunately, none of the living were acknowledging him. Kyle's will and influence over physical matter had proven to be as useful as his *own* physical matter. It was the same with Kyron; it seemed they'd been locked out of the physical world and were only permitted to witness the events unfolding there.

I'm working on it, Matt. Say it! Kyle was beside himself and completely disgusted. He couldn't raise the slightest word of comfort from his unconscious body's lips. *Come on, say it!*

'Hmm bur in m—' Kyle's physical person responded when pushed.

That's going to make him feel so much better! Kyle gave up trying to make a connection and so did Matt.

To Tim? Kyron queried.

With a nod from Kyle, reality spun around and Kyle was standing on the flat land outside Arika's forest, looking towards the mountain, as a sole runner approached; it was Tim.

If anyone is going to hear me it will be you. Kyle projected his thoughts with all the will and imagination that he could muster: *Nivok sent two teams of hitmen up here. I suspect those teams are meant to meet in this place to*

*serve the eviction notice that Nivok and Ivan
failed to enforce twenty years ago.*

Tim's sprint slowed as the entrance to
Arika's oasis came into view, but he gave no
indication that he might have heard Kyle.

It seemed his father was as deaf to his
warnings as everyone else, so Kyle walked
alongside Tim into the thicket-tunnel. The
Matong Bargi Arika was the only hope Kyle
had left of making himself heard. Kyle
observed his father closely, feeling proud to
walk alongside him at last. *You turned out to
be a much better role model than I ever
imagined … I can't wait to get to know you
better.*

'Don't confuse the issue now,' Tim mumbled.

Kyle was startled. *You can hear me!*

'Just shhh!' Tim insisted, holding his head.

*This is not your subconscious speaking. It is
your son!* Kyle understood that Tim might not
be able to tell one from the other.

'If it is my son, then he will know we have
no time to delay,' Tim stated reasonably and
kept walking.

But didn't you hear my warning?

'I heard it,' replied Tim.

Kyle was confused by his attitude. *Do you want to die?*

Tim stopped and looked about, thinking that his subconscious was not usually so blunt. 'Equally as much as I want to live,' he said honestly and walked on.

As intensely emotional as Kyle found the reply, he did understand it. Tim was torn between his desire to be with Alex and his wish to be a father to the son he'd just found. The thought of losing his father, when he now admired him, aspired to know him and be like him, really tore up Kyle's feelings. And yet, having tasted what true love could be like, it was equally heartbreaking to keep anyone from pursuing such bliss.

Kyle raced ahead of Tim, hoping to grab Arika's attention before his father got her distracted. *Matong Bargi!* He addressed the old woman's carcass, nestled in the same tree and position as the last time that he'd seen her. She hadn't moved a muscle.

Matong Bakkare.

Kyle turned to find the young spirit form of Arika standing behind him, and beside his great-grandmother stood his equally youthful mother. *Mum!* He'd never used the word, nor sought a mother's embrace, but both seemed to come naturally in this instance.

My precious one. Alex hugged her boy tightly, stroking his hair and kissing his head.

I can't believe that BOTH my parents are here just when I need you most! He nearly choked on the sentiment engendered by the realisation that his parents were great people who cared about him deeply. *It's a dream come true.* Kyle thought that his physical form would surely be shedding a tear as he looked at Arika, thankful for the part the *Book of Dreams* had played in this reunion.

Your father has a big decision to make today, Arika explained, *and he's going to need the two of you to help him make it.*

What's happening? Kyle looked from one woman to the other, alarmed, and yet he knew the answer.

Hush now. Arika made this sound more like advice than a command. *Trust in the divine order and listen.* She turned to address Tim, who had taken a seat before Arika's old, empty shell.

'Once again I have come seeking your aid, Bargi,' Tim began.

I have been watching all as it unfolds, and all that I can do has been done, she told him and Tim suppressed a sigh of disappointment. *I am not permitted to influence outcomes; that is for a clash of wills to determine at the right time. I may only use my abilities to manipulate circumstances, and I have left no stone unturned in my final masterpiece. Much can happen in a moment ... I would not fear for our cause unnecessarily if I were you.*

Tim could hear the cheeky smile in the old woman's tone. 'Then I trust in your word as always, Bargi.'

The defence took their seats in the courtroom. Many of their key witnesses were still missing.

'This is going to be the shortest case in history if something doesn't give,' Kimba muttered quietly to Zoe, who was checking her mobile again.

'No messages.' She closed the phone, frustrated. 'What is going on out there?'

The two girls gazed at each other, trying not to appear disheartened. 'Why does this feel like the final scene from "Thelma and Louise"?' Zoe tried to make light of their tragic situation, but her nerves were starting to make her feel a bit queasy.

Kimba cracked a smile. 'We ain't going over that cliff, honey,' she promised Zoe, as the court was called to attention.

Rising, Zoe spied a strange little otherworldly creature sitting on the judge's bench. It was only in Arika's abode that Zoe had ever seen such a creature in a wakeful state, and she rubbed her eyes to be sure she wasn't imagining things. No, it was definitely there, and it was the same little creature to which Zoe had gifted her bracelet, the day she'd learnt the sad truth about the history of the mountain they were now trying to save. In fact, the wee beast proudly wore the bracelet around its neck, and as it noted Zoe's attention on it, it winked at her.

Before the judge entered the courtroom, it was explained to the court that the judge previously chosen to preside, and several other judges, had been taken ill and so a replacement had been assigned.

Zoe immediately looked at her uncle to see if the news made him smugger than ever — he might have had something to do with this change in the proceedings. It was a pleasant surprise to find that James Nivok was looking decidedly annoyed as he grilled his counsel about the change.

Well, this is an interesting development, Zoe thought, hoping that her uncle had paid off a judge to no avail. Back on the bench, the wee creature dangled its feet over the edge, swinging them merrily as it chuckled with delight.

'All rise! The Honourable Judge K. Rupert presiding.'

Every jaw in the courtroom dropped as the replacement took the bench, for Judge K. Rupert was a middle-aged female, her skin a deeper shade of black than Kimba's.

Zoe looked at Kimba, who had never worn a smile so large as now, and James Nivok had never appeared more devastated. 'Things are looking up.' She looked back at the wee creature watching over the proceedings from the judge's vantage point, and mouthed the words, *thank you.*

You have greater concerns this day, Arika told Tim, as if he already knew this. *I await assassins who have been sent to finish me off, and you must not be seated with me when they arrive, or you WILL be killed along with me, Tim ... I have foreseen it.*

Tim closed his eyes and a great weight seemed to lift from his shoulders; it seemed the news of his imminent death brought the sweetest relief to him. 'I will stay and protect you, Bargi. You know I will.'

Arika was heard to laugh with great affection. *You are certainly an original for your breed, just like my dear Lance, and I treasure your devotion dearly. But you cannot stay on my account,* she said, well aware of Tim's desire to join his wife, in spite of his love for his son. *It is important that my time in this world ends now. It is meant to be, and you must* not *prevent it.*

'If that is your wish, Arika, I will respect it,' although Tim really couldn't bear the thought of losing her counsel, 'but what to do about my own plight ... that is a harder question to answer. I *love* my son. I want to live on and teach him and support him, because I did not have the chance to do so in the past. However, Kyle has come so far on his own that his wisdom will soon outgrow any that I can offer.'

No! Kyle reacted, but was silenced by a gentle shake of Arika's head. The look on his mother's face conveyed that she understood it was hard for Kyle, but Tim had to make this choice himself.

'When I consider another twenty years without Alex. Another day even!' Tim shook his head, unable to find the words to express his pain. 'The last twenty years without her have left me little more than a walking corpse, whose spirit has perished for want of release. I know Alex will wait for me. I just don't think I can stand being in this world without her for much longer.'

Your time as a husband and lover was short-lived and cherished, it is true, Arika said, *but you have never had the chance to be a father and therefore you cannot underestimate the effect it will have on your quality of life henceforth.*

'And what if our relationship sours, or I cannot live up to my son's expectations?' Tears of desperation began to start from Tim's eyes, for his psyche could sense danger approaching, 'And I pass up this gift of a swift death for a loveless and lonely existence without her?'

Arika held a finger up to silence Kyle's comment before he'd even made it. *And what if I tell you that your son is going to have a great responsibility put on his shoulders and will surely benefit from your guidance?*

This 'responsibility' was news to Kyle. He'd never much liked that word; its implications were daunting. Who in their right mind would bestow a huge responsibility on his shoulders, anyway?

Then it occurred to Tim to ask, 'Is Kyle here, Bargi?'

He is, she replied, to Tim's great distress and relief. *Alex is here with him and they are both ready to support whatever decision you make. But destiny is fleeting, Tim, and fate is hot on its heels … choose, or the choice will be made for you.*

Tim could hear the paces of a small force advancing slowly down the only approach to the forest dwelling. Tim smiled and clasped both hands to his stomach. '*An ungune*, Arika, and happy journeying to you. I shall miss you as much as I miss your granddaughter.' He threw his arms wide. 'I choose life.' Tim scampered for cover behind Arika's tree.

Right. Bargi's youthful spirit turned to face Kyle and Alex, who were both pleased by Tim's decision. *If your father is going to make it out of here alive, you're going to have to do the saving.*

Kyle was horrified to discover that Arika was looking at him. *Me! But I've been completely useless today.*

Because your power stems from the restrained Turramulli, but I have some inheritance for you, young warrior. She smiled reassuringly, her eyes fixed on Kyle, as her assassin raised his gun and took aim at his target. *Any moment now.* The bullets caused Bargi's spirit form to reverberate with each impact, but her pain and distress were fleeting and again she smiled. *Now they've done it.*

Kyle noticed Book's creatures stirring in the shadows; he heard them too and they didn't sound happy.

'The old bugger was a sitting duck!' commented the sniper to his three mates, who left the cover of the tunnel and came out into the open. 'What the hell was the boss on about? That was *easy*.'

Arika turned to her physical body. At the crown chakra, located at the top of the old woman's head, her remaining life force was coming together in a ball of sparkling energy. With her fingers Arika beckoned the mass to her and she regarded it fondly for a moment, before turning to Kyle. *This is the blessed gift given to me by the Great Spirit a lifetime ago. It is mine to pass to whomever I choose ... and my elemental friends agree that the inheritance must go to you.*

Me! There was a time when Kyle would have been excited by this gift, but instead he felt overawed, surprised and humbled. 'I am not worthy, Matong Bargi, or ready for such a responsibility.' He took a step backwards only to have five sets of hands push him forward. Turning to investigate, Kyle found Kyron, Crystaleyes, Adreana, Blue and the fiery girl child, Burn-a-debt, all nodding in encouragement. Book's elementals were gathering around the otherworldly guardians of his being, in vaster numbers than Kyle had ever known.

Wee-y-teena wundurra, the creatures of the nature kingdoms chanted in perfect unison, as they emerged from their union with the surrounding flora like the chameleons they were.

Kyle didn't have to ask what the words meant, as their meaning presented itself in his mind. 'Rainbow warrior,' was the chorus.

It's responsibility you fear. Think of it as respond-to-ability ... put that way it doesn't seem so daunting now, does it?

Kyle shook his head; indeed it did not.

You must be careful with the English language, Arika shared her experience. *Try not to be blinded by the connotation of a word and miss the deeper meaning. Book has taught you much,* and by 'book' Arika referred to those gathered entities which had played out the characters and story so well, *but no amount of learning can qualify you to believe in yourself. Only the self can achieve that for the self, to the betterment of all there is.*

Kyle immediately thought of the unfolding court case. The hunters were now headed around the far end of the waterway; it wouldn't be too long before they discovered his father. 'Then I guess I've graduated from Book's school of life ... *I do believe* I can take it from here.'

Kyle bowed his head in acceptance and Arika placed the glittering orb upon his crown, whereupon the ethereal matter was absorbed into his energy field.

Kyle felt as if a stream of light-filled lemonade was pouring into his body, and for a moment the sparkling silver and gold bubbles blinded him as they poured through his being.

For the child you have created and her children ... use the knowledge wisely and pass it on.

Everything came sharply into focus for Kyle, and he was not surprised to find that Arika's spirit form was no longer present.

'Look!' cried one of the killers, all of whom had been oblivious to the supernatural gathering until now. 'There's a thicket growing around the old witch.'

At least, that's how it appeared to their eyes. What Kyle saw were the creatures of the forest lovingly wrapping Arika's remains in nature's blanket, which they spun industriously while also weeping for the departure of their guiding light and dear friend.

'Jesus!' Understandably, the sight of the corpse being eaten by the vegetation freaked the intruders into a retreat.

Tim gave a silent sigh of relief as he

couldn't have breathed in much more; he had been as hard pressed to the tree as he could possibly be.

Kyle focused on the entrance to Arika's dwelling and willed the thicket to close over, blocking the escape of Nivok's hired muscle, and the elementals of the forest flocked to their new master's bidding.

'The tunnel is collapsing!' one of the men cried on his way back into the clearing.

'It isn't collapsing. It's growing!'

They attempted to shoot their way out, but Kyle willed that the men see all their weapons turn into reptiles. Discarding all the offending items from their persons, they watched as the weapons were swallowed by the earth.

'What's going on here?' One of the men became quite hysterical, and his mates weren't much calmer, except for one of them.

'Calm down,' the bravest of the bunch demanded. 'It's an illusion of some kind — maybe gas?'

Kyle chuckled with delight. *Yes! I'm back!* Directing his thoughts to the intruders, he made his announcement in the voice of a horrid old witch.

Nothing worthwhile is ever easy. Kyle gave permission for the many angry nature elementals converging upon the four intruders to keep them amused for a while.

A cement-like substance poured over the boots of one of the men and he became stuck fast to the spot; as the three remaining hunters backed away in fear, a second man was entwined in the branches of a nearby tree and drawn into a hollow in its trunk.

The fellow who had first reacted hysterically was whisked into the air, where he was whirled and thrown so violently that he lost his voice.

Even the bravest of the men, the one who had shot Arika, couldn't fail to be daunted by the screams of his comrades. He had relinquished his weapons to the earth, but he refused to relinquish his body. He edged around the waterhole and away from the commotion, but the reeds took a fancy to the man's ankles, and having hooked their victim, they reeled him into the waterhole kicking and screaming.

Play nice now. Kyle made light of the proceedings and the creatures of the forest laughed at his jest.

Kyle noticed that his father had emerged from hiding and was watching the proceedings with great amusement. How weird must the activity be from his perspective? Alex was standing beside Tim revelling in his amusement; Tim so seldom smiled and now Kyle knew why.

I have a present for you both, he announced, sure that Tim could now hear him clearly. *You'd better sit down, Dad.* Kyle was getting used to bestowing that term on Tim now. His father was intrigued as he obeyed his son.

'What manner of gift does one have to sit down for?'

Yes, what are you up to? Alex grinned, excited by her suspicions.

A present is supposed to be a surprise. Kyle moved Alex out of his path and squatted in front of his father to focus his will upon him. *Just once in my life I will have all my family together in the same place at the same time. Bring him out!*

At Kyle's words, Tim felt a stirring within himself that he'd only ever felt once before. '*Book of Dreams,*' he mumbled as his sight blurred.

Tim's torso fell backwards, leaving his spirit form seated upright in the wake of his physical form's collapse.

When Tim's etheric sight kicked in, his wife and son were both crouching before him waiting for acknowledgement. 'So this is heaven?'

'Or the closest thing you're going to get to it for a while,' joked Kyle, as he was swept into a group hug.

'We have more company.' Kyron alerted them all.

Immediately Kyle received a flash vision of the exterior entrance to Arika's dwelling and he saw men approaching on foot and in vehicles from all directions. 'Something or someone must have alerted the clan,' he commented to his parents, issuing the silent instruction to the elemental creatures who controlled the entrance to raise the natural blockade and allow Bargi's extended family to enter. As Bargi's murderers were so exhausted from their punishment at the hands of the elemental creatures of her abode, Kyle requested the men be released from the taunting.

The elder who had led Kyle's initiation ceremony was the first man to enter Bargi's dwelling, and upon seeing Bargi dead, and the hunters lying about half dead themselves, he beckoned his relatives to make haste and seize the intruders.

Kyle wondered if he could will that he be seen by the elder, whereupon the aging fellow fixed Kyle in his sights.

To him, Kyle appeared as spirit, but the whirling colours of Kyle's fully functioning chakra system were all too apparent. '*Wee-y-teena wundarra.*' He repeated the chant that had summoned him here today and bowed his head to Kyle, knowing he was responsible for the containment of the men answerable for the oracle's death. 'Arika's prophecy is fulfilled.'

'At Matong Bargi's expense, regretfully.' Kyle motioned to a piece of earth, which opened and spat forth a gun. 'The murder weapon,' he advised. 'These are the men who attacked Felix's place earlier today. Forensics should be able to establish that easily enough.' Kyle then noticed two of the clan attempting to revive his father. 'Tim does not wish to be disturbed.'

The elder called out to his kindred to leave Tim be, and then looked back to Kyle. 'You're done here, we shall accompany these men to justice. I feel you will be of far greater service to the Great Spirit and our forefathers elsewhere.'

Kyle's eyes shot open. 'The court case!'

Kimba was in the process of presenting evidence to establish a case for dispute between James and David Nivok over the development of the piece of land still being argued over that day. As the basis of David Nivok's objection to developing the land when he inherited it, Kimba presented the attachment to Barnett Nivok's will, which had been handed down with the Nivok's family estate over the ages. Kimba then raised the supposition that James had tricked his brother into signing the forms for an exploration permit. To bear testimony to this claim, Kimba called old Charlie from Nivok security to the stand.

At the time in question, Charlie testified he had been aware that David Nivok intended to sue his brother James for fraudulent misrepresentation, but David had been persuaded to refrain from legal action.

Nivok's lawyer attempted to discredit the witness as someone who had been recently fired by Nivok Industries and thus bore James Nivok malice. To which Charlie had pointed out to the court that he'd been dismissed over Zoe Nivok's reported kidnapping, which had turned out to be a false charge. The security guard intended to take up his wrongful dismissal with Nivok Industries presently.

After advising the court of the history of Turrammelin mountain, which explained Barnett Nivok's reasons for writing the attachment to his will, Kimba was just about out of monologue. The story had clearly captured the sympathies of Judge Rupert, but without Ivan to place on the stand, Kimba could not make her case-altering allegation against James.

'This history lesson has been most enlightening indeed,' granted the judge, 'but I fail to see where your case is leading the court, Miss Nura-Jirrand.'

Kimba had been expecting this prompt from the judge for the last hour. She looked at Zoe, who was checking the message bank on her mobile phone, and with a huge smile of relief, the heiress gave Kimba the thumbs up. The young lawyer drew in a deep calming breath, before turning her sights back to the judge. 'Your honour, as I have already established, this piece of land has a long and bloody history. I refer not only to the bloodletting of my Matong Bargi's people, but to numerous other unsolved murders that all have some relationship to this piece of land and the man who has wanted so desperately to develop it these past twenty years.'

'Objection, your honour.' Nivok's lawyer was on his feet and sounding outraged. 'This is a land dispute hearing, not a witch hunt!'

'Overruled,' the judge decided after a moment's consideration. 'Still, I will have the claim struck from the record if you do not have very strong evidence to support a case for suspicious circumstances.'

'I have a key witness on the way to this court as we speak, your honour,' Kimba appealed for patience. 'If I could beg the court for five minute's grace.'

'Objection.' Nivok's lawyer was on his feet again. 'Are we to have the courts time wasted —'

'Sustained,' the judge reluctantly granted; she ran the risk of appearing biased if she indulged the young lawyer's request. 'I'm afraid...'

Kimba's heart sank, as she realised her request was about to be denied. And yet, her hope did not fade, for she felt in her soul that Kyle would not fail; she sensed her cousin's haste, he was close.

'If you cannot produce this key witness —' the judge was distracted as the doors to the courtroom burst open and in charged Kyle alongside Ivan, with Matt and Rex in tow.

Kimba's heart was pounding ten to the dozen with relief and exhilaration; finally the truth could be known. Kyle was grinning as he waved, gave her the thumbs up and took a seat near Charlie, with the rest of the late arrivals. Her eyes met those of James Nivok, who was looking very worried at how chummy his bodyguard seemed to be with his enemies. Kimba served the tycoon an unnerving wink and a grin, as she turned to advise the judge. 'The defence calls Ivan Zevron to the stand.'

As soon as Ivan took the stand Nivok's life was all over: Kimba had plotted her defence to get a full confession out of her witness with very few questions. 'Did James Nivok trick his brother into signing the forms for an exploration permit for Turrammelin mountain?

Did James Nivok plot to murder his brother and sister-in-law in order to obtain access to the piece of land? Did James pay a considerable amount of money to Ivan to arrange the explosion that claimed the lives of David Nivok and his wife? And is it not true that another large sum of money was paid by James Nivok to Ivan recently, to have a similar explosive device placed in a vehicle of Harry Nura-Jirrand — the target being Timothy Burke, who James originally attempted to frame for his brother's murder?'

The court erupted with conjecture and shock when Ivan confessed everything on all counts and the judge agreed that the evidence shed an entirely new light on this case.

On suspicion of the murder of David and Elizabeth Novik, and Harry Nura-Jirrand, the court detained James Nivok and Ivan Zevron for questioning by police. A final ruling on the land at Turrammelin mountain could only be given once all charges against James Nivok and his bodyguard had been heard. If the court found James Nivok guilty of his brother's murder, however, Judge Rupert would be recommending that all rights held by James Nivok in regard to Turrammelin mountain be removed, and that Zoe Nivok be awarded full ownership, to dispense with the property as she saw fit.

As the court was dismissed, a victory cheer sounded from the Turrammelin mountain team.

'Looks like you're back in work.' Kyle turned to Charlie and shook his hand, ahead of being pulled into a hug.

'I might even put in for a raise,' Charlie sat back to wink.

'I'm betting you'll get it too.' Kyle granted that the old bloke had more than earned it. He stood to go congratulate his girls, who were currently hugging each other and doing a victory dance. 'The bushfire from hell,' Kyle said in praise of Kimba as he approached. He'd never seen Kimba teary-eyed before, and he was delighted when she embraced him tightly and with great affection announced, 'I was never so glad to see anyone as I was to see you coming through that door, you really came through for us.'

'No.' Kyle couldn't take the credit. 'Our great-grandmother came through.' The longing underlying Kyle's statement conveyed the news of her death perfectly.

With a gasp and a sob, Kimba collapsed into her cousin's arms and was tempted to cry like a baby. The loss almost outweighed the gain in her eyes.

'*But* ... I'm still here,' Kyle said in a bright and quirky tone, which served to stoke Kimba's spirits. 'And, on a happier note, it gives me great pleasure to inform you that the men responsible for our losses are being accompanied by our kin straight to the closest police station, where they will confess their crimes and blow the whistle on their employer.'

'Aw.' Zoe squeezed in under Kyle's free arm to give him a hug. She was very proud and grateful.

'Why does Kyle get all the hugs?' Matt objected, throwing his arms wide, and Kimba broke away from Kyle to oblige.

'Matty, me mate.' She gave him a huge cuddle, which came as a lovely surprise to Matt. Kimba didn't usually go in for grand displays of affection.

As Matt and Kimba's hug turned into a quiet comforting session, Kyle and Zoe distanced themselves a little.

'I guess it's time to set the date for our

wedding,' Kyle commented and Zoe looked at him, as if he was taking the piss out of her again. 'I only say that because with your uncle behind bars, you might need me to help transform the old family business.'

'So you don't think a woman is capable of successfully running a company on her own?' Her smile was challenging.

'Not with a baby on the way.' He suspected that he knew what Kyron's message from Baiame — that Kyle was here to protect the new guardian of the land — meant now. This prophecy didn't refer to Mount Turrammelin but the whole country — under Zoe's guidance, Nivok Industries would now benefit the land and not destroy it.

His grin was so confident that Zoe thought better of flatly calling it a joke. 'Arika told you.' She struggled to repress her mounting excitement and panic.

Kyle nodded, thinking his face would break if his smile grew any larger. 'It's a girl,' he announced casually, and Zoe jumped on him with a hug and a squeal. There was some bouncing and a bit more squealing.

'Steady on. You'll damage her.' Kyle had never imagined joy could be so intense; so this was what happiness felt like.

'Right now.' Zoe stopped still to announce her intentions.

'What?' Kyle pretended to misunderstand her. 'I suppose we could just drop down under the bench —'

'I meant *I'll marry you* today!' Zoe informed him with a slap of caution to his shoulder. 'We've already got a judge.'

'But don't you want the full wedding, reception, dress thing?' Kyle's hand kept winding even though he'd stopped speaking.

'No.' She grabbed Kyle's hand to still it. 'Just you,' she vowed with a kiss.

The fight for Mount Turrammelin monopolised the news headlines that evening, exposing a hundred years of murder. The spontaneous wedding of the controversial heiress of the Nivok Empire came a close second in the story stakes and Matthew Ryan got an exclusive interview with the heiress and her husband on both counts.

'Well, I have to say this is one hell of a way

to work,' Matt commented, sprawled out on the lounge in the honeymoon suite of the most exclusive hotel in the city. He had a glass of champagne in one hand and with his free hand he was sorting through several newspapers that had run his story on the court case.

'Gosh, you look so pretty.' Zoe kissed her husband's cheek, as they watched Matt's footage of their wedding on the late news.

Kyle cringed; his wedding was his first appearance on television, and he'd been obliged to wear a tuxedo. 'You've gotten pretty damn good with that thing.' Kyle changed the subject, pointing to Matt's camera, now lying idle on the coffee table.

'Well, it helps when you have a camera that shoots broadcast quality.'

Zoe had secretly purchased the new camera for Matthew in anticipation of their victory. Then, as the day had also turned out to be her wedding day, the camera had become the perfect gift for their best man.

'Thanks, guys.' Matt held up his glass to the newlyweds, who raised themselves to clink glasses once more.

'The very least we could do,' Zoe replied.

'Where did Kimba get to?' Kyle noticed her glass sitting unattended on the table. 'Is she still on the bloody phone with those land project people?' He rose to go and disconnect her. 'We're supposed to be celebrating, not working!'

'I'll go,' Matt offered, retrieving Kimba's glass and taking it with him out to the balcony, where Kimba had retreated to take the call.

'You know, I suspect there might be something going on there.' Kyle raised his eyebrows a couple of times in suggestion as he slid back up alongside Zoe.

Zoe chuckled at this. 'Oh, you *are* psychic,' she joked, having suspected as much for weeks.

When Kimba spotted Matthew with two glasses of champagne in hand, she quickly wound up her call. 'I'll get back to you first thing,' she assured. 'I will. Goodbye.' She folded her phone away, and gave a heavy but satisfied sigh. 'Three point one million dollars,' she announced with a huge smile.

'That's fantastic!' Matt placed the glasses aside to hug her.

'That offer ought to be more to Zoe's liking.'

Kimba took up her glass and raised it to Matt, before taking a long gulp.

'How are you doing?' Matt asked in all seriousness. Kimba's world had spun around many times today and she'd not been given a chance to sort through the matted web of emotions.

'Well, let me see.' Kimba considered her day. 'My ancestral lands have been saved and my father's murderer is fast on the way to being brought to justice. I've won my first major court case, seen two of my best friends married and with child, but I also lost my great-grandmother, the most amazing spirit I have ever known and I lost a dear friend in Felix, too.'

'I am really sorry about Felix.' Matt felt somewhat hypocritical saying this, since he had been harbouring feelings for Kimba all this time, but he honestly meant what he said. 'I only knew him a short time but he was a good friend to me and I know he was a good boyfriend to you.'

'Well, actually,' Kimba took another sip of her drink for courage, 'we split up before I came down here for the court case.'

Matt's heart leapt into his throat and he felt guilty to be so delighted.

The moment of truth upon her, Kimba raised her large dark eyes to meet Matthew's baby blues. 'I didn't think it was right to be with Felix, when I was constantly thinking of someone else.'

'Hey, check this out.' Kyle made his way on to the balcony to inform Matt and Kimba that the news broadcast had just confirmed that four filthy, dazed, but unharmed, men had been brought into North Queensland police by the local clan of Mount Turrammelin. They had confessed to being commissioned by James Nivok to kill an Aboriginal elder, and to destroy some video footage which had resulted in a second death. This upped the tycoon's tally to five suspected counts of murder.

When Kyle found Matt and Kimba in each other's arms, lost in a kiss, he backed up quietly.

'What is it?' Zoe rushed to see and was delighted by the development. 'Now that's the perfect ending to a perfect day.' They returned to the lounge, and Zoe picked up the remote to switch the television off.

'Hold on ...' Kyle caught sight of a picture of a Tasmanian Tiger, and relieving Zoe of the remote, he turned up the volume to hear the tale of how three fishermen had taken an extraordinary photograph of a Tasmanian Tiger. Kyle couldn't help but chuckle. 'Could today be any more perfect?'

'I can think of something that would make it so.' Zoe hit the off button for the television, and kissed her husband seductively.

Kyle needed no further prompting. He stood and swept his bride into his arms to carry her to bed. 'It seems that dreams do come true.'

CHAPTER
FOURTEEN

BOOK'S EPILOGUE

That is the end, young warrior. There isn't any more. The words have all been read, their wisdom imparted.

The book's narrative voice, which Kyle heard in his mind as he read, was now that of an old woman and not male at all.

It was a shock to emerge from the spell that the words had cast over his reality. 'It was all fiction,' he realised. 'But there has to be some fact to it, surely? It was so … elaborate!' He sat upright and clutched the book to his chest. 'Oh, my God!' Kyle realised he was a changed person and placed the book aside to run both hands through his hair. 'Is this me, daring to believe in something?'

He did believe.

Kyle believed in himself and that anything was possible for him. It may only have been a story, but Kyle felt an inner confidence that he'd never known he had. He knew it was imperative that he aid Zoe and Matt through this Nivok business.

'Zoe and Matt!' he said aloud.

What was the time? What day was it?

'Christ, Book, how long have I been ...'

The book had gone.

'... out for?' His heart sank. It felt like his best friend had just died.

No time has passed. You haven't lost a second.

'Ron?' Kyle roused himself from the lounge to find Kyron standing not far afoot. 'You're back!'

Never left.

'It's *so* good to see you, buddy, I can't tell you how much I missed having you around.'

Kyle would have given the beast a huge hug, but he was still lacking in the physical substance department.

I missed you too, but we have a mountain to protect, a friend to save, women to woo!

That's when Kyle noticed that he was not the only one to have had a huge change in attitude now that Book's tale was over. Kyron wasn't huddled in a corner fearful of the physical world around him; now that Kyle felt stronger and more confident, so did his guardian.

'Damn straight.' Kyle clapped his hands, feeling they were both up for the quest. 'Now, what the hell did Matt say he was doing today?' It seemed like weeks since he'd had that conversation. 'He said something about going to a television station … I've got no chance of getting to see him there. But, if my dreams serve me correctly, he'll be running around getting keys cut tonight, and he'll be visiting Zoe first thing tomorrow morning.'

So, you've got to make sure you get to Zoe's apartment before him and warn her that her uncle is coming over to surprise her and Matt. Oh, and don't forget to tell her to hide her keys.

'How do I know all that stuff is going to happen?' Kyle started picking dirty clothes off the floor to replace the dirty clothes he already had on his body.

Kyron shrugged. *The same way you believe I am standing here?*

Kyle caught a whiff of himself. 'Maybe I should grab a shower before then? And find my wardrobe?' He tossed all the clothes back on the floor. 'And the washing machine?'

Could be for the best, the beast agreed.

'Why are you taking me into Bargi's abode?' Kimba queried of Kyle as they alighted from her car. 'When you said you had something to show me, I didn't realise I'd be coming all the way out here! Do you have any idea how much work is involved in setting up this land fund and marrying that to the memorial project?'

'Yes, yes, we all know you are a regular superwoman.' Kyle managed to sympathise and mock her in one!

The *Book of Dreams* had proven quite accurate — Kimba had indeed executed her role in the preservation of Mount Turrammelin masterfully. Other aspects of the story had proven far more difficult to manifest in real life, such as Kyle's marriage to Zoe on the day of the court case. The couple had been forced to settle for an engagement, as, in reality, there were forms to fill in and waiting periods — tracking down Kyle's birth certificate alone delayed the happy event for months.

Kimba and Matt were still getting around their guilt over Felix's death, but they had finally started dating.

Zoe was not yet pregnant, either, but Kyle had no doubts that they would one day be blessed with the daughter his Matong Bargi had predicted. Kyle figured that the fairytale ending in Book's tale was not meant to be an accurate account of events, but more a prediction of how circumstances would eventually unfold. However, some of the more fantastic aspects of Book's yarn had, surprisingly, come to pass.

Kyle grinned winningly at Kimba, and beckoned her to follow him to the entrance of Bargi's one-time abode. He missed his great-grandmother, and he knew that Kimba missed her desperately too. But Kyle still carried Bargi's essence with him, and that was a comfort to him and he wanted Kimba to be similarly comforted.

'Oooooh ...' Kimba faked frustration as she stomped along after her cousin. 'You're getting as bad as the rest of our clan when it comes to time schedules, you know that?' she posed, arms crossed, as she caught Kyle up at the tree-lined entrance.

'Good,' he decided, his mind on something else. 'Watch this.' Kyle held his hands together, and focused inwardly for a moment.

Kimba rolled her eyes and was about to comment on not having time to stand there and watch him meditate, when she observed that light was starting to emit from between her cousin's hands. He parted his hands and a ball of glowing energy sat suspended in mid air.

'What is it?' gasped Kimba, awed by his little trick.

'It's a present from Bargi ... a little inheritance that I believe she'd want you to have.'

'But what is it?' Kimba giggled away her apprehension; she still didn't understand.

'I can't really tell you what it is, but if you wish it, I can show you,' he prompted, and Kimba couldn't resist.

She confirmed her acceptance with a nod and as she did, the ball rose and met her head with a blinding rush of golden bubbles.

'Whoa there.' Kyle caught Kimba and helped her to stay standing while she regained her wits.

'Golly.' Kimba was a bit dazed for a second, but it passed. 'What did you just do to me, rainbow man.' She laughed when she saw all the colours his body was emitting. 'I can't believe what I'm seeing!' She backed up, hand on mouth, to observe him better. Then she noted he was not the only thing in close proximity that seemed to be radiating colour and light-energy. 'Everything is glowing green and gold, it's like a really beautiful trip!' she joked, and then denied ever taking any sort of hallucinogens. 'But this is what I *imagine* the world would look like on a really good trip.'

'The voyage hasn't even started,' Kyle advised with a smile as he took her by the hand and led her down along one side of the tree tunnel that arched over the little stream.

'Kyle?' Kimba's gaze was darting about the canopy, and she was looking a little wary. 'This place is crawling with …' Kimba obviously wasn't too sure about what she was seeing.

'Yes?' Kyle grinned, as the tunnel parted and he spied Kyron standing on the other side of the waterhole.

Kimba screamed, jumped and gasped for breath when she spied a huge yowie standing across the way. But her fear dispersed in a flood of joyful tears as the beast just calmly waved at her.

'Meet Kyron.' Kyle rubbed her back to comfort her, but she hit him all the same.

'You could have warned me ... damn!' she cursed, and then laughed.

'How come every time you show up, I get hit?' Kyle queried his guide and Kyron shrugged.

But, you usually get hugged too, it replied more hopefully.

'Oh my God,' Kimba gasped, upon realising she had a telepathic connection with the beast, whereby she hugged Kyle, excited.

There you go.

'The telepathy gets them every time!' Kyle agreed, pulling Kimba off him. 'And before you yell at me again for not warning you ... there's a mass of wee earth elementals gathered around our feet.'

Kimba looked down and her wary-cum-horrified expression inspired a round of laughter from the creatures.

'Don't fret, I'll handle this.' Kyle strode away from her, whistling to the creatures. 'Come on, I've got a mission for you lot.'

Kimba relaxed when they all scampered off after him. 'Well. This certainly gives Doctor Dolittle a whole new slant.'

'Doesn't it,' Kyle quietly agreed, very proud of the achievement. He sat himself in front of the Matong Bargi's tree, allowing the creatures to run amok over him as he focused on the earth.

'What are you doing with them?' Kimba wondered at his intent.

'We're making another present, but this one is not for you. It's bound for another old friend of ours.' He held up a finger to request her patience, and looked back at the empty patch of ground. '*Warrawee, bimble thambaroo, yappulum nganauwe peggeralin.*'

Kimba's eyes opened wide as the creatures began hurling themselves into a glowing mass of energy that had erupted in response to Kyle's chant. The glowing mass began to take form as the creatures enhanced the physical volume of the manifestation.

'*Warrina yetni tumpinyeri!*'

By the time the legal system got through with James Nivok no amount of money was going to save him from serving a true life sentence; the day he would get out of prison would be the day he died.

His money didn't get James any special privileges in prison, either. In his cell there was a bunk, a toilet and a bench. Nothing to do, nothing to see, nothing to gain — this was his life from now on.

Despite the court judgement, James still believed that he'd been betrayed — first by his father, then his brother and finally his niece. He resented them all, but none so much as that half-caste wizard that Zoe had married. If there was one person he wished he'd disposed of, it was Kyle Burke.

Every waking minute since he'd been in confinement, James had been pondering how he might exact his revenge; there was precious little else to do. He had limited access to reading material — he had been denied any financial publications or anything to do with the business world — and the literature that he did have access to didn't interest him.

But today when James was returned to his cell for lock-up, there was a brown paper parcel on his bunk. It was simply addressed to 'James'.

He was rather surprised that the warden didn't comment, confiscate or at least investigate the package.

When he opened the parcel James could hardly believe his eyes. The book looked like a grimoire with its strange little creatures, although the title read *Book of Dreams*.

'I don't read fiction,' James scoffed. 'Who the hell left this here?'

Still, as he had nothing better to read, and there was some time until lights out, James thought, *What the hell.* He opened to the foreword, written in an unusual rainbow typescript. James had never seen anything quite like it before.

We bid you welcome, James. It has been brought to our attention that you seem to be completely lost. If you wish to come to know what it is that constantly eludes you in life ... I am your transport to seek within.

BIBLIOGRAPHY

Butt, P., Eagleson, R. and Lane, P. *Mabo, Wik and Native Title*, 4th edition, Federation Press, NSW, 2001.

Healy, T. and Cropper, C. *Out of the Shadows: Mystery Animals of Australia*, Ironbark, NSW, Australia, 1994.

Hope, M., *Practical Techniques of Psychic Self-Defence*, Aquarian Press, UK, 1983.

Reed, A. W., *Aboriginal Words of Australia*, Reed Books, NSW, 1965.
— *Aboriginal Myths, Legends and Fables*, Reed Publishing, NSW, 1982.

Reynolds, H., *The Law of the Land*, Penguin Books, Vic, 1987.
— *This Whispering in Our Hearts*, Allen & Unwin, NSW, 1998.